by DAVID JOHN COOK

Published by
QUOIT MEDIA LIMITED
www.quoitmedia.co.uk

This edition first published in 2020 by Quoit Media Limited,
Brynmawr, Llanfair Caereinion, Powys, SY21 0DG

For more copies of this book, please email
quoit@quoitmedia.co.uk

ISBN 978-1-911537-13-7

Cover design by Alan Hayes
Cover illustration by David John Cook
Metal mesh vector by Vecteezy.com

A CIP catalogue record for this book is available
from the British Library.

Printed and bound in Great Britain by Clays Ltd, Elcograf S.p.A.

To John Francis Cook,
Dawn Beverly Cook
and to Patrick McGoohan:
Rebels, Prisoners, and now totally Free.

To Kathleen:
My 'Mrs. Peel' in White Horses.

Preface

Patrick McGoohan and his "new" series *The Prisoner* burst upon me during its first run on American television on CBS in 1968. I was already a big fan of McGoohan through his work in the Disney films *The Scarecrow of Romney Marsh*, and *The Three Lives of Thomasina*, and his great work in the series I knew as *Secret Agent* (or *Danger Man* as it was known in the UK). *The Prisoner*, though, simply blew me away! I've been an avid enthusiast of the series ever afterward.

Over the years, through the "magic" of cable television, offering all three networks (CBS, NBC, and ABC) and the independent stations available to us back then, I was slowly introduced to other series provided to us by the British television and film industry. Men and women of mystery, espionage and intrigue began to delight and fascinate me. Vampires and monsters would crawl out of Hammer studios and grab my attention. Later, videos, DVD and Blu-Ray sets of a variety of British Television series and films have been lovingly collected and viewed repeatedly.

The Village of Portmeirion, Wales, where *The Prisoner*'s exterior scenes were filmed, was a "dream place" for me in 1968. I hadn't even realized there was actually such a place in our world until 1973! For decades after, it was a dream for me to be able to afford, perhaps one day, to get there. In Spring of 2014, that dream became reality.

In Portmeirion, one of the attractions is the Stone Boat "Amis Reunis" (or Friends Reunited). On our "Arrival" to the Village, that spring night in 2014, my wife Kathleen and I stood on the Stone Boat, simply thrilled to be there at all.

It was then that a germ of a plot for a story formed in my head. A tale involving mysteries, espionage, daring, and, ultimately, freedom (for some), which would unite beloved characters from those wonderful British television series of long ago.

As author David Stimpson accurately states in his excellent book, *The Prisoner Dusted Down* (a book also available through Quoit Media Limited), "Enthusiasts for the (Prisoner) series have considered, interpreted, speculated, discussed, and debated. Indeed, over the years and decades much has been written about every aspect of *The Prisoner*."

Stimpson's book, along with many other works, informed my understanding of the series, and also informed me as to how I might want to present my story. As I fleshed the story out, I tasked myself to ensure that, even if you were *not* familiar with these characters, that you were given enough information to still find the tale an enjoyable introduction to them.

In my "What If...?" story presented herein, I have attempted to investigate some questions posed in *The Prisoner*, and to provide some possible alternative answers. My intent was to delve more into the narrative aspects of the series, rather than the symbolic or allegorical aspects (although some of those present themselves as well). It is an interpretation of events in *The Prisoner* put in the context of a world as was presented to me through the work, craft, art and care of a great many British television and film producers, writers, directors, casts and crews.

My tale involves a number of beloved characters whom I enjoyed reuniting with in the writing of it.

My hope is that you enjoy either meeting them, or reuniting with them, in the reading of it.

David John Cook
September 2020

Hi(s)story is prologue

Free! Good God, finally, once again, free.

Here on the deserted plain, the Lotus roaring, air pummelling his face...

Alive, free!

It had taken perseverance and patience. A matter of time and tenacity. But he had *beaten* them. Beaten them all. His life was once again his own. Back to his home. His car. His reality.

He had frequently come here to race. To be at one with the car. To clear his mind and sharpen his focus and resolve. To be as objective as he knew how in order to chew over a problem without distraction.

He had time, now, to relax a bit. To 'clear the cobwebs' and to begin anew.

Certainly, there would be some residual effects from the hell he had just escaped. One couldn't go through what he had and not be affected in some manner. It would take time to ascertain. To gauge. He wasn't fully sure exactly how long a time they had held him...

Prisoner.

Now he had allies. Or, at least, one. The butler (could/should he really count on the others?). The silent little man who stood next to him... No, that wasn't right. Was it? Wait a minute...Why was he not there with him before?

He'd left him at his home. Was that wise? It had just now struck him! What if that butler had all along been Num...?

In, in an instant, there it was. ROVER! A 'guardian'. The opaque sphere creature. Whatever one wished to call the thing, there it was, some distance directly in front of him, bounding toward him. Its roar drowning out the sound of the Lotus's engine.

Here? *Now?* How could that possibly be? He had destroyed them (or, at least, one of them?).

Suddenly, his senses were much more focused, as if he had somehow driven out of a mist. He'd been a *fool!* The Lotus hadn't felt entirely 'right', had it? He'd built it with his own hands. He *should* have noticed. The air pummelling him, somehow 'off', as though this wasn't...real, but that idea seemed impossible. Yet the trip with Nadia seemed real enough, and he knew how *that* ended up! The butler...could he have...?

Instantly (impossibly) ROVER engulfed him and the Lotus, bringing everything to a cold dead stop. He knew that was impossible. He was speeding at 74mph. A sudden stop would have killed him immediately. 'How could any of this be happening?' was his last thought as he sank into blackness.

1

By Santa Monica Pier, CA; late summer, 1969

She knew it was him.

There was no doubt. Despite the incredible improbability of it and despite his appearance, it *was* him.

And the funny part was, she would never have noticed him if not for a woman's infectious laugh. "Wow, man! You *really* captured him!"

The hippy caricaturist manning the little open tent kiosk, responded in a low, half-mumble. "I'm obliged, er...thank you. Glad you like it." That verbal exchange stopped Emma Peel in her tracks. Her audio memory vaulted back six or so years ago; to a party she and her then fiancé, Peter Peel, were attending, in Rome, of all places. The tall butler, helping her on with her wrap at the party's end, whispered a barely audible, "I'm obliged. Thank you."

She had recognized him then, too, as she and Peter had arrived at the party. Yet she knew better than to ever let that knowledge show on her face.

Emma Knight had taken the reigns of leadership of her father's industry some years before, shortly after his passing. There were government and military contracts to contend with. One project required security clearance for four members of a small staff of engineers in her employ. That was the first time she had met the handsome and enigmatic John Drake, the agent who would conduct the investigation required.

She never forgot his beautiful eyes. Clear ice blue, though a profound ice blue, and so multi-faceted. One could drown in them were one not cautious. At that time, she very seriously considered throwing caution to the wind, but he was all business. He had concluded the investigation process in less than one week, he and Emma had only worked jointly for approximately ninety minutes. Polite, efficient, and unfortunately (she thought then), strictly official.

It was his eyes that she immediately recognized at the party in Rome years later. In a split second, the ice blue multi-faceted eyes of this alleged 'butler' told her all she needed to know. He knew she recognized him, and his eyes emphatically stated, 'Yes, it is me, I am on assignment. It is of utmost importance you keep this completely to yourself!' Emma never let on and held that trust sacred. He admired and appreciated an intellect that could 'read' that information so instantaneously. He had thus decided to 'chance' a quick whisper of thanks during the noise of the guests leaving the party.

Here now, at this alleged caricaturist's kiosk, she wandered closer to the young couple who were finishing their transaction with the artist. She quickly scanned the half dozen drawings pinned to a board on their left. To their right, the tall artist stood, putting cash into his wallet. He wore a yellow flower print shirt, tan shorts, and sandals. A panama hat topped a head of shoulder length hair, shading a bearded and moustached face. Well-tanned, he looked for all the world like just another 'hippy' vendor on and around Santa Monica Pier. He blended in perfectly.

Two more women were walking up to the kiosk as Emma pointed to the pinned drawings and spoke in a higher than normal registered Mid-Atlantic accent, "You amaze me, how you can get the personality of someone with just a few well-placed lines!"

"Oh, thank you. It's simply a..." the 'hippy' started conversationally but then he looked up at her. Their eyes met and locked, for an instant.

It was him. She'd already known. His eyes immediately confirmed it.

He *was* John Drake!

What was also evident, without doubt, was that *he* had recognized *her* and she saw something else in his eyes which alarmed her. There was a sudden tension in the air between them. One could have cleaved it with an axe.

"Oh! Can you do one of us next?" asked one of the women.

"Ahh...I'm...I'm afraid I...must close, er, early today, dear ladies..." he stammered, quickly turning from Emma, beginning to gather his art equipment into a large case.

"Ohhhh...awwwww," started the other woman clearly disappointed.

"You see, I have a...rather, aihhm, important doctor appointment pending, and, if I close up shop now, I, er, I can just make it. I'm *very* sorry about that," he faltered, hurriedly gathering.

Closing the flaps on the kiosk/tent set-up, he said over his shoulder, "I'll tell ya what! If you can be here tomorrow, I'll be sure to draw you both fer, ahh, half cost! Howzat sound?"

"Hmmm...okay, that'd be great! We'll be here! Thank you so much," the woman replied.

"Not a 'tall. Be seeing you!"

He attempted to somewhat slow the 'shutting down' of the kiosk, as he recognized (too late) that his actions were betraying him. He quickly glanced toward Emma. Damn!

Well, there was nothing to be done for it now! The other women wandered off. The tension remained thick.

"Look, ahh... Miss..." Drake fumbled, turning away from her.

Emma cut him short. "Mister...Wolf is it?" she enquired, pointing to a sign above the pinned examples of his craft. '*Get drawn in!! Caricatures* by *Joey Wolf* $5.00 per person Couples at $7.50'.

"I'll make you the, ahh, the same offer as the others. Half cost to you if you're by here tomorrow..." he continued speaking over his shoulder, a slight edge to his voice.

"I imagine family caricatures would be in the vicinity of twelve fifty? Or do you have a limit of two people per?" her voice fully carefree and conversational.

She was staring into him. He didn't need to look at her to know. He'd never met another woman with such intellectual agility, combined with such accurate instincts. In fact, he'd only met one other man who had these qualities in the quantity that Emma Knight...Peel possessed. His 'act' was utterly useless on her; a waste of effort.

He turned and looked at her eyes. They held no levity at all. Though guarded, he saw concern. Yes, curiosity as well, but primarily he saw concern for *him*.

She walked straight up to him and obliterating all pretences, whispered closely in his ear, "Are you free to talk? Are you in danger?"

He made an instinctive immediate full scan of the area with his eyes. He nodded slightly. "Would you mind helping me get my gear to my wagon, Miss?"

As they walked toward the parking lot and Drake's station wagon, he carrying a large suitcase and she a beach bag and easel, he was saying, "The beach is patrolled and I've never had any real problem leaving most of my...set up right where it is. I'm paid up for the season, so I needn't be concerned with someone claiming my 'spot'. Oh, there is the occasional pilferer who will avoid detection but they generally aren't the destructive sort and they're normally after goods that can be readily fenced. There's not a large market for art supplies. Still, there are a few times those, too, get taken and the cost of art supplies being what they are..."

She had had quite enough of his inane 'cover' drivel (thank you very much). It was becoming insulting!

"I think we both realize were I not here with you right now, your kiosk would be packed up and away. Hundreds of miles from here, come tomorrow. Those women would never have their drawings done, at least not by you. I doubt you would ever set up shop here again."

She said quietly yet firmly. "You're stalling. Babbling until you can think of something to say that will get me out of your..." she noted his 'mane' which just touched his shoulders, "...hair." She walked two paces ahead and turned facing him, halting him.

"John, how is it that you are here? What is happening?"

"Oh..." he began as he stepped around her, feigning a light disposition, "It's all a bit difficult to explain, really..."

She stepped in front of him again, set the bag on the ground, and drilled her eyes into his, effectively willing him to a standstill.

"The last I knew, you were still 'active'. You are legendary, typically galloping into danger where no one else will tread." She paused, lowering her voice while raising the intensity. "Years ago, at that party in Rome, despite every reason why they might have, indeed *should* have, your *eyes* never once showed a hint of what I've just seen in them."

"And that is?" he snapped, but furtively, his eyes still darting about the landscape.

"*Fear, of me*, when you know better. You *know* I'd never blow your cover," she snapped back in a harsh whisper.

"What is wrong? You've just used three different accents while trying to extricate yourself from me and those women! You are *not* on assignment, nor are you canvassing for one upcoming. You are *not* doing 'background'. You are about something else." She spoke quietly, yet with an urgency that may as well have made her voice thunderous.

He grunted "Have me 'figured', do you?" his voice a low gravely rumble.

"I do. You are running. In danger. Hiding! I believe you thought, still think, that I am a danger to you. That I was 'sent' here to find you. I'm not, and I haven't been!

"Now, you are confused. You *are* very much off your game and you *are* afraid. And I wish to understand why."

He stood there, stunned. She had him. She nailed it all perfectly.

He let his anger grow. Anger at her knowing. Anger at himself for not being able to *stop* her from knowing and anger for not being in control of the situation.

He growled quietly, "And, how is it, Mrs. Emma Peel, that you are *here*? Exactly in *this* place and time? *What* is your explanation for so unlikely a... reunion?" his voice rising in volume with every syllable.

She was silent for a time. Then, with a characteristic smirk and slight turn of her head, she asked, "Do you know where two confused people might get a drink?"

Drake considered, and then said, "My...wagon...is about seventy metres that way. I *do* know a place, Mrs. Peel, where a drink might just be the thing."

Hi(s)story is prologue 2

The foot bone connected to the leg bone. The leg bone connected to the knee bone. The knee bone connected to the thigh bone. The thigh bone connected to the hip bone...

Slowly, he was aware, aware he was whole. Not dashed to pieces in the horrific auto accident that assuredly *had* to have taken place *if* ROVER had, indeed, taken the car and him in one full swallow (was 'swallow' the right word?). No, he was whole. He could feel his extremities. He could feel his body, neck, head and face, all intact. His heart beat steadily. That was all he could hear. But, the blackness...so thick and...total. So, he could feel (in a manner of speaking) and hear. He could 'sense'.

Okay, he thought. That much was true. Rebuild. Start with what's true as blueprint. The blueprint gives us the framework. Build from the framework. Then let's see what our situation is. Think of nothing else except what is true now.

Wait! What was that? A glimmer... *yes!* A minute sliver of light! Gone? No, an aspect of it is still there. Ever so slight... but, thank God, it *is* still there!

Red light? Blue? Doesn't matter. The blackness not as 'thick' now. Not as total. Fight. Fight them. You didn't come all this way just to... just to...

...hip bone connected to the back bone. The back bone connected to the...

2

Frankie's Joint, Topanga Canyon, CA.

Drake and Emma entered the small bar. More like a house really, with a neon sign in the picture window, the 'T' in the word 'Joint' shorted out. It was 3:20pm, and there were only two other people in the place. A large strawberry blonde woman in her mid-forties behind the bar, watching television and a man slumped over a small table, snoring rather loudly, the squeaking and slight slam of the screened door not jarring him in the slightest.

The woman got off of the stool she'd been sitting on. Smiling at Drake warmly, she greeted "Joey! Hey, it's been a while! How are ya, hun?"

"Good, good, Frankie. I'm good. Yourself?" Drake returned the greeting.

"I'm great, honey! Things are good. Oh! Hey! This is great! Ya hungry? Yer *just* the guy I've been meanin' to test these on! You're so smart about food an' all..."

Frankie tapped a menu item scrawled on a chalk board hanging on the wall by the bar. "I got a new thing I'm tryin' out here. It's a recipe from my sister, lives in that little town in upstate New York? I told'ja 'bout her, right?" He nodded that she had.

"Spiedies! Its cubed chunks of marinated meat; beef, pork or lamb, don't matter, grilled and put on Italian bread. The way you are with food, I'd love to get your take on 'em. I'm thinkin' of maybe callin' them something else. Getting' tired of havin' to explain 'em, ya know? You let me know what you think. On the house, okay?"

He had to smile. Frankie was a good honest woman, with a heart as big as she was. Hard to get a word in edgewise with her. But, if there was something...unusual going on in the area, she'd be the first to know, and first to tell about it. There were always tourists and travellers going through, with Malibu and Santa Monica about five miles away on either side, though they never stayed long. Still, if some did stay a bit longer than 'normal', if some seemed to be snooping around maybe, Frankie would know about it. She was a fortuitous advance guard, an 'alarm' of sorts. Just in case...

"So, you're here kinda early. A good day?" Frankie asked, rubbing thumb and forefinger together indicating an influx of cash. Then she noticed Emma, standing slightly behind him, looking somewhat amused.

"Whoa! Whozzis? A *real* good day for you, huh Joey?" kidded Frankie, winking at Drake. "Hi, hun! I'm Frankie, and you are...?"

"Famished and thirsty!" Emma replied, finding herself smiling, enjoying Frankie's benevolent verbal onslaught that had, for the moment, pushed aside the seriousness of matters between she and Drake.

The ride in his station wagon from the parking lot had been in total silence. She had started to speak, when, finger to his lips, his stern glare halted all communication. '*What*', she thought, 'has he gotten himself involved in'?

"Two Buds, two double shots of your best whiskey, and we'll try two of your...spiedies, are they? Two of those," he ordered, then leaning across the bar and lowering his voice, he asked, "Might my friend and I use your...facilities and then your back porch?"

"Oh, sure hun. Perfect day for it. I'll bring out yer spiedies when they're done."

"I'm obliged."

"Yer funny! Yer the only one I know who uses that word!" remarked Frankie, chuckling, looking at Emma and hitching her thumb toward Drake, "He does this killer British accent, ya know. Sounds just like that David Frost guy on TV! *Funny!*"

After having used the facilities, they carried their drinks to the back porch, a pleasant spot where they would be able to talk freely.

He had considered hightailing it while Emma was in the WC but it simply wouldn't do to strand her there and besides, Frankie would be liable to raise hell about it, creating a mess he didn't need. No, best to hear her out, figure what to do afterward.

They sat opposite each other at a small table, Drake leaning back, steepling his fingers to his lips. Waiting.

Emma sighed, and drew herself together. She sipped her whiskey, set it down and lightly slapped the table top with both hands.

"To the tale. How is it that I'm here," she paused and then began. "I'll assume you know of my association with John Steed, how that association ended last year when my husband Peter had been found in the Amazon and returned to England. You may recall Peter. We were together at that party in Rome. We were engaged at the time."

"Yes. In fact, I knew Peter Peel somewhat prior to *our* first meeting."

"Ahh, did you? Mm. Not surprising. Well, having been reunited, we had five wonderful months of globetrotting, being darlings of the jet set and all that, after which we settled in. Peter's wanderlust seemed to cool. We'd thoughts of starting a family, things of that nature."

"I began taking a more active role in Knight Industries. Not to the extent I had when you and I first met, but active." She paused, gathering herself, steeling herself.

"Well, our wonderful reunion was cut short!" she uttered, bitterness obvious in her voice. "Things grow wildly in the jungles of the Amazon. In Peter's case, what grew unchecked and undetected was pancreatic cancer. '*We*' found out Peter was terminally ill this past June. I believe he'd known all along and kept it from me. Little things he'd... well, no matter. The cancer took him very quickly. Peter died in July," she concluded, and then drained her double shot of whiskey.

"I'm very sorry, Mrs. Peel. You have my sincerest condolences."

Drake had previously *worked* with Peter, actually. Peter's extraordinary piloting abilities had gotten him out of more than one sticky spot back when he was working with NATO. Peter was a good man; a man who could be trusted, as so many turned out not to be. Drake was honestly sorry to hear of his passing. "I, aihhm, I've endeavoured to keep up with current events. I'd have thought I would have heard."

"Mm. We kept it relatively quiet, for any number of reasons," she explained. "Peter's family has never been fond of his notoriety. Publicity and promotional business dealings for a national hero and daredevil can be...problematic. Especially for me, as I've some notoriety of my own."

"I tried managing those concerns, keeping the plates spinning...coupled with my more active role in my father's company, well, it was all a bridge too far. And then..."

"Here ya go!" interrupted Frankie with the spiedies. "Let me know what ya think, okay? Anything else I can get ya?"

"Another double for my friend, please."

"You got it, Joey! One more for yer lady friend," Frankie confirmed, accenting the word 'lady', giving him a conspiratorial wink.

Emma waited until the double shot arrived and sipped it. It occurred to her that getting inebriated was something she'd been doing far too frequently lately and it simply would not do any longer. Especially now it seemed.

"And then," she continued, "my beloved Steed popped in for a visit. As delicately as he knows how, he suggested rekindling our...partnership."

"The last thing on Earth you would need in your life at that time," Drake stated with some disdain.

"Indeed!" she agreed. "My poor Steed. There he stood, looking for all the world like a slightly older version of Peter. They did resemble each other, you know. Yes, Peter's elder doppelganger, doing his utmost to cheer me, to uplift me! 'Pip, pip, cheerio' and all that sort of rubbish."

Drake couldn't help but smirk at this. Major John Steed was, of course, legendary.

There were two assignments that he and Steed had worked on together. They ran as smooth as clockwork. And these were no cakewalks. They'd been complicated and quite dangerous.

Yet there was something about Steed that rankled him. Steed never gave the impression that he took matters seriously, playing things as they came along, never really having a plan of any sort. As if he thought an assignment was merely some temporary 'romp' to pass the time until something either more important or more *fun* came up!

Of course, that theory couldn't be wholly accurate. One couldn't be as successful and as trusted an agent as Steed was for very long, were that the case. All the same, it seemed to Drake that he went out of his way to present himself as a twee supercilious dolt. Perhaps that all was part of his genius.

He was unsure of Steed's moral compass. Steed could be utterly ruthless, and his propensity for bringing in amateurs and civilians into the often dangerous world of intelligence and espionage; how foolhardy! Odd that Emma would mention Steed as being Peter Peel's 'doppelganger'. He had to smirk at that little bit of irony!

"I...I had something of a breakdown," Emma continued. "I was furious at him for his suggestion. I about bloodied his nose. Threw things at him. Broke a rather expensive antique figurine over that insufferable bowler of his. Metal rimmed you know."

She appeared to be 'somewhere else'. SomeWHEN else. Tears began forming in her eyes. "It...hurts to recognize now how seriously...he took and kept my advice..."

Drake handed her a napkin. She dabbed her tears and discreetly blew her nose.

"He'd collected pieces of the antique figurine as best he could. Said he'd have it repaired, apologized for 'intruding' on my time of 'mourning' and left.

"Afterward, a dear old friend, Cordelia Winfield, stopped by. I hadn't seen her in a while but we had kept in touch. She works for an antiques shop. Part owner, actually. Steed brought the broken figurine there for repair and they had a chat. He urged her to call on me. Ahh Steed! My 'knight in shining armour', always was trying to care for me."

"Anyway, Cord suggested *thee* perfect 'getaway' for me. More precisely, demanded I go. Would *not* take no for an answer. She owns a beach house here in Santa Monica. A peaceful place where I could 'get away from it all' and 'get myself together' as they say these days. She 'ordered' me to go be by myself, for as long as I needed. I've been there for about two weeks now. Today, I decided to take a stroll to famous Santa Monica Pier. That was when I happened upon your kiosk and you and that, as they say, is that! *That* is how I came to be here for our unlikely reunion."

Neither Drake nor Emma had eaten. He was moved by her story, very moved by the trust she showed him, invested in him. How she had completely opened up to him. He noticed how calm and...unafraid he was with her. He felt like they'd known each other all their lives, like it was the most natural thing in the world to trust her implicitly. Something of a shock to him how entirely comfortable he was feeling these things. He began the process of making an important decision.

"Shall we...dine, Mrs. Peel?"

"Yes. And then, your story."

"Yes. My...story."

Hi(s)story is prologue 3

He was standing alone in the abandoned airfield he knew so well. There was no sound save that of his own steady heartbeat. He heard no wind, yet wisps of sand, like miniature tornadoes, would occasionally form, drifting skyward and away. He stared ahead, not moving.

Eventually, one wisp of sand formed just ahead of him. How far ahead it was impossible to tell. There were no other points of reference in this flat plain of sand and concrete that was, essentially, a desert. It seemed to go on for eternity.

One wisp of sand gained volume and mass. It corkscrewed out of the ground and slowly rose into the air as it gradually morphed into a water spout, as if from some underground spring, or fountain. From the bottom of the spout formed a bubble, which, too, gained volume and mass as it rose to the top of the spout, growing more opaque as it did so.

At that point, a combination of sounds came from the large opaque sphere as it was lightly buoyed by the water spout. The sound of air, as from some type of breathing apparatus, coupled with an odd almost musical sound which reverberated. Finally, a roar. A roar which combined that of a lion with the terrorized scream of a man.

Guardian. Sphere Globe Balloon Monster. It didn't matter. It no longer frightened him. His heartbeat remained steady. ROVER. Stupid name for this abomination.

'I destroyed you once, and I'll do so again!' he thought, a wicked smile slowly creeping across his face. 'You can't harm me here. My life is my own!' He mentally taunted.

As if in answer, ROVER abruptly landed on the ground, the water spout ceasing to flow behind it. It bounced up and down a few times, and then landed firmly. It seemed to bifurcate, then immediately split into two Rovers of equal size.

They moved apart from each other horizontally, stopped at one point, again bouncing up and down a few times and then lowered into the ground. 'Wild!' he thought. 'But no matter. Nothing matters here. They may as well be Dali's melting clocks for all the harm they can do me.'

From the exact spots where the Rovers sank into the ground, rumbling occurred and cracks formed on the surface. Quickly, something was rising out of the ground. 'Rocks? Shafts of stone? No! They...they're...buildings!' he marvelled.

The process, though not immediate, was quick. Throughout, he knew the ground was rumbling and shaking as the buildings rose but he could neither feel nor hear it. Within moments, two large buildings stood in the exact spots where the Rovers had sunk. To his right was London's Clock Tower, Big Ben, while to his left stood the Village Clock tower.

Now, he was starting to hear...voices. Very faint voices, nevertheless they were there, along with his heart beat. He could not discern words, only the sounds of consonants and an occasional vowel. He narrowed his eyes, trying to concentrate on what the voices might be saying. They were growing louder, overlapping each other, resulting in gibberish.

His eyes popped fully open as he was startled by the sudden loud chiming of the clock towers in unison, the large majestic chime of Big Ben equal in volume with the quaint church bell chime of the Village Clock Tower. After eight chimes, they both stopped. All was silent save for his heart beat, which had grown a bit faster now. 'Well of course!' he thought. 'Why wouldn't it, with the synchronized chimes of the towers at such a loud volume...Eh? Wait a moment...synchronized! How could that be? That would mean the two towers were within the same...'

Then the voices started in again, louder this time. He immediately noticed the colour of his surroundings had changed hue. Reds and browns. Blood red, in fact. He turned and surveyed the entirety of the plain. The same. A deep blood red. He turned back to view the clock towers. They were aflame, smoke rising from them, burnt sections falling from them. How…? The voices were rising in volume. He would have tried to discern content and context from the gibberish, but he stood transfixed, staring down at his hands. *Blood* was dripping from his *hands!*

3
Such Men Are Dangerous

John Drake and Emma Peel finished eating and drinking. Frankie's Joint had started to fill up with a few more patrons. Drake suggested they go for a walk while he told his story. They ordered two more spiedies to go.

"These "spiedies" of yours are marvellous Frankie! Thank your sister in New York for us. Er, a bit of advice?" He moved forward and in a quiet 'confidential' voice advised, "The thing'll be to maintain quality in the cut of meat you use for dicing. Take care to maintain subtlety with the marinate. You don't want to overdo. Don't be afraid to charge two bucks a piece for 'em. You've got a real winner here. You'll be turnin' customers away before long!"

"Aww thanks Joey. I'm real glad ya liked 'em. You think I should stick with the name?"

"Hmm." he considered. "Change the spelling. S-p-e-e-d-y-s. Because they'll go fast! There's your promotional angle, 'Come and get 'em *now,* cause they go *fast!*'" He smiled, winking to her while he spread his hands forming the imaginary sign.

"Hey! Great idea Joey! Yer so smart. Don't stay away so long. And you, hun..." Frankie addressed Emma, "...never got yer name, but I hope I see you again soon. You've got a good friend in Joey here! He's a great guy."

"Thank you Frankie. You can call me 'Em', and I believe you're right."

"Okay! Take care you two."

"Be seeing you." said Drake.

They walked for about five minutes before he began his narrative.

"At precisely 14:00 June third 1968, I was approached for an assignment by my superior, a man named Hobbs. My mission was to impersonate a person. Oh, I'd impersonated people before. That wasn't a problem. But...you mentioned the word doppelganger. Well it appeared I had one. He was said to be my 'spitting image'. Now, normally the scenario would be to secure this person being impersonated. He is put away, I go in, do whatever I need to, and get out. At that point the unfortunate is released and usually finds himself in some sort of trouble. With me so far?"

"Mm." she nodded.

"So, I asked, 'What is it we're after? What has this man done?', that sort of thing. I was told my double was being held in a protective facility. Hobbs specifically said, 'A facility, The Village'. Those were his precise words!

"This 'doppelganger' of mine was being questioned regarding his loyalty as he was a possible turncoat. He was extremely important and had information in his head that could be very dangerous to us. Very helpful to our enemies. I asked what type of information. Hobbs refused to say.

"Well, how was I supposed to impersonate him without some idea about what information he was alleged to have?"

"You'd have been flying blind." she interjected.

"Precisely."

Emma smirked, "I was my own impersonator once you know. So was Steed. Twice, in fact, that I'm aware of."

Drake stopped and stared at her for a moment. Frowned, but decided to proceed.

"I'd have been flying blind. Now, not only was this man my double, but we shared a number of talents and interests.

Boxing, shooting, fencing, a number of shared skills and hobbies. I was essentially being tasked to 'fully immerse' myself into this man's identity. Become him for a time.

"Not unheard of, I suppose, but again, with no background or understanding about what it was he was being held *for*, other than possible 'disloyalty', how would I be able to be remotely successful in this mission?

"And here is where the penny drops. I was to confront this man, face to face, and do my best to convince him that I *was* him! Convince him that *he* was an imposter, an inferior replica of himself! He would then crack, doubting his own sanity and identity, and would give us...the information '*we*' were after."

"What on earth...?" Emma asked utterly confused.

"Quite!"

"What evidence did they have to suggest his loyalty was at question?" she queried, trying to wrap her head around the plot.

He turned away, walked a few steps, and stopped, his shoulders sagging from an unseen weight. "He had...*resigned*...his position."

"And...?"

"That...was *all*." he snapped. "They had...nothing more."

"They had to have *some* sort of..."

"'*They*' had *nothing*!" he fumed. "He'd resigned, that was enough for them. I was to go on this ludicrously complex mission, never questioning 'their' reasons. But they *had* no reasons that I could discern."

"How odd! Devious. Diabolically so!"

"Yes. I kept probing for more details. I'd *have* to have more on this man than what Hobbs was telling me. I'd need to know more to do the job right. Hobbs clearly acted as though I was sticking my nose where it didn't belong!"

At that point, the words poured out of Drake, as if a great dam had just been blown loose. "I told Hobbs I'd have to think about this one. I told him I felt strongly the plan would fail, and, regardless, it would take at *least* a full month to even *try* to prepare for such a charade. I did *not*, however, mention how *monstrous* I thought the very *idea* to be. How detestable. And yet, my 'superior' Hobbs felt it not only workable, but entirely appropriate! What's worse was someone, or a host of someones, levels above him, thought likewise.

"I felt like I'd followed Alice down the rabbit hole! I was tempted to resign right then and there! An 'alarm' went off in my mind and informed me that *that* was the *last* thing I should do."

"I agree! Something insidious was afoot certainly." Emma affirmed.

"That thought was firmly in my mind, yes. For all I might have known, they could have done the same to me! Whisked me away to this 'Village' for being 'insubordinate' or who knows what!

"I told Hobbs I would need time to mull the whole plan over, and that I'd talk to him the next afternoon. I could see he wasn't pleased with me, but he said nothing.

"Immediately afterwards, I cautiously started an investigation of my own. A few general enquiries through various connections I had made over the years, relationships I had nurtured, to find out this man's identity; his name, his position, what he did, *anything! Any* piece of data I could get my hands on before I went back to Hobbs about it.

"That evening and night, within a matter of *hours,* my sources began drying up. Avenues of investigation were being systematically closed off. Telephone calls were not being answered. Two contacts who lived close, two men whom I'd never before had difficulty reaching were now unreachable. Unavailable!

"Working alongside Steed as you have, you're aware we often use informers outside the system. I found that even these people were shutting me out! I'd never run across anything like it. I suspected where it was all stemming from! I'm certain Hobbs was, still *is*, involved in some way. I've never trusted him, and for good reason.

"I believe as I didn't immediately accept the assignment, he grew suspicious of me. He may well have had surveillance ready to dog my every step the moment I left his office.

"In any event, from the few dwindling sources I *was* able to grab, I was able to piece together this much:

"One: this was a man of high importance, though not high ranking. Not military, most likely *not* part of our Intelligence communities or networks. Possibly even a private citizen, though that prospect put the entire mission in an even *more* hellish light.

"Two: the phrases 'The Village', 'Project Six', and 'Number Six' popped up. Well, 'The Village' was a term Hobbs had used himself. As far as the others, they could have been a project this chap was connected with or something along those lines. They could be referring to the man himself. Or none of those.

"And Three..." Drake motioned to a fallen tree in a small wooded area. They found it large and comfortable enough to sit on side by side.

"Years before, I had had an assignment behind the Iron Curtain. I was under cover as a defector, and where I found myself was in a little perfectly British village. That is, a Russian village mocked up to look like a British village, where communist spies were being trained on how to act 'British', taught by British defectors who were there as teachers. These spies could then infiltrate our society flawlessly. It was a pretty fascinating set up. I did my bit to upset the flow of agents, both to and from. We named this place 'Colony Three'."

"Mmm, I'd heard Steed tell about it." Emma related. "One of my first 'outings' with him was uncovering a cadre of enemy agents who had taken over Little Bazeley by the Sea, a village in Norfolk, right on our very doorstep."

"Ahh, yes. Quite so. I recall reading that report. Your 'outing' caused quite a stir. Put us all on high alert for a while.

"A 'Village'. Yes, point number three; a place called 'The Village'. Wherever that is, that is where they are holding this man.

"What concerned me, haunted me, was that this 'Village' concept was...*my* idea."

Emma sat, dazed. Drake looked at an empty piece of tin foil he had absent-mindedly been playing with, twirling it about. He realized she had eaten both of the spiedies they had taken with them. He felt a twinge of disappointment, but it quickly passed.

"Not specific to this man mind you, but rather, suggested in my report regarding Colony Three. You see, I had suggested, as an effort to quell the exodus of our British defectors to Colony Three, or places like it, that we could create a 'safe town', or 'village', whereby we could 'hold' agents who may be exhibiting a 'weakening of resolve', or who may be merely wearing down.

"A place where one might be able to relax, go fishing, what have you. A 'holiday camp' of sorts, where one is actually under guard, though not obviously so. A place where in a relaxed atmosphere, we might 'coax' rather than interrogate."

He looked at Emma and found comfort in the fact that she looked a bit more confused about the matter, than disgusted.

"Oh," he hastily insisted, "it's not at all Orwellian as it may sound at first blush. My focus had to do with my perception that we were working our people too hard. Gradually grinding down people we should be nurturing and helping in a *very* nasty environment. The agents we were counting on to hold top secret information vital to our liberties and way of life were quite often being thought of as machines, or cogs in a machine, treated horribly. Used up and spat out! I'd witnessed good men and women turn sides by just adding a few hundred pounds to their bank accounts!

"As many of us had military backgrounds, we were all being treated as though we were still in the military. 'Shut up and follow orders' and that sort of rubbish. Problem being Intelligence work is vastly different, as you know. You're dealing with people, getting involved in their lives. Making enemies friends for a time and then betraying them. Being betrayed by friends you thought you knew. A *very* different game than merely storming the ramparts and shooting, wouldn't you agree?"

"Mm." she acknowledged.

"My thinking at that time was, if, say, agent Dickie Smith began showing signs of carelessness, recklessness, growing discontent or what have you, we might have a way to get him to a place where he could be cared for, or retrained, hopefully rejuvenated and ready to go back to work. Rehabilitated.

"Give him a place where he could go have a 'night on the town' and not have to be so concerned he might let something slip to an enemy agent in a local pub. Possibly go to a spa, or seek psychiatric care without being drummed out of service for it. Meanwhile, he would be secured and not represent a danger to other agents or missions. My concept was suggested with an eye toward possibly salvaging a career, rather than destroying one.

"We were seeing a great number of defections back then. And we indeed *did* have lodges and camps and that type of thing for agents, both during and after the war. Probably the most whispered about being Inverlair Lodge in Scotland. Quite an open secret! Retired agents who had information about ongoing missions were sent there and held until that information was no longer dangerous. Not as prisoners, necessarily, more as wards of the State. They were well treated and cared for. All this was just a concept, really. This was my thinking as I wrote my suggested course of action."

"A road to Hell paved by good intention. A prison is a prison, whether the warder brings treats and smiles at you or no." Emma's disapproval was clear, yet had understanding attached, more reasoning than judgment in her position.

"Ahh, the John Drake of six years ago was more...idealistic than...Joey Wolf of today." he sighed heavily, hunching forward laying his hands on his knees. "This poor bastard had simply resigned his position, and he had been abducted by *our side*! Our *own people* did this! And I'm *horrified* to think a suggested course of action made in a report by an idealistic imbecile six years ago might have played a part in it!" he pronounced, slamming the tree trunk with his fist.

Emma reached over, placing her hand on top of his closed fist, which was bleeding at the knuckles. "When every person in our world becomes just as I am" she gently joked, "'practically perfect in every way', we won't have all these ethical quandaries troubling us."

He raised his head to look at her face, seeing her tongue firmly in her cheek. He relinquished a smile, and her hand still atop his, he unclenched his fist, laying his palm on the tree trunk. "Till then, we'll always have this 'jolly holiday' to remember?" he teased back with a wink.

Shortly, she withdrew her hand from atop his and wiped his blood from her hand onto her slacks. "What did you do then?"

"It was early morning. I thought I'd chance a visit to a retired colleague of mine, my old superior during my time with NATO, Hardy. We hadn't always got along, but I trusted him. He wouldn't always tell me what I wanted to hear, but he wouldn't dance about the truth. He'd let me have it. Like it or not. And we would 'cross swords', believe you me! Still and all, he had experience and intelligence. He knew how to guide we young 'firebrands'.

"With that in mind, I went to his home hoping he could shed a little light, or perhaps advise me. He wouldn't see me. His wife answered the door. Wouldn't let me in, closed it on me. I was about to leave when I heard Hardy himself calling to me faintly behind his door. He said, I gather as loudly as he felt was safe, 'I can't talk to you now. You need to run.' I asked him if he was alright. He said, 'Yes, but you're not! Run, John. Run like hell, now!'"

Emma felt chills shoot up and down her spine.

"Hardy was gotten to. So scared he wouldn't even let me into his home. That terrified me. Hardy had *real* connections. No small thing to get to him like that. Whatever was happening, it was big, happening quickly, and I was alone. Hardy gave me all the light and advice I needed. I ran like blazes."

After some moments of silence, they stood from their fallen tree perch, and started their return to his car. "So, back on the beach, you were afraid I was still 'active' and that 'we' had found you." she confirmed.

"I was." he admitted.

"I'm not, and 'they' haven't."

"I know, and I hope not."

"There's only one way to stop them from finally finding you, John."

"John Drake is dead. Long live Joey Wolf."

She laughed. A deep and delightfully resonant laugh which he found amazingly attractive. "You're not fooling me! Mr. 'Wolf', anagram of fowl. An undomesticated 'Drake'?" Emma stopped, grabbed him by the upper arms and looked him square in the eyes, drilling into him once again.

"You *are* John Drake. You have a reputation, and a strong moral compass. As do I. I presently have standing and connections. We've been forces for good, and for what's *right*. We still may be able to do what is *right* for this man who may or may not be this 'Project Six'. If not, we can try to make certain there'll be no 'Project Seven'. 'They' will *not* 'find' you, you and I will find and confront *them!*"

John Drake looked at her, the decision he began making at the table on the porch at Frankie's Joint now made in full.

He *would* go back and hopefully *fix* this. An unexpected bonus being that this amazing woman would be at his side. "Very well, Mrs. Peel. It appears we're needed."

Hi(s)story is prologue 4

"Why did you *resign*?"

"No!!" he screamed suddenly (seemingly?) awakened, in a large round room, secured in a chair, electrodes attached to his head and arms.

"Why? Why resign?"

Not again! How many times would they force him to relive this? Why replay this? God *damn* them! He had *won*! Why was he back here? *How* was he back here?

The surrounding walls displayed a panorama of grotesques. Flashes of phantoms, snippets of a very vivid unreality. The pure *stench* of the man screaming that question repeatedly, over and over and over again, spit landing on his face. Images of ROVER (on a horse? What in *hell*??), a woman on a roller coaster, a lighthouse by the sea...

He's standing by the sea now. He must be, see? Sea that is not a sea, I see, I don't see, be seeing you...

And now, machine gun fire? Faint, but... there! Again! Hands clutching at him. Scratching him. Another woman laughing at him. One slapping him, three wavy lines...lights flashing and sounds circling him at a frenzied pace.

Vote for me. I am in control. Sleep now. Obey me! Sleep...

Die! Die! Die! Again, more machine gun fire. Under attack? *Why?*

"They lack your initiative." *Die! Die! Die!* I! I! I! I-I-I! I-I-I! IwillnotbepushedfiledstampedindexedbriefeddebriefedornumberedI willnotbepushedfiledstampedindexe*"NNooooooooooo!!!!!!!!!"* he shrieked.

4
Cordelia's Beach House; Santa Monica, CA

The ride back to Emma's friend Cordelia's beach house was silent, as the ride to Frankie's had been. As they entered, Drake immediately took what appeared to be a transistor radio out of a shoulder pack he was carrying. He inserted an earpiece into it, the other end in his ear. Raising a finger to his lips, he methodically searched each room. The phone, windows, door frames, lamps and appliances were all searched, then the back veranda. He nodded saying, "All clear."

"Is your wagon bugged?"

"No, but it wouldn't be a difficult matter to aim a directional mic at the car. I've done that myself a time or two. Marvellous technology being invented these days, and I'm over a year behind in my...familiarity with most of it. Fact is I'm a bit uneasy feeling free to talk even at this moment."

"Ah, I can see why. Hmm, 19:40. That would make it, what? In London?"

"Eight hours ahead. It's the middle of night now. 03:40."

"So, we get some sleep, and afterwards I'll ring Cord."

"My caravan is only a thirty minute drive. I'll..."

"You'll not! You are safe here. This wonderfully long divan will serve."

"You think I'll run." he stated. It wasn't a question.

She walked up to him, put her hand to his cheek and, once again, drilled him to the spot with her eyes. "If you had truly wanted to, I would never have been able to stop you. I've faith you won't now." She turned, crossed the room, jogged up a short flight of stairs, and returned moments later with bedding and a pillow. "It's the divan for you." she decreed, taking a seat in the chair next to it.

"Your friend wouldn't object to you entertaining a male guest overnight in her beach house?" he asked, with sudden levity and mock prudishness.

"I would not be at all shocked if my friend Cord didn't have that prospect firmly in mind when first she made me the offer." she smirked ('Take *that* Mr. Drake!' she thought).

He blushed but continued the game. "Ah, an...emancipated woman I gather!"

"Within reason and good sense."

"Well good for you! Fear not, dear lady. I am no gadabout."

"*That* became readily apparent when first we worked together years ago."

He had little choice than to smile, and to capitulate.

"So, what's it to be tomorrow then?" he asked, turning serious to the task before them.

"I'll ring Cord in morning. She'll need to get a message to Steed. It may take a few days for him to respond. He'll need to be told of our return, and of our complete need for secrecy."

"I'm not fond of the idea of contacting him." he stated firmly.

"We'll need to. If I know Steed, he's had me "looked after" since Peter took ill. Likely more so since his death."

"Could he be 'looking after you' now?" he asked, somewhat alarmed at *that* prospect.

"I sincerely doubt it. He may be aware I'm here in the States by this point, though not where, precisely. At any rate, we will need to have him pull all surveillance from *me* personally. He may also be able to reduce surveillance at Heathrow at the time of our flight's arrival."

"No, absolutely not. We cannot ask that of him. With the IRA bombings in London still fresh, especially now as our...esteemed Prime Minister Williams sent British troops into Northern Ireland last week, the airports along with rail and bus terminals will be on raised alert. As well they should be."

"Mm, well, my thought was there may still be people searching for *you*, specifically. Your long hair, beard and moustache puts paid to most of that concern I should think. Sunglasses are a must for those eyes of yours, though."

"Sometimes the best way to avoid detection is to invite it. I'll wear a head bandage which covers one eye, a hat, and sunglasses. Crutches and a foot cast to accent the bandaging, and a belly belt adding fifteen or so pounds ought to suffice. A bit obvious perhaps, nonetheless you'd be surprised how often that has worked.

"I've confidence in Joseph Wolf's passport passing close inspection. However, if I might touch on another concern; no matter how...quietly your current marital state has been kept; being the male travelling companion of the recently widowed Mrs. Peter Peel might spark more interest in who I might be than any other item I can think of. We'll need to reckon how we might travel together separately. As regards meeting Steed, for my safety and possibly even his, he is not to know who I am until we are face to face, and, hopefully, free from monitoring."

"Precisely. Agreed. Resolutely. Without doubt and amen! And, if you are as weary as I am right now, yet able to consider all that, it will be a kick to watch you scheme when you're wide awake and fully alert!" she kidded.

He blushed. "Er...I'm obliged. Ehh, by the way, which branch is Steed with presently? Still in Mother's house?"

Emma smiled at both Drake's blush and his question.

"Do you know, I'm not certain! Steed and I were very autonomous during our partnership. I rarely ever had to deal with any bureaucracy. I've never had much patience for it. I was never actually sure which 'branch' we were attached to. He was considered my superior, and that seemed enough for them. He would occasionally just happen to mention I had this or that level clearance. Not that any of that ever mattered to me. I usually got what I was after, be it information, tape, weapon, file, villain or what have you."

"Remarkable! I'm thankful you're on our side or, at least, *my* side. However did you achieve that kind of 'Carte Blanche'?"

"I'd wager being my father's daughter had a lot to do with it. Being President and Chair of one of England's largest and most powerful corporations likely offered me a little leverage."

"Ahh, now your being facetious."

"Am I? Hmmm...well, in any case, what I truly believe accounts, was a Russian file on Steed and I. I'd been able to peruse it while sneaking about a Russian embassy during a case. It contained stamped photos of Steed and I. His read 'Dangerous, handle with care', while mine read, 'Very Dangerous, do not handle at all'. I imagine the Poohbahs read the file and *believed it!*"

Slowly, a wave of laughter overtook them. They laughed until their sides ached.

Finally, she stood and stretched. "It's been a full day. I'm for bed."

"Mrs. Pe...aihhm, Emma..." he stammered as he stood, testing his footing calling her by her first name. "Emma, thank you. Talking with you, listening to you, I'm...'centred' again. Focused. Reenergized, though tired at this moment. I'm..."

"Obliged?"

"Ha! Yes. That. And, a good deal more."

She admitted, "Talking to you, hearing myself out loud...I must apologize to Steed. I was angry with Peter for dying. Angry with him for leaving me to mourn *again*! Poor Steed just got in the way of that anger. I'm obliged to you as well."

"Well, if he is half the gentleman I think, half the trusted friend you think, he knew all of that already."

"All the more reason."

John Drake and Emma Peel found themselves standing closely, facing each other, holding each other's hands and grateful one for the other.

"Good Lord!" he exclaimed.

"What?"

"I hadn't noticed before, but you are an unusually tall woman!"

Emma gave Drake a light fisted but solid thump to the chest. "Good night!" she said, grinning.

Hi(s)story is prologue 5

Voices swirling in the madness. Where was he now?

"Hey, get the medic over here. This one's in rough shape!"

"Well then how very uncomfortable for you old chap!"

"Well bloody hell, who's *not?*"

"Yeah but he's alive!"

"...already dead. Locked up... in a long box"

"So's this one!"

"Christ what a mess!"

"Look, we knew it would be a mess goin' in. We're doin' the best we can."

But he had won. They called him 'Sir'!

"What the hell was that 'globe' thing? That 'balloon' thing?"

"Who cares? Thing's toast now. Just keep your eyes open for any others."

Iwillnotbepushedfiledstampedindexedbriefeddebriefedornumberedmylifeismyownlwillnotbepushedfiledstampedindexedbriefeddebriefedornumbered...

"Can SOMEbody *please* turn that God damn thing off, or I swear ta *God*, I'll blow it up myself!!!"

"Obey me now and be free."

"Cor! Lieutenant!! It's him awright!"

Iwillnotbepushedfiledstampedindexedbriefeddebriefedornumberedmylife...

Who are these people? What's all this smoke? Where...Being grabbed again...

"Ives! Ives?"

Who? Who...

"Who is Number One?"

5

London; late summer, 1969

Cordelia Winfield-Mannering had only been awake a mere ten minutes when her phone rang. "Ugh!" she uttered. She looked at her clock again. 08:41. "Hey ho." she sighed, accepting the inevitable fact that her day would have had to start at *some* point. Might as well be now. Could be John at any rate, probably to remind her that his flight would be coming in at 13:30. She lifted the receiver.

"Hello?"

"A bright and wonderful 'Good Morning', Cord! Rise and shine! It's a beautiful day!"

She held the receiver in front of her, staring at it. She peered out her bedroom window. Yep! Rain. "Bollocks, Em. It's pouring buckets! And how in hell would you know?" She heard Emma's laugh. A rich laugh that could brighten the worst weather. "It's good to hear you laugh, Em."

"Cord, you've no idea what a tonic this has been for me. You were spot on."

Cordelia grinned from ear to ear. "I'm *so* glad to hear, Em. Truly!"

It was the sudden change in Emma's tone of voice that really impacted her. "I need to further impose on you. This is important. I need to ask you, is your line secure?"

She knew exactly what Emma was asking, but it concerned her.

"Em? Call me back in ninety minutes, alright?"

"Yes. Thank you. Talk with you soon."

There had been two different successful attempts to bug the telephone in John Mannering's London shop. He frequently had dealings with the government, most of them along with head of diplomatic intelligence, John Alexander Templeton-Green, a liaison, and, ultimately, a trusted friend. Mannering had, in no uncertain terms, told Templeton-Green (or 'Temp', as she, John, their associate David Marlowe, and nearly everyone else called him), that there would be 'Holy Hell to pay' should he find a third. So, Temp had equipped them with bug tracking devices (periodically updated and improved) so they could protect themselves against further attempts.

She clicked the switch hooks twice, then called David Marlowe.

"Rise and shine sleepy head. I'm home, and need a favour. I need you to come over with some pest spray. Right, yes. Wonderful. See you soon."

John Mannering had often chided her saying, "Cordelia, curiosity killed the cat, you know. You have enough curiosity to kill a truck load of cats."

She could not recall a time when her curiosity had ever been as elevated as Emma's phone call had just made her. She looked at the clock. 08:52. The next ninety minutes would take an eternity!

6

Mannering's Antiques, London

Mannering Antiques associate David Marlowe had done a thorough search for any illicit listening/recording devices, or 'bugs', in the Mannering London home and happily found none. He then went to the Antique shop to man business hours as Cordelia Winfield-Mannering would need to be free to collect her husband John at Heathrow airport at 1:30 that afternoon.

Cordelia was sitting directly by the phone when it rang at 10:00. She snatched up the receiver on the first mid-ring. "Hello?"

Emma Peel's laughter was rich and infectious. "Ahh, dear Cord." she happily sighed, "I'm glad I didn't keep you anxious!"

"Right, right, right. So, er, what's up, Em? We're bug free, just had it checked in fact."

Emma was relieved. It didn't strike her as unusual that Cordelia would know how to deal with bugged phones, as they'd been long time friends, and had a number of opportunities to meet and share stories of 'exploits in espionage' with their 'two Johns', Steed and Mannering.

She cut to the chase. "I need you to contact Steed for me, in a very specific manner. Hopefully I'll be able to tell all later, but for now, I must remain 'mysterious'"

"Alright Em. Trust me. Though, making me wait for an explanation is damn cruel you old *hag*!"

"It'd take a full dinner and drinks afterward to explain it all, ya' little *tart*!" Emma retorted lovingly. "Cord, I'm truly in your debt for the kindness you've shown me. Both you and your husband."

Cordelia was a bit awed. Emma had always been *so* sharp! "How did you ever...?"

"Framed photos luv! Plus, a distinct lack of a woman's touch in the décor of this marvellous beach house, which isn't in 'your style' at *all*. *But* yer gaining on him!"

"Clever girl! Alright, now tell me what you need me to tell Steed."

John Steed was at his apartment home when she called.

"Mister Steed, Cordelia Winfield here at Mannering Antiques; I've both bad and good news regarding the figurine you brought us for possible repair. Would it be possible for you to pop in sometime this afternoon?"

He looked at his watch. "Miss Winfield, wonderful of you to call about it so quickly. Might I visit you within the hour? I'm afraid my afternoon is spoken for. Say thirty minutes?"

"Thirty minutes?" she replied, "Yes, that'd be fine Mr. Steed, we'll be seeing you soon."

"Splendid. Cheers."

Thirty minutes later, he was standing with Cordelia in the showroom of Mannering Antiques when owner John Mannering entered. The tall red-headed Mannering stopped, closing the door behind him. He furrowed his brow at Steed's back, then his eyes opened wide as he began to grin. "Major Steed!"

Steed turned about and met Mannering's expression with a grin of his own. "Ahh...Captain Mannering!" The two men warmly shook hands.

"Wait! Don't tell me!" Mannering held up one arm, palm outwards. "You've finally come to your senses and have decided to sell me those Trafalgar miniatures of yours!"

Steed leaned back scowling, taking full mock offense at the very temerity of the suggestion. "My *word!*" he exclaimed, turning his head toward Cordelia, "The unmitigated *cheek* of the man! And offering pence for pound worth I'd wager! Tisk tisk!"

"Okay, okay" Mannering mock surrendered, "a pound per piece! My final offer!" he haggled, as if that were the deal of the century.

"Mmmm" Steed struck a pose as if he were in deep contemplation of the offer. Then he sneaked another look at Cordelia, saying in a stage whisper, "He *does* drive a hard bargain!"

"Yep! No sense in delaying the inevitable." Mannering kidded, as they enjoyed a good laugh together. "What brings you in? What can we do for you?"

"I'm here to speak with your lovely associate regarding a piece belonging to a dear friend."

"By all means. I've a bit of business to attend to, so if you'll forgive me, I'll leave you in her very capable hands. Great seeing you, John."

"Delighted, John." he warmly shook Mannering's hand once again. "Wonderful to see you as well. Do let's try to get together sometime soon and catch up, shall we?"

"Yes indeed. So long." said Mannering, turning and entering his personal office.

She escorted Steed to her office just off from the showroom and closed the door. He sat at the chair in front of her desk.

She began abruptly, quietly, and very seriously. "I've taken liberty of making certain there are no bugging devices in here Mr. Steed. Nevertheless I cannot guarantee the same for our phones for the time being. It is vitally important ours are the only ears hearing this.

"Emma called me this morning. She's been staying in the United States in a home I own. She wants you to call her at this number," she instructed, handing him a slip of paper, "as soon as possible, on a telephone you are absolutely certain hasn't been tapped.

"Emma has explicitly told me to relay this information to you alone. No one else is to know. She wants me to assure you she is in no danger, 'as yet'. She says she's somehow stumbled on a situation with incredibly serious implications for British Intelligence.

"She told me to tell you, word for word; 'Recall both Bazeley by the Sea, and the mine beneath the chapel of the Duke of Benedict. Recall those situations, and what they might have become had they remained unchecked. Now, magnify them, possibly a hundred-fold, and consider the implications'." She paused to let him mentally 'digest' what he was being told.

She knew Steed peripherally at best. In person, he was always a charming, gregarious gentleman, unflappable, without a concern in the world, with all the confidence in the world.

The expression on his face unsettled her. He now showed nothing *but* grave concern, and she got a strong impression that there would be hell to pay for that. She gulped involuntarily and concluded Emma's message.

"Mr. Steed, Emma is with a friend. She said their very lives could depend on her trust in you, and in your discretion. As implausible as it sounds, she swears it is true."

He sat nonplussed. This was the *last* situation he could have conceived hearing about here in an antique shop! "My word!" was all he could think to utter.

She concluded, "I should be able to have our phones here double checked for devices within a day or two, if that will help. My home phone would be available, but John and I won't be there till very early this morning, and..."

"Oh, think nothing of it!" Steed interrupted. "I'm certain I can find one, and from the sounds of it, the sooner the better." After a brief moment, he stood, put on his bowler, and extended his hand. "Thank you, Miss Winfield. Thank you for being a *good* friend to Mrs. Peel. I will call her as soon as I can, with all the security I can. And thank you as well for your discretion in this matter."

"My discretion in what matter, Mr. Steed?" asked Cordelia, without a trace of humour.

Steed let a smile creep in. "That's the girl."

Hi(s)story is prologue 6

There was no way to tell if he could hear them. He assuredly wasn't making any attempt to contact *them*. But the voices *were* there.

"So, what's the story here?" asked a white-haired man.

"Not good, but not hopeless. There's activity in there. He's a fighter. The next 72 hours will tell the tale."

"Alright. That's good then, at least for now. The chopper's set. How long you need? Within reason?"

"We'll be set in ten minutes."

"Great. Well done gentlemen."

The white-haired man stood in the middle of a cavernous room, looking around and up at the ceiling. Another came running up to him.

"Okay Lieutenant, we're set."

"Good." He acknowledged, looking at his wristwatch.

"Almost a shame. Some of the buildings here are..."

"Rebuildable." the white-haired man interrupted, as he unclipped a walky-talky from his belt, raised the antenna, and hit the send button. "Mister K!" he barked.

A blast of static burst through, then a voice. "Yes?"

"Status?"

"I believe we've recovered about half. A little less."

"That'll have to do. How long?"

"Out in fifteen, maximum."

"Great. Good job. Out." Another click on the send button. "Stirling?"

"Yeah."

"Thirty minutes. Last chance for abort in 25. Clear?"

"Clear, Mac"

"Thirty minutes. Then take it down. Take it all."

End of prologue

7
A Very Dangerous Game

'Mrs. Peel, what on *earth* have you gotten yourself involved in?' was the question Steed found himself repeating, his apprehension growing with every sentence Miss Winfield uttered. He took time to sit in his Bentley and ruminate.

Who was this 'friend' she was with in America? A whole village taken over by enemy agents? A 'hundred-fold'? Villages? What had that to do with British Intelligence? Are they involved?

Well obviously. Why else Emma's need for complete secrecy on British phone lines? The extraordinary measure Miss Winfield had gone to "clear" her office, was Mannering aware? Why wouldn't he be? But then, if he was, he would've said so. He would have been in the office *with* them. Thus, apparently, Cordelia was keeping all of this to herself at the moment.

It all seemed so *incredible*, and yet, one thing he and his partners were constantly being made aware of was that the implausible, the highly improbable, indeed the impossible, occurred constantly in their world. For the love of Mike, hadn't human beings walked *on the moon* only a month or so ago? Hadn't he himself actually been in a rocket, for pity's sake?

No, Emma was no paranoid crackpot. She was on to something, something potentially huge. That simply was a fact. If she said no one but him must know for now, that is the way it would be.

Any other rumination on what she was suggesting would have to wait until he talked with her. Now how to do that? And how to do that as quickly as possible?

Given, there would be wiretapping on his personal phone. Steed's primary partner ever since Emma Peel had left to be reunited with husband was a young, beautiful, and uniquely gifted agent, one Miss Tara King. As Tara was attached to Steed in service, her phone would come under the same scrutiny as his. It was simply the nature of the special agent's game. What's more, any attempt at debugging his or Tara's phone would be immediately noticed, and that would raise suspicion.

Likewise any telephone at Department HQ, or at One-Ten's branch, or in any office or branch where Steed had previously done 'business'.

There would likely be taps on any government phones thanks to idiots like Ex-Secretary of State for War John Profumo, and the *so* many who came afterward with this scandal or that. Everyone had gotten used to the idea that *someone* was going to be listening in on someone *else* SOMEwhere! One would've thought a good idea might be to actually conduct affairs as ethically and as honestly as possible, yet government and Intelligence never seemed to catch on!

Well, let's face it, Intelligence and Espionage has always been a game of which lie gets believed first. Who can overhear what, and make use of the information. Or sell it.

No, phones he would normally use without ever thinking twice were out of the question. That left, what? Public phone use? Impractical and costly. Plus, one never knew which of those could be bugged as well. The world was *mad* with spying!

So a private phone would be the best alternative that he could see. It's now a matter of whose. Who did he know who might not be under surveillance?

Men on the moon...love of Mike...Mike...*of course!* There wouldn't be blanket surveillance on agent trainees! Most of them would be drummed out eventually, so there wouldn't be a need. Plus it probably allowed a nameless penny-pincher in accounting a good night's sleep knowing he'd shaved off the cost! Agent trainee Michael Gambit!! He was the ticket!

Of the trainees he had appraised in the last year or so, Mike Gambit had very much impressed him. As intelligence agents so often had military backgrounds, his military record alone was impressive. So, he had more than solid pedigree.

He was quick, ruthless, and sharp, eager and ready to learn. More importantly (at least, in Steed's view), he was ready to unlearn and relearn. He was 'un-locked' as it were. Open to change plans at a second's notice, or no notice at all.

Ready to be ready! That was a quality very few people in general had. Even in his partners! Cathy Gale had that to a large degree; Tara struggled to learn it and wasn't doing too badly at it. Emma had it in surplus and was never afraid to ride with it.

He started the Bentley. He would go about his new 'normal' business of the day. No sense brushing things aside or cancelling appointments for now, matters were too 'delicate' as they were. Making this call to Mrs. Peel was the first very sensitive and important move in what looked to be a *very* dangerous game!

8

Steed's Gambit

Several hours later, Steed parked his Bentley in front of an apartment building in Harrow. He walked in, up a flight of stairs, and stopped first door on the right. Blues music could clearly be heard, though not as loudly as a lot of young people often had it. He smiled; the young man who lived here had a better sense of propriety than most. He rapped on the door using the handle of his brolly.

A young man with longish brown hair answered. "Yes?"

"Hello!" Steed began cheerfully. "Is this the apartment of Mr. Michael Gambit?"

"Yuh, 'Oo'er you?" the young man asked, simply being diligent, not suspicious or antagonistic.

"I'm a friend from work."

Right, 'ang on." The young man closed the door half way.

"Mike? S'fer you." The music was a tad louder with the door open, and Steed couldn't make out a reply, but he knew it was Gambit's voice.

"Wot? Oh. Right. 'ang on." The young man opened the door full again, "Just a tic, e's in the loo." The door closed halfway once again.

Steed grinned. He'd always found it fascinating how the average person could usually be counted on to, unbidden; unthinkingly provide much more information than was absolutely necessary!

"Yes?" The door fully opened again, and a tall, slim yet muscular man in his late twenties with dark curly hair stood bare-chested and bare-foot in the doorway.

His eyes blinked thrice before he next spoke. "M-Major...Steed?"

"Gambit, hello!" he greeted cheerfully. "I do hope I'm not interrupting you. Might I come in?"

Gambit stood stock still. "Of course! I mean, of course not. I mean, you're not interrupting...Yes! Please, come in!" He then remembered that he was standing in the doorway. He moved aside, stood at attention, and sweeping his arm, bid Steed entry.

Steed had thought about the ways he might address him. Not a good habit to be informal on the clock and all that. Nevertheless he *did* feel a certain closeness to the young agent trainee. He decided, 'It'll be 'Gambit' for the agent, colleague and subordinate. It'll be 'Mike' for the friend and the man'.

Gambit turned and addressed the young man who had first answered the door, who was seated by the stereo reading a magazine. "It's Major Steed, Bob! From the Department!"

"Cheers." Bob absentmindedly saluted with his beer bottle, never once glancing up from his magazine.

"Can I...get you a drink, Major?" Gambit enquired, moving some books and newspapers from a chair. "Would you like a seat? Sir? What in the f...I mean, excuse me, what brings you here Major?"

"Mike, Mike, at ease! I'm not here to make a pest of myself." he grinned, while simultaneously motioning for him to stand a bit closer. "Mike, I need to speak with you. Privately." He whispered as quietly as he could with the music still playing, his voice suddenly turning very serious.

Gambit looked about and motioned to a door which opened to the kitchen. "Hey Bob?" he called.

"Yeah?"

"Uhm, the Major and I need to talk."

"Awright." said Bob, obliviously granting permission, not lifting his eyes from his magazine.

They entered the kitchen. The door swung closed, Steed judged the music playing in the living area loud enough that Bob wouldn't be able to overhear them.

"Mike, I need a favour." he began without preamble. "I need to borrow your apartment and your telephone for the next few hours, alone. I'd like to tell you what this is about, but I'm not free at present, do you understand?"

Gambit looked directly in his eyes. Precisely two seconds later, he said, "No sir, but that is perfectly fine with me. Especially as it comes from you, I don't need to understand your request in order to grant it."

He was firm and sincere. He respected Steed immensely and would do anything for the man who had taught him so much so well. Gambit felt he'd become twice the agent he was only a year ago due to Steed's mentoring.

"Remarkable. I knew I could rely on you. I *will* compensate you the expense for the use of your phone, and it *will* be expensive." Steed reached in his pocket and pulled out some cash. "Here's a hundred pounds for your trouble. And another twenty. Go get your friend Bob and have a quaff or three on me, eh?"

"Not necessary sir, but I will accept your generous offer on behalf of my friend and myself." Gambit consented with a grin.

"Two more items Mike. No mention of my being here to anyone. No one is to know until I say so. And, I may well have a special assignment for you within a few weeks, possibly within a few days. I hope my time here will clarify the matter. Are you up for it?"

Gambit's nod was immediate. "I am, sir. And Major...?"

"Yes?"

"You could have given me orders to do this. The result would have been exactly the same. But you asked me. I appreciate and respect that very much, sir."

They walked back to the living area. Gambit walked over to where Bob was seated, turned off the music and deftly took the magazine out of Bob's hands. "We're going down to Nan's for a few, mate!"

Bob looked annoyed, then confused, but eventually comprehended. "Right, right." He got up and retrieved his jacket from the floor by the chair. Gambit finished getting dressed, and soon stood by him, jacket in hand.

Steed, Gambit, and Bob entered the hallway. Gambit feigned locking the apartment door, but left it unlocked.

"Will you join us, sir?" Gambit asked, perhaps a bit too loudly.

"No thank you Mike, busy day tomorrow. Early bird and all that! Nice to meet you, Bob!" "Yuh. Nice t'meet you, Captain Steel." Bob said as he walked down the stairs. Gambit shrugged apologetically, rolled his eyes upward, turned and followed Bob down the stairs and out the door.

Steed sat in the chair Bob vacated, the telephone directly in front of him. He checked his watch. Almost 19:00. 11:00 California time (no great deductive challenge to discern the number Cordelia had given him had a California exchange). He took out the slip of paper from his vest pocket and prepared to dial the number written on it.

'Change is the call of the decade', he thought. We've just had men walk on the moon! First move in a dangerous game.

"Very well, my dear Mrs. Peel. I am here, ready to be ready. No matter what."

Scotland

He stood at the cliff's edge, looking out across the sea.

He never would have imagined! Horrible. He really should have guessed.

All the signs had been there, honestly. But he'd never imagined...

And the hell of it was, if he'd been there, it wouldn't have made any difference at all! In fact, he would have likely been done in himself. He was in no condition to fight anything! He'd been in a horrid state, after what he'd just been through! After what *they* had just been through!

Not as though that was any excuse...

Yet, what earthly use would he have been?

Earthly! Ha!

How alien that seemed to him now. He felt horrible about it.

Likely he wouldn't have made a bit of difference. That stubborn man!

Still, he hadn't even tried!

He'd removed himself from it all. Escaped from it. So he thought...

Let the others continue, if they can. I've had it!

Blind fools! He *had* told them. Repeatedly.

What did he get for it?

'You'll keep your damn hands *out* of things' he'd been told. That's what he got!

"Well! Where are your hands *now*, you pompous sadistic psychotic bastard?" he raged! "You and your ilk!"

It made him sick to death.

Hadn't the affair with Zellaby taught them anything? Bloody hell! Hadn't his own at Winnderden Flats? And there'd even been solid reporting on *that* one too, until they got it quashed as well!

But too many people knew! Not that they'd ever *admit* it!

Oh no! Must *control everything!*' he raged at the sea.

'Delayed bomb explosions' indeed!

If they'd put one *iota* of effort in caring for the people involved rather than a herculean effort to cover up...

Poor Ives. The price he paid. *Was* paying.

Maybe it would all come out now. The truth.

John 8:32, 'Then you will know the truth, and the truth will set you free.' 'Fiat Justitia ruat Caelum.' Ha! At least that much Latin he remembered!

"Let justice be done though the heavens fall."

Ives. Good Lord. Well perhaps, just perhaps...it wasn't too late for him to be of some use. Some good! Perhaps he could serve truth once again. Help in bringing about justice.

He turned. walking away from the cliff's edge.

9

You Aren't in Any Trouble, Are You?

The phone at the beach house rang. Emma Peel and John Drake moved quickly from the veranda. After three rings, Emma answered, holding the receiver so they could both hear.

"Hello?"

No one on earth announced her name like Steed did. "Miss-sehzz Peee-ihhll!"

Emma started to cry, but she quickly took control. She allowed herself a feeling of joy, however short it could be.

"Steed! Dear *dear* Steed, thank you so very much for calling so quickly."

She steamed ahead. "I've much to say, and I'm afraid much of it will need to remain cryptic until we can meet. So please let me proceed as uninterrupted as you can, hey?"

"Certainly."

"We're on a secured line?"

"As secured as I possibly know how to assure it, Mrs. Peel."

"Wonderful."

"Mrs. Peel, two very quick questions if I may?"

"Go ahead"

"Are you well?"

"I am, Steed. Thank you."

"Two, are you and/or this friend Cordelia mentioned in danger?"

"Neither of us, that we're aware of, nor should we be as long as no one is listening in on us. If someone were, I expect my friend would be in some sort of danger before I would be. At least, that's how we have it sorted out."

"The danger to your friend, life threatening?"

"Unknown. Quite possibly."

"I see..."

"One more preamble. I am so *very* sorry for the way I treated you. I hope to explain more about that at..."

"Mrs. Peel, there will never be a need for it. All is forgiven. Fact is, never was there a charge drawn up."

Drake mouthed the words, "I told you so" and smiled.

"You are a very kind and understanding man Steed."

"Please don't let that get around Mrs. Peel."

Emma gave Steed the gist of Drake's story, without specifics save two.

She mentioned The Village, referencing Inverlair Lodge as explanation of what The Village's function might be, and 'Project' or 'Number Six'. She gave him a sketch of the plan to come back to London, the scheme to plan a rescue if it wasn't too late, and then to plan how they might manage any fall out stemming from their actions.

"Mrs. Peel, my one objection has to do with your safety. I know you can well take care of yourself, I will assume your friend can as well. Yet you and I have had to rescue each other far too many times to rely on self-sufficiency."

Drake tensed at this and looked at her. He went to retrieve paper and pencil and sat back down.

Steed continued, "If there is a bad strain or strains in British Intelligence, which seems quite likely given what you've just told me, the shadows will have shadows. Even fighting back to back, you'll never be able to turn about quickly enough. You'll want watchmen to watch watchmen as it were. I don't believe we should proceed on assumption that watchmen won't be there."

Drake had been writing as Steed spoke. He held the paper in front of her. His notes read, 'Making good sense. Forced to agree.' and, 'Like '*We*' should proceed, not '*You*'.'

"Mrs. Peel, you're going to have to risk partners in this. Past getting you home unscathed, we will require a team for what's to be done afterwards, and we can discuss that later. For now, I urge you; let me send two 'angels' to Heathrow the date and time of your arrival. It should be a simple matter to work our tasks in conjunction. My angels' task will be not to identify or escort anyone, but to simply stop anyone who stops a first class passenger."

She followed the scenario through. "Thus if security wanted to stop or detain me, your angel..."

"...would stop or detain that person. Interrupt them from interrupting you or any other passenger really. Check credentials etc. I'm assuming you would fly first class?"

He quickly held up notes again, which read; 'Agreed two 'angels', and 'First class for both'.

"Yes. And we welcome your 'angels'."

"Wonderful, Mrs. Peel. I assure both of you the two I have in mind are entirely trustworthy. All progressing smoothly, you'll never know they're there."

"Steed, we look to do this within three days. Time enough for you?"

"Yes."

"Wonderful! Cord will contact you regarding flight and arrival time."

"Splendid, Mrs. Peel. I'll await your call after you've settled in. For now, any loose ends needs tying?"

"No."

"Emma?"

"Mm?"

"You couldn't have known about this; Mother died mid-July about the time of Peter's passing. I've been tapped to replace him. I'm covering a number of his responsibilities as it is. I'm not sure I'll leap into that fray as a regular diet. But for the present it does offer us a higher vantage point. Please mull things over keeping that perspective in mind. Keep safe won't you?"

"Indeed. I'll be seeing you in a matter of days, Steed."

Drake went to the bar and poured himself a drink. He offered one to Emma, but she declined. Breaking the silence, he said, "Steed has a good head on his shoulders after all. I like his 'angels' contingency plan."

"He's right about extending our trust to the people he trusts." she stated. "We won't be able to do this ourselves. Finding this Village, finding your double, getting him AND us out alive; any one factor a tall order for two people who've been out of 'the biz' for almost two years. It would take more time than we have to get back to fighting trim." She began to laugh, "Neither of us are Simon Templar or James Bond!"

"*That* we can both be eternally thankful for!" spat Drake.

She sauntered up to him. "Ooo! A sore spot?"

He turned abruptly. "Emma. This must *succeed!*" he growled. He stormed past her, paced for a bit, then finally stood still, his back to her, his shoulders drooping. She gave him the silence he needed.

"I've...just recalled." He eventually admitted quietly, his voice hoarse and raspy. "The angels plan. I used...a similar plan six years ago. I...I couldn't recall till just now."

She walked around him, turned and faced him, her hands on her hips. Almost defiantly. "This is not about vindication for you or I. This is about a poor man wrongly imprisoned!"

She moved closer, softening her tone. "John, this...reluctance to risk trust, this...fear, it's crippling you, chipping away at your skills and talent. What you have up here," she tapped her temple, "has been imprisoned as well. You need to free it."

"And I free it by risking trust?" he asked derisively.

"You're not allowing it to fly because it might fall?"

Drake's eyes flashed. "Your choice would be to trust Steed! What if he's part of this? What if he already knows all about it? What if he's been gotten to? Compromised? What if he betrays us?"

"Then we'll have failed! But only because we risked trying! We hope to free this man and expose something diabolical. If we don't try, don't risk, what hope does he have? What hope do any of us have? She paused, "I choose to trust him. And us! I choose to fly and risk the fall. I choose freedom. I refuse to live under a shroud of dread!"

Emma turned, leaving the room, leaving him alone to make his choice.

10
London

The drive from Harrow was difficult for Steed. He constantly had to refocus his attention to his driving. Away from filling in the puzzle with pieces he was able to glean from the phone conversation with Emma. The whole thing was so damn intriguing. Troubling.

'Well', he thought, allowing for an air of joviality, 'at the very least we've confirmed the state of California has not been overrun by enemy agents'. Home at his apartment, he shot a glance at his telephone and thought of the tap that must surely be on it. '...but perhaps *we* have!'

Settling into his chair, he started ticking off the steps necessary for the next move in this game, comparatively much simpler than the first. Tara King and Mike Gambit would be his Heathrow 'angels', obviously. Of course, it was possible Mrs. Peel might recognize Tara, unlikely though, as Tara was recently a blonde.

What Gambit had said to him tonight moved him. He was certain Mike would be a solid 'knight' throughout this game.

A troubling thought surfaced, 'What if Gambit is a plant'?

He immediately and fiercely mentally brushed the thought into the trash bin. 'If I start second guessing every detail, all is lost before we ever start.' No. There would be plenty of extreme caution used but no room for paranoia! He would have little problem surreptitiously contacting both of them tomorrow and giving them their orders.

He had already called off the two 'chums' he had 'looking out' for Emma when she'd left England. Honestly, the way things stood now, he wasn't certain they should be involved any longer. He would have to 'fine-tooth comb' all of his contacts and sources for the time being. Too much could be at stake for half or three-quarter measures.

The identity of her mysterious friend: that could certainly wait for a few days. Given he was a 'he' (one doesn't normally assign a woman to impersonate a man), and an agent. Steed was certain he wasn't from the Department, or 'Ministry'. He wasn't from Diplomatic Intelligence (Temp would *never* have condoned such a plan). His money would be on M9, yet there were still other units that he could be from, military intelligence seeming like a good bet.

He'd really be much better off ascertaining who this mysterious captive was. Getting that piece would allow so much of this puzzle to simply fall together. But the *how* of the getting...like removing a pea from beneath a falling axe!

There was the confounding aspect of this agent's finding two clues amidst that rapid cascade of vanishing sources (which *had* to be a truly frightening experience!). 'The Village' and 'Project and/or Number Six'. He appreciated the instinct of the agent in trusting these were valid clues, but they also could be cryptic red herrings.

The Village: He was aware of places like it dotting the whole of Great Britain, especially during and shortly after the war, yet these were limited in scope and size. He knew of two current 'camps' himself. Department training grounds could be considered a 'Village', he supposed, and that was only five minutes outside of London.

Mrs. Peel had been spot on reminding him of Little Bazeley. Then there was the vast underground compound, beneath a graveyard, where they planned on housing *thousands!* To say nothing of Little Storping-in-the-Swuff, the small village of murderers they'd put paid to. Really, it *could* be a sizable Village almost anywhere.

'Project and/or Number Six'! Good Lord! Valid clue or not, that could mean *anything!* Still, of possible use as a phrase to drop when the timing was right, a tactic he had used before with surprising results. One never knew what would open up a can of worms. Drop a certain word, a miscreant overreacts, and suddenly you're hot on the trail!

Thus, he was left with a few thoughts scratched out and a few blanks sketched in. Next move: 'Steed's Angels' assure a safe homecoming.

Back home, Steed clicked on the telly, purely for distraction's sake, catching about the last half of "On Point" before sign off.

'Oh, splendid!' he thought facetiously. That popinjay author, Jason King, the poor man's Ian Fleming was on. The man seemingly never met a camera he wasn't fond of! Incredible that the man would actually be sought out by law enforcement as a consultant, of all things!

He almost switched it off, but King was saying something that caught his ear. "...conspiracies can never last. There's always someone who knows. An author's difficulty is in finding that person and talking with them. Good journalists understand this as well."

The moderator countered, "Well, surely conspiracies rarely get uncovered until the damage has already been done."

"True, and that simply points to a generally wretched lack of intellectual acuity on the part of investigators, as I've been saying: a deplorable state that needs addressing."

The camera then moved to a third member of the panel, one Claude Eustace Teal of Scotland Yard (retired). "Well we can't all be geniuses like you Mr. King!" he stated drolly.

"Oh, *please*, Inspector Teal," King admonished, "its systematic, isn't it? One can hardly be fully blamed when one must diligently fill out two dozen forms for every action. Initiative and thinking outside the frame are *hardly* encouraged, are they? No, no, no, I *do* fully empathize with the drudgery of your lot. It leads to an erosion of creative extrapolation. You and your colleagues are hardly to blame for it. You *are* however, the victims *of* it!

"Herein lies your conundrum. Your job is to look for clearly defined connections while it's the criminal's primary function to misdirect and obfuscate! Your training is hardly conducive to exercising one's imagination! A man standing over a dead body holding a fired gun is *obviously* the culprit, isn't he? Honestly, how often has that simplistic reliance on the empirical come back to bite you?"

Teal's expression displayed reluctant agreement.

"Well, your novel's fantastical plot lines are hardly run of the mill criminal activity, surely!" interjected the moderator.

King smiled, "Ah, but don't you see? I insist that my Mark Caine novels be *fully* based on reality! Actual crimes! I demand it of myself. I have done what Mark Caine has done, though perhaps not in such immediate chronological procession. At the *heart* of every one of my plots is a *simple* crime. A 'magic trick' if you will.

"The onus of the investigator is *not* solely to connect dots, but to ascertain *why* the dots are there, and to find dots that aren't! A conspirator's task is to present a plethora of dots. It is due to that manufactured complexity that conspiracies unravel. As I said, there is always left a dangling thread, and someone who knows about it. The trick is not looking for the thread, rather it is looking for the person who may know where that thread is!"

"Well, thank you gentlemen for an interesting discussion on the matter..." the moderator said by way of closing.

Steed found himself chagrined. King had a point, a very good point. A number of them in fact. There seemed more to this chap than he thought.

He had to scold himself. Reminding himself of how often it was that he had won the day basically by virtue of being mistaken as an ineffective effete 'dandy' by an opponent.

Besides, how often had he heard, 'Nonsense, Steed!', or 'that's impossible, Steed!' from his superiors, only to have been proven right time after time? How often had a proposal been 'out of the question', not enough in the 'frame' for them? Systematic indeed!

He was uncomfortable admitting it. Jason King was onto something, and it was very likely they were of similar cloth. This gave him an idea.

SOMEWHERE

"Where am I?"
"Where no one can hurt you."
"Who's side are you on?"
"Yours."
"Of course you are. What do you want?"
"You, well."
"Oh. I'm surrounded by benefactors now, is that it?"
"Well, yes."
"Of course I am! Who are you?"
"What do you mean?"
"*Who are you?*"
"That would take some explaining..."
"I appear to have plenty of time!"
"Yes. Yes you do."

11
Kings and Desperate Men

The exchange of flight details between Cordelia Winfield-Mannering and John Steed, the flight from LA to London, arrival and procedure through Heathrow, and the trips from Heathrow to the Peel home in Camberwell Green, all went without a hitch.

Cordelia simply met Emma at Heathrow reception and drove her home. There had been no fuss at the airport or otherwise.

David Marlowe was waiting outside as Drake exited the airport. Drake, in his disguise as an injured person using a crutch, was being helped by an attractive young blonde woman.

Just in case the disguise wasn't enough, he was holding a box of chocolates complete with a green bow, that further indicated to Marlowe that he was indeed Emma Peel's travelling companion.

Marlowe moved to escort the allegedly injured man, helping him with his suitcase. "Thank you, Miss. You've been an absolute angel." Drake risked telling the blonde, insisting on gifting the young lady with the box of chocolates.

Tara later reported this to Steed as he and his 'angels' met at a car park. He got both a chuckle and a chocolate butter cream out of it. This agent, whoever he was, showed a great amount of cheek and a wonderful sense of daring, he thought. 'Absolute angel' indeed!

Gambit reported nothing more than heightened security due to the IRA bombings that had been escalating recently.

Marlowe utilized a longer route to the Peel home than Cordelia had used, arriving about fifteen minutes after her. Drake had used the time to divest himself of the faux bandages and crutch, leaving them for Marlowe to dispose of.

Drake greeted Cordelia with a peck on the cheek saying, "I am forever in your debt." She looked at him in all seriousness, and with a bit of warning, she said, "Just be kind to my Em, old boy." When Drake and Emma were alone, he checked the premises for bugging devices. There were none. So far, all was well. Next was to meet with Steed.

Steed meanwhile had worked on attempting to locate where this 'Village' might be, without using the aid of his normal resources. Of suspected locations the Department already had its eyes on; he had whittled possibilities down to a few dozen. This 'Village' could be anywhere, best to start with the 'knowns' as it were. As for investigating the identity of the imprisoned man, until he had more information to go on, it was a fruitless exercise.

He had much greater success making an appointment with author Jason King. Sweeping aside his preconceptions of the man was a bit of a chore, but there was something about what King had said that tugged on his instincts. He had enough experience to know one *never* ignored one's instincts in this game, and a bit of research on King sealed the matter. This fellow was no 'poor man's Ian Fleming' after all!

It had taken almost a full day and a bit of string pulling, nonetheless he had managed phone contact with King, twice, prior to this appointment.

The first call merely established that he had seen King's appearance on television and wished to discuss the subject in depth. Playing on his ego was enough enticement to secure a second call.

During the second call on Gambit's line, he had supplied King with a precursory description of the mystery at hand and convinced him of the need for secrecy in the matter. That had King hooked.

At 16:30, author Jason King opened the door of his London penthouse apartment dressed only in a magnificently vibrant purple bathrobe, lavender scarf and slippers.

"The Honourable Major John Wickham Gascoyne Beresford Steed! A pleasure. Please do come in!" he invited, smiling.

King's surroundings, though opulent, were much less garish than Steed had imagined. This was, he gathered, primarily a work place. Papers were strewn about, on table tops and crumbled in wastebaskets, filled to the brim. Books were stacked on the floor and laid open in the seats of chairs, and full ashtrays were everywhere.

He offered Steed one of two empty chairs. "A drink Major? I'm having one."

"No, thank you, Mr. King. Thank you for taking time out of your busy day." he said sincerely and cheerfully, doffing his bowler and taking the seat.

King sat opposite him and lit a cigarette. "I will assume Major, that you have checked my credentials and reliability with my good friend Sir Curtis Seretse, as I suggested?"

"That I have Mr. King."

"Oh, please. It's Jason. I'm uncomfortable with a man of your reputation and pedigree referring to me in any other way, especially since I believe we shall be working together on this puzzle of yours for some length of time," King said, his hand waving the air dismissively. "I understand you prefer to be addressed simply as 'Steed'?"

'My!' he thought, 'he certainly has done his homework'!

"Steed is fine, Jason."

"Capital. So, at the heart of your puzzle, we have; a man of some importance being held captive, the purpose being to extract information from him thought vital. An Intelligence agent is given the assignment of impersonating and confronting this man in this place as a means of extraction. What does this suggest to you Steed?"

"Well, that's hardly the manner in which I might go about it!"

"Precisely. There are certainly many easier, more benevolent ways of extraction. This scheme is grandiose. Needlessly complex and malicious. It suggests to me a deeper sadistic motivation much more primary than merely getting information, or 'confirming loyalties'." King nearly spat those last words out.

He sat, somewhat stunned. "You know, that hadn't occurred to me!"

"Well Steed, you are a benevolent gentleman, regardless of your reputation as being somewhat ruthless."

"You flatter me. You've a very keen sense of discernment."

"Th'nk yoh." King replied. "To the task; it's as if said information was superfluous, wouldn't you agree? Moving on to this agent; given an assignment he finds repulsive, as well he should, he abstains from accepting. He starts his own investigation which is short-circuited immediately. This suggests...?"

Steed, mind racing, said haltingly, "...he was..."

"Yes?"

"...being set up."

"Exactly. Never expected to accept the assignment! Why ever would he be asked in the first place?"

"Hmmm...indeed!" he agreed.

"Unless it was to confirm this agent might represent a problem. Leave no doubt, force his hand. Make him act, and then shut him down. Likely all plotted out before he was ever given the despicable assignment. This agent is then told to run, by a 'trusted' source."

"...who could have been in on the whole scheme!"

"Possibly."

"It boggles the mind!" Steed admitted. "Why not simply have him likewise imprisoned, or killed?"

"Mmmm. This agent, a man of notoriety? Of good reputation, high importance? Too 'connected'? His death, if at all suspicious, raising too many questions? No, no, no, much cleaner to manipulate him into placing himself out in the cold, wouldn't you say?"

"Yes. As it stands, I'll know his identity soon. That should clear up matters."

"And should then point to some suspects I would think. Another thought occurs to me, there may be a connection between this agent and the prisoner. Possibly one neither knows about."

"Remarkable! And very disturbing. Well, Mr. King..."

"Jason." King reiterated.

"Jason then. You've been of enormous help." Both men stood shaking hands.

"Not at all. Steed, I urge you to consider possible motivations of this agent's superiors in connection with the functionality of this village. Consider who might benefit from all this. What is the need for these complexities? There is obviously conspiracy afoot here."

"I agree."

"I will make a few discrete enquiries and I'll be in touch."

"You've given me a lot to chew on Jason. Thanks again."

After Steed had left, Jason King stood staring at the door. He stood there staring for quite some time.

By 18:00, Steed was back in one of Mother's old offices. He made a call to Emma welcoming her back home, asking if it would be alright were he to pop in for a visit later that evening (verbalized in 'code' only they two would understand, for the benefit of other 'ears' who may be listening). She stated that she would be delighted.

A light rap at the door, and Gambit entered. Silently he unfolded a map on the desk. 26 points on the map had been circled in red. Four of those had been crossed out in black. He pointed to one which had recently been crossed out, noted '15:00'. He next pointed out an area on the map which he then circled in green. He produced a legal pad, handing it to Steed. The notes on this read, 'Odd place. New construction going on. Construction begun 20/4/69. A Sunday!! Long time! Few locals. Conflicting reports. Some think military.'

Steed nodded once, handing the pad back. Their eyes met, then Gambit folded the map and exited. 'A Sunday!' he thought. 'Curious'.

12

Emma Peel's home, Camberwell Green

Emma greeted Steed affectionately. They hugged, and then beheld each other silently for some moments. Their eyes spoke volumes that simple words never could. They then proceeded to the parlour.

Drake was seated at one of two sofas situated by a coffee table. He immediately stood as Steed and Emma entered. He had tied back his shoulder length hair and had trimmed his beard and moustache a bit. Steed stared hard at him, 'inspecting' him, not immediately recognizing him. Drake walked up to him and shook his hand.

"Drake. John Drake."

Emma could not recall ever seeing Steed so utterly nonplussed. She found that surprisingly refreshing!

"Good God! John Drake! Of *course!*" Steed shook his hand heartily.

"So much clicks into place now!" He was beside himself, staring dumbfounded. He let all decorum flee. He flopped himself into the sofa gobsmacked. His bowler still on, he pushed it back on his head. "I've not seen you since Berlin!" he grinned.

He turned to address Emma, "Did you know Mrs. Peel, Drake and I shared exploits that are required study for Department trainees?"

His surname notwithstanding, Drake was an odd duck. While he obviously had a sizable ego which rather enjoyed compliment and acclaim, he was also uncomfortable in the face of it. "Yes...well, I think we are aware that we have each achieved some... notoriety? I'd like to suggest we...dispense with mutual admiration, so our time could be better utilized discussing more...pressing matters?"

Steed sat forward, removing his bowler. "Drake, how *are* you? You've been under what I would say has been enormous strain! Are you alright?" he asked, clearly indicating certain concerns be met first.

Drake paced a bit, snapping his fingers, then turned and sat down. "I...am, Steed. Obliged. I...hadn't been, but I am well on the mend now."

Steed stole a quick glance at Emma. She was concerned, he could tell. But her expression informed him she also thought getting to the business at hand was more vital.

He addressed Drake. "Knowing *who* you are fills in a lot of holes in my understanding. I think it paramount to tell you that, at least in my circles, I haven't heard one whisper regarding you within the last year or so. Not that you were in trouble, not that you'd run off, and not that anyone was looking for you. No scuttlebutt about you at all. Of course I hadn't been listening for any either, yet given your notoriety, one would think I'd have heard SOMEthing."

Drake was surprised. He glanced at Emma who was still standing by the couch Steed sat in.

"Mind you, that's only in my neck of the woods. Even so, that's a sizable neck."

Drake stiffened slightly. "I see."

"Not to suggest extreme caution and diligence aren't absolutely necessary, perhaps more now than ever. But I hope that at least relieves you of *some* burden."

"Obliged. I...I've been a damned fool!" Drake uttered, letting his anger out. "I've been, manipulated."

"I believe so. Manipulated yes. 'Damn fool' I would take issue with."

Emma sat next to Drake. Steed *almost* reacted, but he'd steeled himself to the possibility that she and this 'friend' might be 'involved'.

"What's next?" she asked.

"Security! Despite what I've just said, we need to be assured of no other ears hearing us."

"I've taken care of that here." Drake assured him.

"I'd assumed that to be the case. And we need no other eyes recognizing you."

Drake gave Emma a quick meaningful look. "I'm comfortable...risking that my passport identity, Joseph Wolf, along with my changed features" his hands indicating his longer hair, beard and moustache, "will reduce the likelihood of that."

"Ha! Indeed! It fooled *me* and I *know* you more than in passing!" Steed remarked. We've no idea how far up or how far wide this assumed bad strain has spread, whether it's a few, a few dozen, hundreds or more. So, until we get a clearer picture of what we're up against, I've taken liberty to have the newest in surveillance detection equipment dropped off for you here tomorrow.

"Next, Communications. We can't continue running a maze solely to converse, relay information, or plan. We'll want one, possibly two, other meeting places. I should think too much new traffic to this home might raise suspicion on the part of your neighbours. We've much to do, and unfortunately my current duties at the Department prevent me from coming and going as I please. Much of my time is no longer my own."

"Cord has proven efficient and effective in communications." commented Emma. "She's offered to aid us as her time allows."

"Which leads us to the third item for discussion." Steed paused here, audibly letting out a breath, "We need to discuss our teams."

Both he and Emma looked at Drake apprehensively.

Drake dove in. "A minimum of four are needed presently I'd say. Two outside of myself and Em...er, Mrs. Peel. Thus far we need at least one person with freedom of movement. I would say two scouts further on. Certainly, we'll need a few 'commandoes' for the eventual extraction, the specific talent sets to be determined.

"I'm sorry putting it quite this way, Steed, but it's logical to presume, from what you've indicated, that your new duties will keep you from any activity in the field. However, I would be in your debt if you acted as coordinator. We'll need and rely on your recommendations. Our...circle has grown to include Cordelia, her associate, and your 'angels', thus far to good effect."

Steed was very relieved in one sense. Given how Drake had seemingly been manoeuvred and used, it would have been a simple matter for him to have fallen into a state of paranoia. This spoke well of Drake's mental state and fitness.

He was also, however, annoyed at the thought of being 'desk-bound'. He found himself being offended. It spoke well of his mental fitness that he found himself being annoyed at being offended.

'After all' he thought, 'Drake is being entirely reasonable, logical, and correct. I am best situated to be operations coordinator. In a way of speaking, I brought it up myself during our phone conversation when they were still in California! So, simmer down old boy.'

Emma was over the moon, though her expression masked it. All she'd allow herself to show was satisfaction with Drake's decision.

Drake let out a sigh. "I am disconnected Steed. I've a few people on a mental list, but I've no idea if they're alive or dead. If alive, I've no idea if they're trustworthy any longer. If trustworthy, I've no idea if they're able to function the way they used to. I'd like to try to contact them, but I've no idea if I should, given the possible risk involved. I am frustrated at every turn. Thusly..."

He stood, walked over to Steed, and looked down at him. Steed suddenly thought of an old print he'd seen; the God of the Old Testament, looking down at Sodom and Gomorrah! Lord, this man could be intimidating!

Drake completed his statement in quiet measured tones, his eyes driving spears through Steed, through the chair, and well into the floor. "...I am risking trusting you. Do not betray me. Should you betray me, you will also be betraying Emma. And should you do that, you will never...be able to run far enough away from me. Am I clear?"

Steed sat still for a few seconds staring directly up at him. As he stood, his eyes never left Drake's, never blinked. Not once.

"You are. You have my word. And you have my word on this, should Emma Peel be harmed in any way, through your action or inaction, through your neglect or incompetence," he moved closer, their noses now only inches apart, with a smile that sent a slight chill through Drake, he said simply, "I'll kill you."

They stood like that for some moments when they heard a loud, "Ahh-eh-HEMMM!" Both turned in unison and saw Emma standing, arms folded, her mouth skewed to one side, looking at them reproachfully. All that needed to be said was in her eyes.

13
From that Point

Emma, after having figuratively hosed down the two lions in the parlour, presented a theory she had been considering. "Steed, I was thinking about the security and surveillance needs of this 'Village'. It strikes me that the types of technology required in such a limited environment would give off some sort of noticeable and therefore traceable energy pattern. Like sonar or radar for example."

"Mm. Yes." Drake agreed, "It's likely located in a minimally populated area. As public utility usage might well be noticeable and suspicious, it'd likely have its own energy generation, which may be traceable."

"Indeed! I'll get on it with one of our Department 'wizards' first tomorrow!" Steed declared excitedly. "I would like agreement on my contacting a man I trust highly from a sister department to 'contact' my superior with a minor mission 'request'. Then I'd be more at liberty to allocate resources to our needs without raising suspicion."

Drake and Emma nodded. They said their good nights and Steed left.

Things began happening in increasingly quick succession from that point; Drake, Steed and Emma were able to check off items on their 'to do' lists.

The next afternoon, Tara dropped off the latest in anti-detection devices at Emma's home. Steed had gotten in touch with his trusted colleague and arranged for the faux 'mission request' (which Steed's immediate superior ordered him to comply with); and had surreptitiously discussed Emma's theory concerning detecting, tracing, and/or monitoring energy patterns with two lads in the Department's tech lab.

Meanwhile, Drake, as artist Joseph Wolf, was able to find a studio close to Steed's workplace. Using cash Emma had on hand, he secured lease and took possession later that day.

Emma, exhausted, had slept in that morning. She later called a photographer friend from her modelling days, hiring her to snap photos of specific locations (to be named later). If they were impossibly fortunate, they'd happen on a photo of Drake's double, and the game would be on. If they were lucky, a security guard might 'shoo' her away, which might help them confirm a location as suspect. If her theory about energy usage detection proved workable, these two schemes might whittle down the prospects.

Knowing Emma's 'mystery friend' was Drake, vastly simplified investigation efforts on Steed's part. He had unearthed some fascinating details.

Whereas M9 was concerned, no one (officially at least) was after Drake. No sanctioning, warning, alerts, alarms, flags, requests for surveillance, or anything of the sort. He was simply classified as 'inactive'. One interesting item; Drake's superior, Hobbs, had apparently died of a heart attack about six months ago.

This raised the spectre of an obvious question. What if they were chasing a ghost? What if this imprisoned man had died, or been killed? That he had been imprisoned was given. Drake was not the sort to incorrectly understand even scant mission details. But what if they had ascertained loyalty or gotten whatever they were after in short order, and just released him? A troubling thought.

It was here where Steed's trust of his colleagues' instincts (and his own) had to be made manifest. Until he had hard evidence to the contrary, he had to trust well trained instincts that had proven themselves many times before.

Most importantly however, had this man died or been killed while wrongfully imprisoned, then that was a further injustice. A crime against the people, and the state, that had to be avenged (regardless of whether the state itself might be the perpetrator).

Were that the case, he was a firm believer in the words of Sir Winston Churchill at Harrow in 1941, 'Never give in--never, never, never, never...'

SOMEWHERE. NIGHT

He ran, but it was no use. The damn globe thing or balloon thing was rolling after him, the distance between them closing fast.

At that moment, he tripped over a low edge of some sort of fountain! Falling into the water, he tried getting up, slipped and fell again.

The thing was getting closer. He found footing and started running again. He stopped, just behind a structure. Perhaps, if he could get to that balcony above...

The bizarre décor of the place! So bloody strange!

He ran up a small set of steps to the balcony. The globe thing bounced over the fountain, stopping just below.

He tried to catch his breath. He was too old and too out of shape for this. He expected any number of things, but nothing like this spherical apparition!

He heard a jeep again. No, not a jeep, a Mini Moke or cart.

Someone drove up a pathway and parked next to the fountain.

A man in the Mini Moke stood at the wheel. He was dressed totally in dark grey, complete with cap. He held his hands to his mouth, stating loudly, "Stop! Walk slowly toward me and you will not be harmed. You have entered a government instillation. It is restricted, and you're here illegally. Comply *now*!"

What to do, what to do? The balloon thing was 15 metres away down below, the chap in the Mini Moke some thirty metres away at the side of that ridiculous fountain.

"This is your final warning. Come out, and slowly move towards me." His accent was American! Perhaps Canadian. Certainly not one of ours!

Suddenly the balcony was filled with bright light. Blinded, he stumbled backward, falling down the steps. Just as he reached the landing, the balloon thing bounced onto him, 'enveloping' him! He started to scream but the thing covered his mouth. He was tightly bound, encased in it. He couldn't move a muscle. His head, from his top lip upward, was left free. Even so, breathing was difficult.

The man from the Mini Moke walked up to him, shining a flashlight in his face. "What's the matter, pal? You got trouble hearing? You speak English?"

He could see enough to make out that the man was holding something else besides a flashlight. Some type of small box. The man clicked (a button? buttons?) on it.

The balloon thing somehow 'loosened', or 'lowered' itself until his mouth was freed, though the rest of him was still encased as tightly as before.

"Who are you? What are you doing here?" The man asked.

"I...I'm a...journalist, a...reporter." He mumbled, barely able to get the words out.

"Sir, you're in a restricted area. You're here illegally. I'll have to take you with me. You won't be harmed unless you resist. Do you understand? Do *not* resist."

He nodded. He had no choice.

"Do you have ID on you?"

He nodded again. The uniformed man once again clicked on the box. Within seconds, the thing holding him started to dissolve away into the ground. He'd felt as though his body had been dipped into a bottle of seltzer! He could breathe fully again. What had just happened was unfathomable!

Before he could get off the ground the uniform man held out his hand.

"ID please. You got a name?"

He struggled to get his wallet out of his back pocket. "I...I'm a journalist." He stammered. "Mmy n...name is...Mac McGill." He relinquished his wallet.

The flashlight immediately blinded him again, the light glaring right in his eyes. He didn't dare move.

"What? You gotta be joking!" the man uttered.

The man leafed through the wallet, found McGill's press credentials, and started to chuckle. "Well, I *will* be damned! So you *are*!"

The man pocketed McGill's wallet, bent down, took him firmly by the arm, helped him up, and escorted him to the Mini Moke. The man's grip was strong and assertive, but not painfully so. Just solid enough to inhibit any thought of resisting.

"You...you have to let me call...call my..." McGill started to say, as he was seated in the Mini Moke.

The man turned to him, grinning. "Well I don't wanna be disagreeable with you Mister...McGill," he said starting the Mini Moke, "but I don't have to let you do ANYthing!"

14

London: The Studio

"This will work wonderfully!" remarked Steed, surveying the studio. He turned, indicating the young man to his right. "Mike Gambit," and the woman on his left, "Tara King, may I introduce Mr. John Drake, late of M9, Mrs. Emma Peel, Tara and Mrs. Peel have already met briefly I gather, and Miss Cordelia Winfield."

"'Miss'!" Emma quietly snickered at Cordelia, who in return gave her a slight elbow jab to the ribs.

Tara walked over to Drake, her eyes wide with admiration. "I'd just like to tell you personally what an honour it is to work with you, Mr. Drake."

"Thank you. This is...uncharacteristic of me, but might I say to each of you I am indebted to you for your willingness to help us. I will never forget it. Now, let's proceed with the business at hand?"

"Gambit?" Steed summoned.

Gambit began by thumb-tacking three maps to a large canvas on an easel. "Mrs. Peel made the great suggestion of looking at odd amounts of energy usage in areas where there wouldn't normally be. One of our special weapons lads came up with a way for us to do just that, using a modified infrared camera. We flew over most of England, Scotland and Wales using this camera set up and created this map using the photos we got. Notice there's eighteen locations circled.

"Map two shows known locations of decommissioned military installations. We thought maybe someone may have unofficially reopened one or more. Here we've got a number of locations circled.

"Map three shows various places that have been known conclaves of criminal activity or espionage over the last few years. One being a certain 'Murderville' that Steed and Mrs. Peel squashed a few years ago."

He withdrew another larger map from the inside pocket of his suit jacket, unfolded it and pinned it up over the first three maps, "This is a map where each of the separate components coincide. This gives us sixteen circled locations."

Steed commented "Drake, you're free to peruse these of course. You may find or know of something we overlooked. For now, I feel concentrating effort on these sixteen is the most efficient way forward."

"Certainly." Drake agreed. "As it could be any or none, it's movement in the right direction."

Tara spoke next. "I've been going over past cases of ours and noticed a number of them initially got our attention because of some bizarre occurrence. Well, I happen to have a friend who's an absolute *bug* about odd police and news reports. UFOs and ghosts and things of that nature. As I've shown her a keen 'growing interest', she keeps giving me clippings of articles every so often, almost weekly in fact. I'll bother her to see if she has any more for me. It might seem silly, then again one never knows what may turn up, perhaps pointing to the very thing we're on the look-out for."

Both Drake and Emma smirked at this. However, Emma verbalized the remainder of the thought they'd each had, "We've all indeed solved cases before through that *very* kind of thing, Tara. It's a unique approach and a wonderful idea."

Emma offered, "My photographer friend is snapping shots by some of these places. I told her she may run into a military instillation or two, and that she may be shooed off. I told her to obey the rules and not to be sneaky or try any heroics."

"Yeah!" chided Cordelia, "Like that ever did you or me any good, Em! I suspect the same holds for Tara here as well!" It wasn't only the women who found that amusing. "It's a shot in the dark, but we never *do* know." Emma admitted, giving Tara a wink.

"Well done." Drake congratulated Gambit after his presentation. "A pleasure working with you."

"The honour's mine, sir."

"Well then," Steed prepared to conclude, "is there anything else?"

Cordelia said, "Yes. I'm happy to continue to relay anything you wish as needed for the next week, but Joh...Mr. Mannering and I will be in Hong Kong for two weeks after."

"Cordelia, you've done us an *enormous* service. We've managed to come up with an efficient communication network that doesn't require jumping through quite so many hoops. So, thank you. Please extend our thanks to your Mr. Marlowe as well, won't you? Thank you, all." Drake closed as Cordelia, Gambit and Tara took their leave.

Later, as Steed, Drake, and Emma sat in a circle on three overturned crates, Steed told of his findings regarding Drake and M9.

"Hobbs is dead? Well well..." Drake remarked simply. "Still, I don't feel that adequate enough invitation to come galloping back to the corral."

"Assuredly." agreed Steed, "nevertheless, I wonder if we might feel a bit freer attempting deeper probing."

"Hmmm." contemplated Drake, his finger rubbing his lower lip. "I would say 'steady as she goes' at the moment.

I'm...satisfied with our progress thus far, and don't want to upset anything."

"Understood. I've other candidates outside of Gambit and Tara regarding an extraction team in the works. Had you further thoughts on that?"

"Yes I had. I'm sad to say one of my operatives is dead. Two others I've made overtures to connect with. I'm very impressed by Gambit, and unsure of Miss King, to be honest."

"Well, she's no Mrs. Peel" Steed smiled at Emma, "but by the same token, she's a wonder to behold in her own right, and I trust her with my very life."

Drake replied, "For now, I'm asking for final refusal. But, she's gainin' on me."

"Splendid old boy"!

Emma got up. "There are a few items in the car I want to bring in. You boys behave!" she admonished, wagging her finger at them.

Steed was about to leave, but he sensed Drake wanted something, just to chat perhaps. He had always appeared to Steed as a tightly wound coil. Well, that was true to his nature, wasn't it? Here, now, it was good seeing him unwind a bit. Especially good to see him willing to do so openly. Steed had known too many tightly wound coils who'd suddenly snapped. He recalled working with Drake on those two occasions years ago. They worked together flawlessly. He felt it was the 'Yin and Yang' of their personalities and styles that won the day. He liked to think they had learned from one another.

Drake had been staring at the maps. "Steed, you and I, anyone who served during the war, would see the obvious. These...kids wouldn't.

"Occasionally, even we...elder soldiers sometimes forget a thing *is* obvious? What are we looking for here?"

Steed squinted. "I'm not sure I follow you."

"We're searching for a...?"

"A 'Village' I gather."

"Right. A Village, when we should be looking for a prison, with four walls. What's easier to guard than that?"

"A prison with three walls?"

"Or two." Drake pointed, "Which of these represents *that*?"

"*Ahh yes*!" Steed suddenly comprehended. "Mountains, and/or Water!"

Drake walked to the easel, picked up a paint brush, dabbed it in yellow paint from the trough, and painted eight circles on the map. "Let's concentrate effort on these eight first."

"You're right. I should've seen it too."

"It's getting late." Drake smiled, and then looked back at the map. "I just hope not *too* late!"

15

Within two days afterward

Target: Chittening, Bristol: A refinery. Checked off.

Target: Croyd, by Exeter: A resort area with inefficient power generation. Checked off.

Target: Mucking, Stanford-le-Hope seemed way too close to the London Gateway shipping lanes to be viable. Checked off.

Target: Stolford, Bridgewater: *That* was an oddity! It was the point on the map Gambit had shown Steed days ago, the area where construction started in April, on a Sunday, and was apparently still going on. Five months? What could they be building there? Demolition and rebuilding? Fine, so, what *had* been (may still be) there? Responses to enquiries weren't readily forthcoming. Locals gave conflicting reports, and there was no Intelligence on the place. Whatever the case, it warranted watching.

Target: Gower, Wales: That looked promising. In fact, there were three points in the Swansea area of Wales that looked promising. Odd energy patterns were detected in places with low population. An old decommissioned airfield was located near there, beaches, cliffs, it just 'felt right' as Drake put it.

Drake had gone over each of the maps, circling other areas he found of interest, a number of places in Scotland and Wales. Emma's photographer friend was headed to Wales. Each was doing what they could, and he felt they were making good progress, considering what they'd been able to accomplish thus far 'under the radar'. Yet Steed wondered how to speed up this investigation. It was damned tedious. It was just that he had a feeling...they were getting close. He was getting itchy. Impatient. He was sure Emma and Drake were feeling likewise.

For now, Steed attended to securing two drivers for the upcoming mission, as he called in two agent trainees. He told trainees Brian Gordon and Helen Merrow that he would have a special assignment for them, likely within a month. They were to provide transport for other agents in a highly secret operation. They were to tell no one, and he wouldn't be able to officially acknowledge their part until months after the fact. The operation would likely be a late night/early morning situation, and they would engage in no other component save the transportation aspect. Full details would be provided them within 24 hours before the mission. Could he trust them, and were they 'ready'? Gordon and Merrow eagerly indicated that he could, and that they were. He thanked them and dismissed them. Another item checked off.

Keith Turnbull sat drinking coffee when Drake showed up at the café and sat across from him. "Tom! Good to see you again!" Drake began.

"Joey! Wonderful to see you too!" said Turnbull. "Sell any of those weird paintings of yours yet?"

"No, not yet. I've been working at a studio I'm renting, getting a few pieces together for an exhibit comin' up. I'm hoping that'll be successful."

"You know, I think you'll do pretty well here. A lot of folks are suddenly very much into your style these days." Turnbull kept the charade going.

"I wanted to get with you about framing specifically for the exhibit. One in particular could really use your eye. Like the one I sold that woman in Prague. Do you remember that one?"

"Ahh, Joey. I didn't tell you on the phone because I figured the best way would be just to show you." Keith lifted his arm which had been under his coat. His entire arm, from fingertip to elbow was in a cast.

"Damnedest thing. Car accident a month ago. Can't use my hand at all. Busted almost every bone in it. The doctors say it could take six months just to start getting useful again."

"Ahh hell Tom! That is a real shame. It really is." said Drake sincerely as he stood. "Tell ya what. I'll give you a call in six months. See how you're doin'."

"I'd appreciated that Joey. Honestly. Hey! I like the beard and hair. Makes you look more like the nutty artist you always were! Don't be a stranger, eh?"

"Be good to yerself Tom. Be seeing you."

Drake walked out of the café thinking, 'Well, that was unexpected! Good to see him though. A busted arm is better than being dead. 'Twould appear Steed will need to secure us a trustworthy electrics wizard.'

Later in the evening, Steed left his office and had started the Bentley when Tara came running, calling to him. She quickly jumped into the passenger side. "Drive me around a little while, I've still work to do, but I had to tell you this! Bubble Ghosts!" she exclaimed excitedly!

"'Bubble Ghosts'?" he repeated, not sure if he'd heard her correctly.

"Bubble Ghosts! Huge Bubble Ghosts! In Swansea county of Wales! You see, earlier today, my zany friend popped in for lunch and gave me her latest rundown of odd news 'finds'! Listen to this!" she entreated as she pulled out some papers and started reading.

"'County of Swansea: We can put to rest fears some of our local neighbours have been harbouring regarding nocturnal 'Bubble Ghosts' invading our region, particularly around Gower and Oxwich. Our very own intrepid reporter Mr. Mac McGill went snooping at our behest. Reports of sightings of large 'bubble-like creatures' are not unfounded, but rather, misattributed. After a thorough investigation, our Mr. McGill informs and assures us these 'beings' are actually weather balloons, some which can reach up to 2.5 metres in diameter when fully inflated. These large balloons are opaque and appear bright white and rather 'ghostly' when viewed at night. The balloons carry meteorological devices skyward to measure various weather patterns. According to Mr. McGill, there has been an uptick in weather research in the Swansea area...'." She stopped reading, and beamed at Steed, proud of herself.

He stared at her. After a moment, he said, as gently as possible, "Tara, my dear, I'm afraid that the obvious connection between this vital piece of reporting and facts regarding the prison village we're searching for is beyond my capacity to discern at this hour. It has been a busy day..."

"Well, alright. I'll...admit there may not be a...a *direct* correlation that is...readily apparent. Or...apparent in the long term, or...apparent...at bloody *all* in the bloody *slightest!* Ohhh Steeeed!" She slunk down in her seat pouting dismally.

Witnessing the incredibly rapid disintegration from the jubilant, excited woman to this depressed, dejected woman on the verge of tears was more than he could bear. He exploded into a long fit of laughter, to the degree that tears were flowing down his cheeks. Her expression changed as she began to see the humour, then she too laughed until the tears came.

In between laughs, she tried to explain, "It's just that...only a few hours...after Gambit gave me our location updates, I read 'Gower, Swansea'...my friend handed me these ridiculous pages...and *again* I read 'Gower, Swan...Oh *hell!* I don't know *what* I was thinking!"

He leaned over and gently kissed her forehead. "There, there, there now! Perfectly alright, Tara, I understand. We're all anxious to have this case solved and away. Besides, I can't recall the last time we've laughed together like this. I believe I've needed that more than I ever knew."

She rested her head on his chest. "I'm happy to hear that Steed. Truly!"

She then quickly pecked him on the cheek, exited the car, waved and ran back into HQ.

'ReMARKable girl!' he thought. 'And it *is* rather an interesting coincidence...'

16

The London Apartment of Jason King

On the sixth ring, Jason King picked up the receiver, took a quick drink of his champagne, and took a drag from his cigarette.

"Yes, yes," he answered, clearly annoyed. He searched the room. Where the *hell* were his strawberries?

"No, I haven't ..." Ah! There they were! He stumbled over the half dozen or so newspapers lying on the floor as he made his way to the bowl of strawberries perched precariously on the arm of a chair. Realizing his hands were full, he turned and sat in the chair, stabilizing the bowl with his arm.

"Indeed?" he exclaimed, his eyes widening. "And?"

He listened for a moment, his expression slowly shifting to that look he often had when his marvellous brain started hitting on all cylinders. As though he were staring at some fascinating horizon far away.

"What was his answer?"

"I see." he said, picking up his flute of champagne from the floor by the chair, "Yes. Well done."

"No, I don't think we'll have..."

"I don't see how that would matter. Especially since you were..."

He dipped a strawberry into his champagne and took a bite. "Ahh, wonderful! Yes, I think it was the best possible course. Agreed. Thank you for letting me know. Yes. Ta."

He hung up. He looked around for a clock...

Ah! On the floor by the couch! Oh, my! 10:30. Steed would be here within a half hour. Had best tidy up a bit. The place looked a bit more dishevelled than he was comfortable with, especially as he was expecting guests.

"Steed! Do come in."

"Good morning, Jason"

"How goes your puzzle?" King asked, indicating the chairs they'd sat in during Steed's previous visit.

"Falling together."

"Indeed?"

"We believe we've boiled down the location of this 'Village' to a handful of possibilities."

"Splendid."

Steed went on to describe the process of elimination they'd followed. Without getting too specific he discussed various other theories and information they were sifting through.

"Steed, this issue of this agent simply having been 'discarded' as it were, apparently without any further surveillance assigned to him after he ran, don't you find that notion at all troubling?"

"I had, Jason. But I tend to manage by exception. My, 'reach' has been limited by our own security needs, thus as nothing further has 'popped up', I merely remain eyes and ears open while we proceed."

"Mmm, wise. Still, I wonder why manipulate him so thoroughly? What is his connection with the imprisoned doppelganger?"

"If one there is!" Steed said somewhat dismissively.

"It would be of immense help to me were I to know who this 'agent' is, Steed."

"*That*, old chap, is out of my hands. I risk speaking to you about this as it is. You have my apologies along with my appreciation of how much aid you've been, 'blindfolded' as you've been."

"None necessary, Steed. I understand completely. So, you wish to proceed as if these two issues were separate?"

"I don't see that there's much choice. Our primary concern is finding this man and freeing him if at all possible. Time enough to address other questions later."

"Ahh. I see. Your course of action, though. I'm trepidatious. Personally, I'd wish to have matters more... settled?"

Steed sat silently in consideration for a moment. "Jason" he began, "You're an outsider. Yet you're smart enough to realize that the whole of 'Intelligence' rests on rapidly shifting ground. We've nearly as many agencies as we have agents, working at cross purposes. It disturbs me. Somewhere along the line, our noble cause seems to get confounded. It becomes a power struggle. Information I have on you is my power over you. I can get you to do as I please. I become the very thing I'd sworn to protect you from!"

King leaned forward in his chair, his expression changed from mild curiosity to intense scrutiny.

Steed continued "This mission ostensibly is about infiltrating and exposing a diabolical enemy faction in our government. But, at its heart, it's about saving isn't it? We hope to save a man. We hope to right a scurrilous wrong, to do our utmost to prevent the wrong from happening again."

King stared at Steed with naked admiration. As with most people, he was reminded, there was much more *in* this man than he'd thought.

Steed's reveries ended, he snapped to the subject at hand. "Whatever the reasoning or motivations behind this man's abduction, or the manoeuvring of...the agent, grave injustice was done. As you've said, a simple crime was committed. *That* must needs be addressed. The long view must be that justice is done. The devil take the hindmost."

"Would that I had recorded that Steed, I would love to have Mark Caine utter it. I would, of course, credit you in the footnotes..."

Steed smiled, "Of course. So! What do you have for me, Jason?"

King sat silent for a moment, like he was trying to decide something.

"I have four possible locations for you, Steed. I forbid you to enquire as to how I've gotten them." he announced, walking to the table on which his typewriter was stationed. He leafed through a number of papers, and finding one, presented it to Steed.

"Mind you, I cannot personally verify these are this 'Village' you're looking for."

Typed in the middle of the paper were the words, 'Ramsey Island', 'Stolford', 'Porthmadog', and 'Oxwich'.

It took all Steed had, not to appear as astonished as he truly was. He fought to look unimpressed. A faint alarm began telling him that something seemed...'off'.

He attempted to make light of it. "Ahh well and good! Tell me, would you send your 'Mark Caine' to look into these?" he smiled.

King wafted his hand dismissively, "Oh, he likely would be at the true location already, being romantically involved with a woman who was in on the plot from the first."

"Undoubtedly!" Steed chuckled warmly, shook King's hand, thanked him, and took his leave.

Once again, King stood staring at the door. After a few moments, he moved to his telephone, picked up the receiver, dialled and waited.

"Hello, King here." He waited another few seconds.

"Hello. I believe we need to chat." He declared simply, his face a stolid mask.

17

That Night at The Studio

Emma presently had the floor. "...so, we've some beautiful shots of Llanmadoc, Wales, which were taken unimpeded, and which reveal nothing. She went to take more around Gower earlier today. I'll contact her again tomorrow; ask her to get shots at Oxwich specifically."

Tara King sat on an overturned crate, looking inordinately pleased with herself, making occasional furtive glances at Steed, who merely smiled back at her.

Gambit proceeded. "I've asked a buddy to make a reconnaissance flight tonight, as close as feasible, using the modified infrared equipment over the Swansea and Snowdonia areas in particular. There are a number of spots that fit our criteria. As Steed mentioned though, that Porthmadog area seems a bit too populated. We'll see.

"Stolford, that place is a real puzzle. Something is wrong there. Bluntly, I'd vote we go there if we can't get better confirmation about these other areas.

"As we've discussed, the Ramsey Island location is a possibility, but the geography and terrain makes it seem very unlikely."

Drake let out a long breath, stood up and began pacing, snapping his fingers absentmindedly. "We're embarking on an extraction mission, missing key personnel. We've little idea what types of security we could run up against. No guarding schedule, layouts or blueprints, no inside information of any kind."

"And" Steed pointed out, "no certainty our man is actually being held there in the first place!"

"Yes." Drake had to concede.

Suddenly Tara stood, wide eyed. "I just got the strangest idea! Steed! The Bubble Ghosts! I'd like to go talk to this reporter, McGill!"

"The *what?*" Emma blurted.

Tara and Steed went on to share their humorous exchange earlier that day regarding the odd newspaper item.

Drake was the only one in the room who didn't find the story humorous, the only one who didn't react to the idea with incredulity.

"Correlate the timing of this man's investigation with documented weather readings...find out who has been doing these recent weather experiments. See if you can contact who might have made the reports this man was investigating...*yes!* Absolutely interview him! See if he can't narrow down our search."

His brain was galloping forward. "...weather balloons could certainly be used as a means of security and..."

"Detection!" Steed snapped his fingers.

It was decided Tara should proceed forthwith. Again, they each had to admit, from personal experience, that cases had been solved utilizing flimsier methodologies involving even more ludicrous likelihoods.

Gambit walked up to Drake, murmuring. "I may know a man from 'outside' with the electrics and demo skill sets we need."

"Do you trust him?"

"Um, well sir, as far as him yappin' to anyone, yes. As far as trying to run off with our equipment..."

"Can ye put the fear o' God in 'im, boyo?"

Gambit grinned. "I believe I can, sir."

They adjourned, agreeing that they would reconvene at Emma's home the evening after next, or sooner if necessary.

Outside the studio, Gambit stood by Steed's Bentley, waiting. Steed strutted forth, twirling his brolly, a good sign that he was pleased, confident of their progress.

"Mike!" Steed greeted.

Gambit nodded toward a pub down the street. "A word, sir?"

"Of course, Mike."

They entered the pub, secured a few pints, and went to an empty booth between two booths which were likewise empty.

"What can I do for you?"

"Bluntly sir, I have doubts this man we're after is even alive."

"Mike, please, it's 'Steed' when we're away from the office." He winked. His expression immediately turned serious, "And, I know precisely what you mean."

"According to Drake's own timeline, this chap has been incarcerated for over a year, apparently without cause. I mean, he could have..."

"Been released, killed, or died long ago. Yes, I know." Steed interrupted, finishing the thought succinctly.

"Exactly sir."

They sat in silence for a few seconds.

"Sir..."

"'Steed'."

"Steed. Yes, Steed... sir, I have the utmost respect and admiration for Agent Drake and Mrs. Peel, to say nothing of Miss King and, well, certainly you. But I can't help the feeling that what we're planning, what we're doing is..."

"A fool's errand." Steed once again interrupted succinctly.

"Yes sir. Steed. Sir."

Steed considered his next words very carefully.

"Gambit, there will be many times in your career when you will be asked to put your life on the line purely on someone's say so. Every scrap of information, instinct, intellect, and intuition you can bring to bear will be used to make a decision within a microsecond. Risk believing them or not. Risk trusting them or not. Risk trusting part of yourself or not. Risk going with the one when thousands are telling you not to. You're a Navy man! You already know that risk is our business.

"Mike, I'm about to tell you something I will never tell another living soul. Ever! Something I've never quite put into spoken word until now."

He had Gambit's complete attention. He huddled across the table between them and stated very quietly but emphatically, "I love Emma Peel with a love that defies description. There aren't words for it. I would trust my life and the lives of every man woman and child in the nation on her say so. Do you know why?"

Gambit looked directly into Steed's eyes. He gulped once, then answered, "Because you already have a number of times, and she was proved right."

Steed cocked his head ever so slightly, grinned, and winked at him. "Well, there *is* always *that!*"

18

Emma Peel's home

"Hello?"

"Emma?"

"Anne! Hello! How are you?"

"Pretty good, Emma. I've got some great shots around here. It's really very beautiful."

"Where are you now?"

"Oh, back at the Gower Hotel. Nice place. Nice people."

"Mm. Were you able to get shots of the beach there, ohh...what's the name of the place?"

"Oxwich? Tor Bay? There's a few nice spots through there. There's Oxwich Green, that's like a mini Cliffs of Moher, like in Ireland? Only it's like they shrunk it down and moved it here. It's beautiful though. There's a wonderful old church up there, but I can't pronounce the name of it. You know Welsh! It's not pronounced at *all* the way they spell it. But that was pretty. Then there's the cliffs. Then, I think, a Navy place, and further down are the beaches."

"Mm. Sounds wonderful!"

"Yeah. It's kind of weird, such a beautiful place, you'd think there'd be more people here. It's like almost in the middle of nowhere. But the people who do live here are beautiful. One woman invited me into her home for tea!"

"Oh! How lovely."

"Yes! Louise is her name. We had a really nice chat."

"Anne? What did I hear you say about a 'Navy place'?"

"Oh, yeah. About two kilometres from the church. It's posted and all. It's a Navy station, I guess. Or maybe Air Force. I can't recall now. Louise mentioned it."

"Oh, you didn't see it?"

"No. I guess you can see it by the beach by the cliffs, but I came from the other way. Why?"

"Oh, just curious. Perhaps just as well you didn't snoop around there anyway."

"Oh. Yeah, probably. Okay, any other stops you'd like me to make before I head for home?"

"No, thank you Anne. The photos I've already seen from Llanmadoc are absolutely perfect for this project I have in mind, and I can't *wait* to see what you have in store for me."

"So happy you like them. Thank you. I'll give you a call when I get home. I'll put a rush on these, okay? Talk with you soon."

"Mm, so long, Anne. Thanks again. "

Emma walked past the parlour where they'd moved out furniture and set up a makeshift gymnasium, complete with mats on the floor, parallel bars, a spring board, barbells and other physical training equipment. She walked into the drawing room where maps and photos had been pinned or taped to the walls.

Drake sat up on a sofa, writing in a tablet. Five other tablets were near him on the floor. At his feet were reconnaissance photos taken the night before, which Gambit had dropped off a few hours ago. He looked up at her enquiringly.

She grinned as she leaned on the door frame, her arms crossed. "I think we may have just struck gold!"

19

A pub in London

Gambit sat in a booth with his buddy Terry O'Neil, empty booths on either side.

"...you've been staying out of trouble then?" he asked.

"I'll tell ya this Michael; it's not as easy as you might think." Terry replied.

"Oh?"

"Right. There's a lot of opportunity for someone like me these days y'know."

"I'd suspect. But then, there's always been. I mean decent opportunity. I've tried to tell you that. It just takes a little longer."

"And, y'know, I've listened. I really have."

"I believe that. I told you to keep your nose clean for a year."

"It's close to fifteen months now, Michael." Terry boasted smiling, obviously pleased with himself.

"Great, Terry."

"Y'know what the thing was?"

"What?"

"I know you'll find this funny, but it's one thing that keeps popping up in my head. Your 'arithmetic lesson'. Ya remember that?"

Gambit searched his brain. "The thing about the hundred quid?"

"The same. Here, I thought I was really somethin', with what I made from that one job. One hour's work. Bam! One hundred quid."

"And at that, you sold yourself cheap." Gambit reminded him.

"I did. But you told me, 'Y'know, you coulda been workin' part time in old man Tyler's shop for about a month for that, and ya wouldn't be in a soddin' cell, *and* Charlene would still been with ya, *and* your lawyer wouldn't have *that* money *plus* what your Ma had to give him on top of it'."

"Good Lord! You memorized all that?" Gambit marvelled, genuinely touched.

"I did. I've christened that speech the 'Arithmetic Lesson'. You're a good friend t'me Michael."

"I'm... honoured Terry. Seriously, I had no idea. Y'know what's funny?"

"What?"

"I'm not that good at arithmetic."

The two friends had a good laugh, then Gambit took the plunge.

"You're keepin' in good shape."

"Aye. I been at the gym. Instead of taken the odd job, I been workin' out. It helps sometimes."

He smiled warmly. "Okay Terry. This is gonna be... wild comin' from me. Please, just hear me out on this, okay?"

"'kay." Terry narrowed his eyes, suspicious.

"Do you have any idea what I do?" Gambit asked, double checking their surroundings, insuring there were no eavesdroppers.

"You're a government guy. James flippin' Bond. I dunno. A kinda copper."

Gambit grinned. "Okay. Yeah, close enough. Uhh...do you think you might like to work for James flippin' Bond occasionally?"

Terry eyes narrowed even further, then widened, then narrowed again.

"Doin' what, exactly?"

He grimaced, scratching the back of his head. He should have thought more about how to explain this. "Ummm..."

"A hundred quid jobs?" Terry verbalized Gambit's thought, putting it in a nutshell.

"Uuhhh...yeah." he muttered uncomfortably.

Terry thought long and hard about the offer. For about four seconds.

"Awright. Only it can't interfere with my reg'lar work, right? Old man Tyler took a chance with me. I'm not about to muck it up."

Gambit was, frankly, overjoyed. Not that he'd let it show. Just enough to let Terry know he was pleased. "How 'bout this? I'll clear it with Tyler myself, beforehand, when I need you."

"You can do that?"

"I'm pretty sure I can. I'll confirm."

"Cool!"

"Great. Okay, there's a few things I'll need to...there's people I'll...Oh, hell. Are you free tomorrow evening?"

"I am."

"I'll call and pick you up."

"Awright."

"One last thing Terry, No one, I mean no one, not even your Ma, is to know about this, right?"

"Right. Else ya'd have to kill me." Terry acknowledged, slowly nodding his head.

Gambit couldn't believe that Terry absolutely believed that and was still willing.

20

The Offices of The Herald of Wales

Balding, overweight, upper middle-aged and tired, Mac McGill, was almost annoyed with himself. He'd just put his most recent article 'to bed', and was about to head home for a well-deserved ale before figuring out what he might want for a late dinner. He was getting too old for this sort of thing. The 'incident' last week at that... whatever that place was ('Sanctuary'?) went a long way in convincing him of that!

"I really can't thank you enough for seeing me on such short notice Mr. McGill!"

The attractive young redheaded woman seated by his desk was oddly dressed in an outfit which looked as if it had escaped from a Pop-Art display. In the final analysis though, McGill would have had to admit that it was her legs, framed as they were by her ludicrous mini-skirt and go-go boots that convinced him to agree to her interview, even though it was well past working hours.

"Not at all, Miss..."

"Rosewood, Pandora Rosewood." Tara King announced.

"Miss Rosewood. And you're associated with?"

"'Other Worlds Weekly'."

"Indeed!" Or 'weakly' he thought, sighing inwardly. "How may I help you?"

"Mr. McGill" she began, pulling out a Steno notebook and pen from an oversized paisley bag she held in her lap, "You are the Science Editor of the Herald, correct?"

"Well, yes, I suppose. I'm simply a journalist, but my background is in science, and I mostly report on things pertaining to science, yes." he answered.

"I've done research on you Mr. McGill. Didn't you once work for our Atomic Energy Commission?"

'My word' he thought, clearly surprised someone involved with a publication as silly as 'Other Worlds' might put themselves through all the torture of actually doing a bit of research. "Well, yes, years ago when I lived in Scotland. Purely a temporary assignment for me at that time, but yes I did."

Pandora looked at him, *very* impressed, her beautiful eyes flirted, "Well, one would have to be awfully intelligent to work for *them*, I would think!"

"Well, quite honestly, my work on the commission was more along security lines. It stemmed from my Navy service on nuclear submarines. I really shouldn't go on about it too much. I was more cop than scientist."

"You *see?*" she yelped. "I've been saying to my editor, 'This man has background and standing! Intellect! *He* would *certainly* know a hoax when he saw one. If he says these are weather balloons, then by God, they're weather balloons!'"

"I'm afraid I don't..."

"These 'Bubble Ghosts' or 'Bubble Aliens' or whatever, we've been getting reports of these things from *all* over!" she complained.

"Oh." said McGill, suddenly comprehending what she was leading to. He began looking a bit peeved and/or troubled.

"And when I happened across the item in the Herald regarding your investigation, I was *thrilled!*"

"Really?" he asked surprised, now not at all certain where this was heading...

"*Yes!* I mean, it makes sense doesn't it? These things going about supposedly attacking people and killing livestock and all, disappearing into thin air; tosh, I say! Utter nonsense! 'Why are they only seen at *night?*' I was asking!"

McGill was clearly befuddled. "Killing livestock?"

"Yes! Weren't those among reports you received about them?"

"Well, no...there was only..."

"Really?? Well we've received *dozens* of reports like that! What were *you* hearing?"

"Ehh...these were only...sightings actually..."

"*Right!* In Oxwich, correct? *Not* the *whole* of Swansea, like my buffoon of an editor thought at *all!!*"

"Uhm, yes, but...No, not..."

"So *you*, being the reasonable, *responsible* and *brave* scientific journalist you are, went to investigate!"

"Ah...well, more or less, uhh...but, seriously, it was only..."

"By the shoreline, correct?"

"What?" he asked, trying to make sense of this woman's babbling

"The shoreline here. The beach! There's no livestock on the beach!"

"Uhhh...yes, by the beach, and...uh, no there's no..."

Suddenly, McGill came to, and snapped his mouth shut. He was angry. This had to end *now!* He couldn't afford to 'slip up'! What a fool he was, allowing himself to be distracted by her legs!

"Look, Miss Rosewood, it was all...they were just weather balloons! Weather research, that's all they were!

Nothing more!" he stated very emphatically indeed. He stood abruptly from his chair. "Miss Rosewood, I...I'm afraid I must conclude our interview. I have..."

Tara noticed he was beginning to perspire. Something was wrong. It was obvious that something had scared this man. He was hiding something.

"As I suspected!" she announced triumphantly. "*Your* brilliance *proved* I'm right!!! All these nonsense reports and sightings! *Tosh!* They're distracting us from investigating, from finding out the *truth* about the *real* menace!!"

This caught McGill slightly off guard. 'Does she know anything else?' he wondered, as he gently but firmly helped her from her chair, beginning to guide her out of the office.

"The...'real' menace?"

She turned and grasped him by the shoulders, cautiously looked about the room, leaned close and whispered to him confidentially, with eyes wide, "*Yes!* From *Venus*, Mr. McGill! The *Stone* Creatures from *Venus!*"

He stood stock still for a moment, just staring at her, his mouth slightly agape.

He then continued to guide Pandora Rosewood to the door. "Yes. I see...from Venus...thank you for stopping, Miss...Good bye." he mumbled, quietly closing the door behind her.

Tara drove an hour's trip to Cardiff, where she then flew a chopper to Bristol. From there she flew another chopper back to home HQ. She smiled for most of the trip.

It occurred to her that, once again during her career thus far in the Department, the most absurdly obscure clue was proving to be something very important. The key was to keenly observe *people*.

Steed had always taught, "Watch their eyes," whether with regard to investigating or physical altercations, or what have you. McGill's eyes had given away far more than he could imagine!

She was happy that, all told, even with the inconvenience of clandestine exchanges of information, the staggered entrances and exits from the Peel home and the studio, the precautions they'd taken in every step of what would have been a difficult investigation in the norm, things were coming together.

She wasn't a church going person, however she did profess to a basic faith. Right now, she was thankful, praying that they would remain productive. She also prayed for protection and wellness for each of the members of their team. Gambit was the only one of them who was regularly active (as active as a trainee could be that is). She and Steed had been sidelined when Mother passed on; their duties being primarily Department bound since and hadn't been active for months. Mrs. Peel and agent Drake hadn't been active for about two years (that she knew of). It would be a risky mission at best. With 'rusty' operatives involved, they'd need all the prayers she could make!

21
Emma Peel's home

Drake, Steed, and Emma sat in the drawing room sharing drinks, Tara, having informed Steed of her findings in Swansea just one half hour prior, and all pertinent information having been shared.

Drake summarized discussion to that point, "The question stands; do we first send one of us to Oxwich to obtain needed information to best insure a successful extraction, risking exposure and/or capture, thus risking the *entirety* of our mission? Or do we attempt a full mission without insurance? I side with the latter."

Steed and Emma sat opposite each other while Drake paced between them.

Emma finally broke the reverie. "We are *too close* to this! Too invested. Honestly, save for Tara and Michael, we each have emotional attachment. That always proves myopic if not dangerous." Drake and Steed slowly nodded in agreement. They were loath to accept it but could not refute her logic.

"We need new eyes." She stated simply.

Drake sat down while Steed said, "Early exposure of what we know could also cause our ultimate 'foes', if you will, to go even deeper 'underground'. We'd be worse off than going back to square one.

"The complexities involved are not easily packaged and presented as a hypothetical. Our need for secrecy has prevented me from doing just so with the minds at the Department, no matter how loyal to our cause they may turn out to be. I'll be first to admit that that particular wrinkle has irritated me to no end."

Drake added, "While I haven't contacted anyone I thought could be of help for the very same reason, save one who is physically *unable* to help us. It echoes ominously of the sudden 'unavailability' of contacts that was instrumental in my running in the *first* place. I'll be first to admit that has me a bit 'off'.

Emma stood, hands on her hips. "We need someone unencumbered. Someone with a reputation for answering to no one. When all is said and done, our mission boils down to this! We are *stealing* something!"

Steed immediately recalled the words Jason King had said during the television panel show, 'At the *heart* of every plot is a *simple* crime'.

"We need new eyes located in a front of a devious mind, and a devious mind located above a noble heart."

Emma turned and looked at her 'two Johns'. She couldn't help letting out a warm and loving laugh. They both sat looking up at her, the exact same expression on their faces. A pouting eight year old boy look which implied, 'But...but I can be devious if I wanna be!'

"Oh, my steadfast lads! Look at you. Yes, you both can be devious and ruthless cads. But not quite like whom I have in mind. My late husband was acquaintances with a person who fits the bill precisely. I will take our problem to him; get his unbiased perspective and any help or advice he may have for us and have it ready for our meeting tomorrow evening."

Drake was firm, "Emma, watch yourself with this...'person'. We've worked too hard, come too far..."

She walked up and touched his cheek. "I know. Trust me." She turned, wished Steed good night and went to bed.

Steed winced at Drake, "Any idea who this 'person' might be?"

Drake nodded curtly. "I hate to say that I just might."

22
The Saint Steps In

Simon Templar paced back and forth in the parlour of his luxurious penthouse apartment, his left hand cupping his right elbow as his right hand cupped his chin, his right index finger rubbing his lips much like a windshield wiper.

"My dear Mrs. Peel, let me see if I've got this all fully comprehended correctly: A person of questionable importance is or is *not* being held prisoner in a facility which may or may *not* be located in a location which may or may not be the *real* location where this person is being held prisoner, *if*, indeed, he actually *is*."

She nodded.

"You are planning a paramilitary extraction operation in which you haven't the *faintest* idea of the exact layout of the place, no idea of what types of security there could *possibly* be there, and no *real* understanding of what kind of consequences you might face should the operation fail, assuming of course all the other stuff is true."

She nodded.

"You dare not invite people of questionable moral character, or people of dubious loyalty to Queen and Country, though what constitutes *that* these days is debatable, to aid you, as there may or may *not* be a conspiracy of enemy forces deep within our intelligence organizations, that may or may not extend to the *highest* positions in our government, and you *dare* not risk exposure. Is that about it?" Templar stood still and stared at her.

"EeeyYUP!" emoted Emma, disheartened. It was rather crushing to hear how foolish it all sounded.

"Good *Lord*, Mrs. Peel! That is..."

'Here it comes.' she thought, dismally.

"*Amazing! What* an *adventure!* Why, I haven't had fun like *that* in *ages!* I can hardly *wait* to get started!" he exclaimed, grinning, his eyes gleaming with excitement and eagerness.

"I'm yours till the end! What would you like me to do?"

Ninety minutes later, two cars pulled in the drive of Emma's home.

Drake opened the door as Emma stepped in. "Command decision!" she trumpeted, effectively shutting down all opportunity for debate or compromise. She bid her waiting guest enter.

Simon Templar knew how to make an entrance. Magnificently. Grandly. With suitcase in hand, and extending his other to Drake, he announced, "I am Simon Templar. I am *completely* at your service, and *fully* committed to your endeavour. I owe it to my dear departed old friend Peter Peel, his charming wife, and to the survival of all that is good and Godly in our country to do no less!"

Drake slowly extended his hand and shook Templar's. 'This can't possibly be happening' he thought, as he silently followed them both to the parlour. It was unlikely his left eyebrow could have risen any higher.

Templar, looking about the 'renovated' parlour set down his suitcase. "Ah, excellent. A gymnasium. Doing a bit of 'training' are we?" he asked with a wink. He turned once again to Drake, "I welcome your inspection and scrutiny Mr. Drake. I am completely sympathetic to your security needs and concerns."

Drake stated, "Were you or your suitcase...'wired' Templar, I would have known before I opened the front door."

"I see. Very good! Mrs. Peel has given me all the information she feels I've needed to this point. If you and I could go over this extraction plan of yours, I would welcome any further details that you deem fit and proper to give me."

Drake felt numb. He knew he was, in reality, standing there, hearing this man. But the words were so...fantastical. Templar sounded like a bad actor in some horrific play.

'No' he reckoned, 'he *is* here. This *is* real.' So he decided to simply make the best of things, saying, "Mr. Templar, please, don't knock yourself out. You could wind up among friends here. I am acting as 'primary' commander, yes. Regardless, this is a shared effort. All we can ask of anyone is that they tell no one about this. If you choose not to be involved, you could walk out that door, right now, unhindered. Understood?"

"Completely and totally!" Templar affirmed redundantly, standing at attention.

Drake brought Templar to the drawing room, where he began showing the materials pertaining to the mission. "We wish to 'steal' a person from here. Now, how would the 'world renowned' Simon Templar go about doing that?"

23

The Man on the Beach

Emma, Drake and Templar breakfasted. Emma ran errands while Drake and Templar worked out and sparred. After showers and changes of clothes they went to the drawing room to finalize tactical plans.

"As far as these shots show us, this place has one of the most unusual layouts I've ever seen!" declared Templar. "It's as though we're invading a holiday camp as opposed to a military installation. Look here, here, there... these structures seem purely ornamental. That's obviously a fountain or a pool! And this here! Of what use could that possibly be? Highly doubtful they're ruins of any sort. Why keep 'em around?"

Drake nodded, "Entrances to underground passages? Though those could be anywhere. Three groupings of what appear to be apartment complexes, residences all about, almost as if put there as an afterthought. I agree, it's a bizarre layout."

Templar remarked, "I've had my own experiences with a few weird places in Wales! I can tell you that!" He involuntarily shuddered remembering one in particular.

At one point, Templar had strongly suggested that he be allowed to make a personal appearance at this place. Go on a clandestine fact gathering mission. He figured were he caught he could actually play the innocent as he had little information to begin with. Be considered just a nosey tourist type and all that.

Drake convinced him that, if this *was* indeed what they *thought* it was, the risk of them 'showing their hand' to whatever insidious powers that were would be too great. "Besides, Simon" he'd said, "I doubt you've had the anti-interrogation training that many operatives go through. And even *with* that, these people have methods that could break a man permanently. I'm not doubting the strength of your resolve, but your career indicates you've only 'orbited' these kinds of operations. You are extremely good at what you do. There is no doubt whatsoever of that. But, as it stands, this is a different game entirely.

"You could go in and never be heard from again. You'd *need* back up on even such a basic mission, and that being the case, we may as well go 'all in', or not go at all."

Templar couldn't fault the logic of Drake's argument, conceding, "*And*, where's the *fun* in knowing precisely what to expect?"

Drake decided to ignore the fraction of scolding he inferred from the question, as Templar's face indicated no hint whatsoever that he was implying it.

Drake indicated "We'll focus on obvious buildings first. With infrared goggles, searching ought to be quick and simple. I suggest Gambit and Tara take those two, and then work toward these clusters here. You, Emma, and I will divide the remainder into these three sections I've marked."

Templar added "We do this systematically, clockwise in each section beginning at twelve, and so on. Also, a hypothetical; we know people are in at least two of these 'apartment complexes'. Residences, allegedly, connected one to the other. Our infrared shows them, so we then go about, what? Knocking down doors? News of *that* type of activity would, shall we say, 'travel around the neighbourhood' fairly quickly."

"Hmmm..." Drake paused.

"Where would *you* keep Prisoner Six?" Emma asked from the doorway, announcing her return. She grinned and sauntered off.

The two men looked at each other slightly disconcerted. It was obvious she had been standing there for quite some time. Neither of them had heard a sound.

"A remarkable woman." Templar sighed.

"Indeed. Don't get any ideas." murmured Drake, only half-joking.

"Oh don't concern yourself. *That* one is totally immune to my considerable charms."

"Indeed?"

"Indeed! I wouldn't even make an attempt. No... I've met a few 'femme fatales' in my time, and I'll tell you something, thank *God* our exquisite Mrs. Peel is on the side of the angels."

"Really! If she wasn't?" asked Drake, enjoying this exchange.

"Oh!" Templar looked at him from under his brow, shaking his head back and forth, "No one could stop her." he declared with all conviction. "No one!"

Emma came back holding two large manila envelopes. "I've more of Anne's photos here. They really are beautiful. Of course they're intended to be more artistic than tactical, but they *do* give us an idea of the terrain we'll be traversing during our 'hike'. Still, what caught my attention were these two in particular."

Drake inspected two photos she'd placed in front of them.

"The depth of field in these is wonderful!" Templar remarked.

"Anne apparently got closer to our target than she knew. Can we get an enlargement of these?" Drake asked.

"I've just begun resurrecting my makeshift dark room in the garage. I can within the hour!" Emma smiled. "You see anything of interest?"

The photos were indeed of the beach area by their target. Far to the left in each, Anne had managed to capture, though out of focus, three men walking. The middle man looked to be bearded, wearing a panama hat.

Emma went to enlarge the photos while Drake and Templar scanned a diagram of the compound, further contemplating the question she had asked earlier.

Templar asked "What, or who is 'Prisoner Six'"?

"Well" began Drake, "it's a possible clue I was able to snatch over a year ago. It could mean this man, something he was involved in, or it could mean nothing."

"I see. Alright, so, we have this...shall we say, 'important' person. I take it from the scheme in which you were to partake; we aren't concerned with being delicate with him. Or are we?"

"I'm not sure. We've a man we want information from. We'll obviously go through absurd machinations to get it. We can't afford physical harm to come to him. But mental collapse is fair game? Do you see the incongruity?"

"I do. We assume whatever information he has, it has long term potential. I mean, we *have* been at him for over a year now, correct? Anything time sensitive, he'd be dead or released by now, right? So we assume its long term, we assume he's still alive, and we take a giant leap of faith that he's even *in* this compound. I have him, I want him *kept*. I can torture him for months, but he'll eventually die from it.

I want to eat my cake and still have it. So I'll keep him healthy."

"Medical personnel. Possibly even psychiatric..."

"Physical care." Templar indicated the makeshift gymnasium in Emma's parlour with his hand. "Plenty of room for exercise. Keep him fit for whatever I have in mind."

"Like...guarded walks on a beach?"

"My, my! That fits!" Templar exclaimed excitedly.

'He's like a young boy!' Drake thought. For years, he'd had an impression of this man some referred to as 'The Saint'. An immoral cad who fancied himself Robin Hood. A womanizing hedonist who loved tweaking the noses of propriety. He was obviously highly intelligent. Law enforcement from a dozen countries had tried to apprehend the rogue, but never succeeded (at least to the extent that Drake was aware). He was always one step ahead of them. Drake had often begrudgingly gotten a kick out of hearing or reading reports of his exploits. He was happy they'd never tangled. He'd almost hate having to take Templar down.

The one story that changed much of his opinion regarding Templar had been the infamous burglary of a diamond necklace belonging to a countess in Rome. Templar had even widely publicized that he would steal the thing in the bloody newspapers! However, it turned out to be a charade which legally raised millions of dollars, ultimately benefitting hundreds of orphans, while simultaneously decreasing Rome's crime rate for a time. This left Drake scratching his head. How does one figure a chap like that?

Working closely with him, Drake had the answer. Templar was like a decidedly gifted young boy. He liked pretty things. He loved adventure. He was fiercely loyal to his friends. And he hated the truly 'ungodly' as he often called them. Yet, oddly, there was something clearly nonjudgmental about him. Drake decided Templar was a man who believed all but the most 'ungodly' could repent and become agents for good. Just as a young boy might.

"Yes." Drake affirmed, allowing a small smile, "It fits perfectly."

Later, Emma came in with her enlargements. "They're not as I'd hoped, clearer when viewed from this distance..."

She held them up about three metres away from Drake and Templar.

There were three men; two in dark clothing, the man in the middle wearing light clothing, a panama hat, and sunglasses. He was bearded. While not clear, it certainly could have been a photo of Joseph Wolf, Drake thought.

Templar went back to the diagram. "Let's assume this village follows prison format. Complete with laundry, food..."

"A moment, please, Simon?" Drake intruded, thinking furiously. Templar gave him the silence he needed. Finally, Drake took pencil to paper.

"My conclusion. These...complexes let's say, we'll call A, B, and C. We'll assume they're for some type of 'support' as you suggest. As you've made a strong point regarding spreading 'news in the neighbourhood', let's leave those either till last, or investigated by only one of us. That would allow four, or the five of us to divide investigation of the rest."

"North, south, east and west, more or less. What saves our bacon is, though scattered about, we actually have a relatively small search area. Still going systematically clockwise from twelve o'clock, it should take no more than two, three hours at utmost to thoroughly investigate. Might I suggest either myself or Gambit hitting these three?

"There's a few other points I'd like considered. I would say once this man is found, we get everyone acting in concert to get him out of there. We can fill in the details of that later. We've yet to discuss what to do if he; A: is physically unable to be moved, or B: has been brainwashed where he may not *want* to 'rescued'!"

Emma chimed in, "Yes. John, Steed, and I discussed that at length. We five can only do what we can, and those possibilities give us one option. Our position would then be to get out with photographic evidence, get home and rattle some cages. With evidence we might get this place acted upon and fully exposed, and, hopefully, the people behind it."

"Well met. A big 'if', though." Templar said.

"Mm." Drake concurred. "Our plan 'B' should our 'target' prove somehow 'un-rescuable'. Back to this layout, I count 22 structures of interest. About five apiece for each one of us to investigate. And I agree, Gambit should reconnoitre the three complexes A, B, and C. The rest we'll split into these four quadrants."

"Mm. These two areas or structures or...not sure what those might be...One east, the other, north."

"Aerials are unclear..." Drake quickly leafed through the pile of Emma's friend Anne's photos. "Here?" Drake tapped one photo with his fingers "This here, upper north. Possibly Sewage? Containment? Water supply? High shrubs confusing the matter..."

"...a drive leading to it. Very likely. It's too bad we haven't time. One way to go about this would be to render everyone unconscious via the water supply, or better still, create a need for mass evacuation. Or to..."

"All brilliant ideas for a bigger team with greater resources."

"True." Templar conceded.

"I'm satisfied with this...germ of a plan for now." Drake concluded.

"*Concurred.*" Templar heartily agreed, slapping the table with his hands. "On to the probable alarms and security this place might have! Now, as I mentioned before, we can be assured they'll be using a..."

Emma leaned on the drawing room doorway with arms crossed, watching and listening. She always loved to watch artists at work.

24

The Superlative Seven

There were seven at the studio; Emma, Drake, Steed, Gambit, Templar, Tara, and Terry O'Neil. Tara had the floor as she referred to a map they each had copies of.

"Steed was able to secure the availability of four helicopters and two pilots for the mission. We will be flying a bit less than one hour from Department HQ helipad to Little Rissington. Our second 'hop' will be to Saint Athan, which is approximately eight kilometres from Oxwich target. That leg will take approximately an hour and fifteen minutes. The reverse is our escape route."

Drake took the floor. "As it appears likely part of the security utilizes weather balloons equipped with some form of detection devices, any unusual air traffic too close could raise alarm. Landing this distance away should prevent that."

Steed took the floor. "Stationed at Saint Athan will be your drivers, Gordon and Merrow with two vans. They will drive you about an hour's journey to Three Cliffs Bay which as you see is approximately a three kilometre circuitous route from target. As close as we dare by vehicle I'd wager. From there you'll proceed on foot."

Drake concluded, "Obviously the beach would be the more direct route, but we'd be detected with only minimal scrutiny, thus we'll traverse above it. We do not expect to run across land mines, yet we'll proceed under a presumption they are there."

Drake and Templar had semi-finalized the plans for the extraction and would work with Terry O'Neil (electrics and demolition skilled amateur) to tie up loose ends. O'Neil would not be needed on the mission itself.

Steed also would not be going on the mission. He would stay in London to coordinate alternate plans with drivers and/or pilots should the need arise. He would also attempt damage control should the mission fail.

It was decided to totally de-bug his apartment for the night of the mission, and to risk notice of surveillance decommission. "What difference would it make?" he justified. "By morning light it'll be known about and tracing it back to us would only be a matter of time. Of course, any failure on our part would speed the process. If we do fail, I've been working on contingencies which hopefully may keep us from becoming 'prisoners' ourselves."

Templar, who had remained silent during this entire meeting, finally addressed them.

"I have spent my entire career working in and outside of the law. Under it, over it, around it, breaking it as I deemed necessary. I'm pressed to say we have no real legal *standing* here. We know of no illegality done save kidnapping, which was no doubt sanctioned by way of 'national security' or some such. Have we thought about the legal consequences of this action?"

The thought and its consideration struck everyone silent.

Steed said, "Well, our pilots and drivers are in the clear. They were simply following the directives of a superior."

Gambit said to O'Neil, "I haven't mentioned anything to the old man as your involvement hasn't resulted in time away from your job. I really don't see how any of this could be traced back to you at all."

"Right. 'Michael *who* again, inspector?' O'Neil affirmed giving them all a chuckle.

Templar winked at O'Neil "And unless I'm immediately incarcerated to prove differently, I am currently enjoying a wonderful vacation in the Bahamas. Would that I could provide each of you remaining with the same cover, though the thought occurs to me just now that I may be able to help!"

"To be honest" Emma admitted, "I don't believe *any* of us have ever really had to deal with the legal end of any of our exploits. All basically 'handled' as we went our merry way."

"Short of being thrown into a gulag, should we manage to expose the conspiratorial group responsible for this poor fellow's incarceration, we'll need to consider our legal standing *after* this project concludes. This situation has a number of games afoot. I will tell you this, if my collection of brilliant solicitors and barristers can be of service to you noble people, I would consider it an honour to press them into service myself on your behalf." vowed Templar.

After a pause, Steed admitted, "Templar, I am stunned and gratified. You are not at all as I'd heard or imagined."

Drake reluctantly agreed. "Your...reputation preceded you. And though I am personally aware of a handful of your more...'Saintly' exploits, I fear I discounted them. My opinion favoured your more infamous aspects. You have my sincerest apologies, Templar."

Templar grinned, his eyebrow arched, "Infamous? *Me?*" he asked, hand on his chest. His pose provoked some laughter, after which he explained, "To the degree I still have dealings with the ungodly from time to time, I'll admit I *have* purposefully promoted the more 'roguish' aspects of my reputation, so as to enable freer movement among them. I thank you sincerely for your apologies, though they really aren't necessary."

Drake moved back to the task at hand. "Steed, Simon, and Mr. O'Neil here have provided we five 'guerillas' with equipment enhancing our chances of success. They will be here, with instruction on their use provided tomorrow evening. Any amendments will be presented then as well." He stood silent for a few seconds. "This has been a very long road for me. There aren't words to express my gratitude to each of you. I want you each to know that."

Outside, Gambit walked with Steed. "You, Tara and I stand to lose the most if this goes wrong."

Steed turned facing him. "I'm convinced Drake uncovered something very nasty. And potentially enormous. If true, we've *already* lost much. We just didn't know it. Now's our chance to begin getting it *back*."

Gambit nodded grimly, audibly letting out a breath. "Mm. Good night, Steed."

25
Seven, Six, Five...

The next night at the studio, Terry O'Neil was finishing his 'class' on the equipment which would be utilized during the mission. Specifically instructing on the modifications he had made to a few items. "So, ya all know what to do with these things, right?" He received affirmative nods all around. "Any questions at all?"

There were none.

"Right, then. Guys, I want to wish you all the best. Godspeed, and kick arse!"

Steed and Drake approached him to shake his hand. Emma handed him an envelope which he shoved inside his jacket pocket, "Ta, ma'am."

Gambit clapped smiling. He put his arm around O'Neil's shoulder. "You need to consider bein' a teacher, mate. You're damn good at it. Seriously."

O'Neil bid them farewell once more, then left.

Then, there were six. Five returned to their seats.

Steed remained standing. "Your pilots and drivers will be at the ready. Any changes of personnel, Gambit and Tara will hear from me. Run across a change they don't know about, the plan is immediately scuttled. On the return, should they not know a pilot or driver, you are to dispatch the unknown, replacing them with either Tara or Mr. Templar. I'll keep the home fires burning. I'll be alerted at each leg. I'll rejoin you on your return at Little Rissington. Do you have any questions for me?"

There were none.

"Well then!" Steed turned to depart, moved forward three paces and stopped. Not turning, he stated quietly, "I am an uncommonly blessed fellow to be working with such extraordinary people. And if you'll allow this middle-aged agnostic license, I, too, wish you Godspeed. And here's hoping all runs smoothly so that *no* 'arses' need kicking!" He then exited in his characteristic march.

Drake stood. "Alright. Once more around the room."

Templar, Tara, Emma, and Gambit each verbally reiterated the plan and their specific responsibilities therein, Drake concluding the round. He had them each verbalize the responder codes for their mission, again, concluding the round. He felt as if he had a great deal to say. What he wound up saying was,

"Well done. Let's get some sleep. Be seeing you at HQ at 19:00."

26

21:00, 9/6/1969

The team left Department HQ helipad at 21:00 precisely. Forty minutes later they landed at Little Rissington base, switched choppers (complete with fresh pilots) and lifted off at 21:55, arriving at St. Athan base at 23:10. There, the team met their drivers and started on their way to Three Cliffs Bay at 23:27. Steed glanced at his watch. They should reach Three Cliffs within the hour. Once there, the team would proceed on foot to the target.

At 23:57, the signal from agent Merrow came across the receiver Steed had set up in his apartment. They had reached Three Cliffs Bay and were prepared to proceed. At any step along the way, if the team didn't receive the confirmation signal back from him, the plan would be aborted. It would mean something had gone awry. He sent the confirmation signal back to Merrow. Move forward.

23:58. Two minutes to midnight, he settled back with his drink. Whiskey and water, which he sipped. Champagne would be for after he got the signal to proceed to Little Rissington. 'No.' he amended the thought, 'Champagne will be for the *moment* they're all back home safely, with a released prisoner in tow. Not a moment before'. Thus would begin some of the longest hours he would ever endure. It was precisely then that his doorbell rang.

Steed really didn't care for guns. He didn't care to use them and practicing marksmanship with them became a task he'd never enjoyed, though he was amazingly good at it. They were noisy things, and they limited one's choices as to how much damage one wished to cause. He believed strongly that one didn't have to kill or maim to stop a foe, or to get a thing accomplished.

But, he supposed, one couldn't argue with their 'finality', their 'immediacy'.

A pointed revolver invited no further discussion, and generally halted further activity. A pointed revolver settled the argument, at least, for the time being. His revolver was right by his side tonight. And it was in his hand as he went to answer the doorbell.

It could, after all, be anything really, something that had no connection whatsoever to this mission at hand. An emergency, as emergencies would often occur. This hardly would've been the first time he'd opened his door at midnight to find a poor soul either desperately in need of his help, or there to warn him about something.

It was with that in mind that he answered the bell, standing in a way that the revolver was hidden, though ready for use. "Yes? Who is it?"

Steed's door was essentially a large pane of textured glass framed by wood. He'd often been chided by his friends and colleagues for having such a flimsy means of entering his home. Someone in his occupation, one of his position in his occupation, should *surely* have a much more secure entrance to his domain!

He basically felt that if someone wanted to get at him badly enough, a door was just a door, only as strong as the walls holding it. Glass, wood, concrete, what did it matter? He would decorate as he liked, and not feel like he was being held prisoner in his own abode.

However, there were times when he'd wished the textured glass wasn't quite so textured as to completely obscure the identity of whoever was behind it.

"Major Steed? This is Sir Curtis Seretse. May I come in?"

Setting aside the amazement at the alleged identity of his caller, his instincts instantly took over. Sir Curtis Seretse was a large black man. Two men were at his door, and the first was NOT a black man. The second may have been black, but the damned textured glass wouldn't allow for further acuteness of observation. He made a decision, holding the revolver even more at the ready. He swung his front door wide open, putting on his most cheerfully surprised smile. "Sir Curtis!!" he exclaimed, "What on *earth*..."

Steed never got to finish his greeting. Too late, he felt the sting of a small dart entering the side of his neck. Instantly, numbness spread. His motor functions simply froze. His hand dropped the revolver. His legs started to buckle within seconds. It wasn't a matter of things euphorically spinning out of control; it was purely a matter of things suddenly shutting down. '*Astonishing!*' was all his brain could utter.

He was astonished to see that it was, indeed, Seretse at the door. What astonished him more; the man in front of Seretse was an impeccably dressed white man with a moustache and ridiculously bouffant hair style. Steed's eyes closed, and as he fell to the floor, blackness flowing over him, the last thing he heard was Jason King's voice saying, "Forgive me, Steed."

27
Arrival

The team of Drake, Gambit, Tara, Emma and Templar had made their way from drop off point at Three Cliffs Bay to the target at Oxwich, Wales by 01:10. They supposed an imagined parameter about the proximity, having only some idea what to expect with regard to actual fences or security. Alarm systems utilizing infrared or laser beams could have theoretically extended out for about two kilometres, though that was unlikely in practical terms. Still, caution ruled the day as they proceeded toward their objective.

They'd have to make efficient use of their equipment. The equipment would only last as long as there was power, and with only a few battery changes available, power was limited. They'd considered the possibility of landmines unlikely, but still utilized the age old methodology of tossing rocks in front of them, along with occasional modern use of miniature metal detection devices just in case, following one another in single file when the terrain allowed.

They had planned to be able to meet most any contingency, including tranquilizer darts for dogs and human guards, and lenses for light refraction. Yet they would have to be able to move quickly and not be weighed down with an abundance of equipment.

Though each had their own individual back packs, Templar and Gambit volunteered to serve as 'pack mules', carrying batteries and other items that would be dispersed once they entered the grounds.

They weren't dressed in black, like secret agents one normally sees in film or on television. In reality, at night, black attire actually stuck out like a sore thumb. Their clothing was varying shades of charcoal grey, or blue-grey which blended in with the surroundings.

What they were surprised by (and somewhat alarmed by) was the fence. They had envisioned an intricate high security system, not this simple four strand electric wire fence that was actually in place. Above and below the fence were double rows of barbed wire. Posted every so often were signs stating 'Security Area. No Trespassing' or, 'Military Property. Limited Access'. Decidedly benign thought Drake, as he wondered what else might be in store that was more in keeping with what they had planned for.

A number of natural occurrences were aiding them. Foremost, it wasn't raining. Secondly, it was warm enough that one couldn't see their breaths, which could expose them. Third, the moon was at a waning crescent, providing good visibility, but not illuminating the area like a searchlight. And fourth, there was a light fog, the wisps of which would occasionally betray the presence of motion detectors.

Each member of the team donned special goggles provided by Templar, and 'tweaked' by young Mr. O'Neil. Drake and Templar made quick work of the fence, and they were inside. Simple motion detector locations were sighted and noted. And that was pretty much it!

They were all taken aback by the apparent lack of forms of security they'd prepared for. It troubled each of them. Lifting their goggles, they all silently looked at each other. A quick nod from Drake settled matters. 'Proceed to your assigned designations and tasks'.

It was understood that, under these circumstances, analysis of what was encountered had to wait. One had to act according to plan regardless. As far as any feelings of over-preparation may have been concerned, Emma had put it best; "It's always preferable to have surplus and no need, than to have need and be at a deficit."

Thus, they split up, and the search for the prisoner was on.

28

A, B, and C

It was very tempting to allow oneself to be bewildered by the surroundings of this odd place, Gambit thought. He found he had to remind himself not to rely on preconceived notions regarding, well, *anything* really.

They knew this would be different. But it was all so...disorienting. He found himself thinking it might be nice just to visit during the day and relax! He shook his head. 'Stop it!' he inwardly scolded himself. 'On task! Quit daydreaming!'

He reached his target, and hit the transponder belted around his upper left arm. One beep transmitted 'have arrived at destination'. One low beep responded via Mission Commander Drake, 'acknowledged'. Gambit donned his infrared goggles and began inspecting the first of three large long complexes.

There are few cases where infrared goggles might not pick up the heat signatures. Glass effectively blocks imaging, as do some alloys, such as aluminium. One can temporarily throw off body heat imaging by throwing on a blanket, but heat starts building again fairly quickly. A thusly covered sleeping body is readable, for example.

Standing close by a similar heat source can confound imaging. Common attempts at masking can actually create 'negative' imaging, as what's being 'masked' doesn't blend in with the ambient heat of a given area. The image reads 'too cold', creating a 'black hole' in the overall view, and thus must be human, or highly suspect.

Circumnavigation of complex 'A' revealed three heat sources of a mechanical nature, all on the first floor.

His investigation of complex 'B' revealed three mechanical heat sources on the first floor, and two sleeping bodies on the second. It took a bit of time to investigate further, but he was able to ascertain that neither of these sleepers was the 'objective', by cautiously climbing up to a second floor ledge, and peeking in the windows via binoculars.

Complex 'B' thus crossed off his mental checklist; he switched goggles and was able to locate motion detectors on the surrounding grounds which he easily skirted. Climbing a wall brought him to the elevated front of complex 'C'. He switched back to infrared goggles again and found them beginning to short out.

'Damn! These things take up a lot of battery power *fast!*' he thought. He sprinted to another wall by the entryway and crouched down by a shrub, opening his backpack. He replaced the battery pack for the IR goggles, harnessed his backpack, put the goggles on, stood and turned to begin his investigation of complex 'C'. He turned a corner and...

Mike Gambit never knew what hit him.

29

Simon Templar; North-East Quadrant One

Transponder signal sent and acknowledged, Templar began his task of scanning and investigating the five small buildings assigned to him. IR goggles in place, he viewed the first. These were small living spaces, much like flats he'd known elsewhere. One person awake on the first floor, moving about in a kitchen. Another awake on the second, apparently preparing for bed as the figure stretched.

'And *what* a figure!' Templar mentally noted. 'A woman! In fact, yes, both were women! Interesting.

He scurried around a decorative structure, some sort of tall archway leading to nowhere in particular ('Odd place' he was continually commenting to himself), and came to his next objective, a one-story circular building.

These places had absolutely nothing in common with any type of structure one might use to imprison someone, he noted, growing more perplexed with each observance. 'And I should know. I've been held prisoner more often than I care to admit!' he mentally admitted. Large windows, ornate landscaping; one could easily escape, concealing themselves in the shrubbery and odd corners of the place. It simply made no sense.

IR goggles read one person asleep in a lounge chair. A peek in the window would serve to see if this was their 'Prisoner'. He removed his goggles when he noticed a tiny flash of light.

"Ah! Here we are!" he thought. He took a tiny spray bottle from his backpack. Holding it back from the window, he sprayed twice. A fine mist of coloured water revealed a matrix of very fine laser lights crossing the window pane.

'Of course! Spend the money on refined systems for the displays holding the treasures, and we can forego the expense of a great deal of security for the museum itself!'

This went a long way in explaining why it had been such a simple matter for them to gain access to the grounds. 'Aha! And there's our magnetic tape on the sill.' It was a relief to him to find such measures in place after all, as the sheer *lack* of what they had been expecting was rather unsettling.

Finishing his examination of the window, he replaced the spray bottle in his backpack, and withdrew a penlight from a small pack secured to his side. A precisely aimed flash from the penlight confirmed this sleeping man was not who they were looking for. He quickly moved from this structure, stealthily cleared a waist high wall, and crept up to the next place.

He made a full scan of target three and found no heat source at all. On to number four.

Here, he stopped, then crouched beside a small ornate well. *Yes!* He *had* heard a sound! That of a Mini Moke, located twenty metres in front of him. The sound came a bit closer, slowed and continued for a bit, then regained speed and drove away.

'And here, *finally,* we have the ground crew.' A grim smile formed, as he found humour in the incongruity of his being relieved that there *was* more security here than met the eye. He cautiously circled the well, and slowly stood.

Three metres directly in front of him stood a stunningly attractive blonde woman, looking straight at him! He couldn't help himself. 'Oh no!' he thought, 'Whatever would Drake and Steed make of *this?*'

The woman looked at him passively. She spoke in an even, quiet, firm tone.

"Please make no sudden moves. I do not wish to harm you. Do you understand?"

After a moment, he nodded slowly.

"Good. You are illegally trespassing here. You are obviously aware of that. Again, I wish you no harm, but I *do* insist that you comply with my directives. Is that clear?"

This was *fascinating*, he thought, dumbfounded. The woman was completely unarmed. There was no weapon bearing down on him, no gun pointing at him. Yet this woman had all the confidence in the world. As though there were no question, at least in her mind, that she had complete control over the situation. He slowly nodded once again.

"Thank you. Very slowly, please divest yourself of your backpack and of any weapons you may have. Toss them some distance from you to your left."

He drew himself up, lifted his shirt, and slowly pulled out his revolver. He suddenly aimed it at the woman, who just as suddenly was no longer in front of him.

The next thing he knew, he was lying on his back on moist ground four metres from where he'd just stood, his gun simply *gone!* He winced in pain. He could feel a number of items in his backpack, some shards of broken equipment stabbing him, though not seriously so.

The woman stood in front of him once again, peering down at him.

"Please! I'd really rather not resort to this. I insist you comply to avoid further harm. Now undo your pack and stand up."

He unhooked the harness and did as he was told. Confused, he tried shaking his head clear. '*How* had she managed to *do* that?' he wondered. Slowly he got up.

"Now walk forward. Please follow my directions." He discerned no animosity in her voice whatsoever.

He did as he was told. After a minute, she spoke again, "Please turn left at this pathway, and proceed along it."

He turned, and as he did so, he could see that she was less than two metres away from him. He purposefully 'stumbled' to a crouch and kicked out with his right leg.

...and connected with nothing but air.

She wasn't even in *sight!* Remaining in a crouch he turned his head. There she stood four metres in front of him once again, glaring at him. He could *not* believe his *eyes*. 'That's *impossible! No* one could move so *fast!* She was just...'

"This is becoming tiresome." she stated simply, as the lights suddenly went out for The Saint.

30

Tara King; South-East Quadrant Two

Their mission was to investigate 24 buildings, or structures contained in what they called 'The Compound'. If they had not found the man they were after (easily identifiable as he looked like Drake) within the first 22, they would then investigate the remaining two questionable structures (if structures they were) in some fashion.

Once one 'cleared' their quadrant, they would return where they had first gained access, exit, move to a grouping of trees twenty metres outside the fence, beep twice on their transponders, and wait.

Tara's quadrant had only four buildings, but they were scattered farther apart.

This was the most unmilitary looking place she had ever seen! The seemingly random placement of these residences was quite puzzling. There were paved pathways between some, and cobblestone stairways to others. Pathways that went to or came from nowhere, tables set up in odd spots near nothing in particular, miniature patios here and there, decorative edifices and structures seemingly in place merely to look pretty, serving no other real function that she could discern.

She supposed that, in the light of day, it would've all been pastoral, quaint, and picturesque. Viewed now, in relative darkness, it was just eerie.

What's more, the overall *quiet* of the place unnerved her. One might be tempted to refer to it as tranquil, were it not for its unproven but very likely insidious nature.

She was half-way through her quadrant when she was surprisingly 'relieved' to hear the sound of a vehicle. Then, very quiet voices. They were quite off in the distance, no cause for immediate alarm, but certainly cause for intensified caution. She was relieved in the sense that she was finally hearing what she expected under these circumstances. She waited by a tree until the sounds faded.

Scampering over a thigh high wall, she approached her third building. Like the first two, this one was bereft of heat sources. It bothered her. While it was a blessing to find empty buildings, it was also not producing their objective. She resolved that eliminating possibilities would have to be enough.

Directly across the lawn stood her final target. Her IR goggles revealed a sleeping figure. She gingerly reached the tiny balcony outside of where they slept and climbed onto it. Again, she couldn't believe her luck! One tiny window had been opened just about an inch! Without having to move closer, she could clearly hear snoring. A woman's snoring! That being that, she furtively made her way to the assigned waiting place.

It was starting to get cold, and it had gotten decidedly foggier. From her viewpoint here, she could see a large section of the compound. She thought she could hear voices at times but couldn't be certain. It could just as easily have been animals nearby.

Tara had very acute hearing which had saved the day on any number of occasions for her and Steed. She recognized the occasional sound of a vehicle. A cart or Mini Moke she guessed. Not particularly alarming as it was expected, guards patrolling the area and the like. And again, it was, in a way, reassuring to hear these sounds as opposed to the dead quiet.

She became suddenly alarmed at what she thought was a flash of white off in the distance. She strained to see. 'No. Nothing. Wait, *yes!* There it was again!' She decided to risk using binoculars, placing her hand over the top of the lenses to decrease the possibility of light reflecting off them. 'No, gone again.' But she *had* seen it. She thought, 'A weather balloon? Their 'eyes in the sky'?' that's probably what it was. Let's hope it's too dark or too foggy for them to be useful.'

She thought of Steed, manning the ramparts at his home in London. What a dreadful watch for him. At least she was *here!* Poor Steed. As often as he was fond of breaking rules, his sense of duty was immense and unflappable. It would do no one any good for him to be here. He understood that. Even if she had bristled at the thought of him being unceremoniously 'sidelined', he would attempt to be their 'safety net'; their last line of defence should this whole enterprise result in crushing failure. 'He also serves...'

'...who sits amongst these trees and waits.' Tara sighed silently.

31

John Drake; South-West Quadrant Three

He was honestly pleased his IR goggles showed no heat signature coming from Target Three in his quadrant. He felt he had spent an inordinate amount of time breaking and entering into the first two structures. It had taken little time to verify that neither of the two men in the first building was the man they sought, but it had taken deft manoeuvring to verify the same for the one man in the second. He had been sleeping, but just as Drake entered the bedroom, the man awoke, arose, shuffled to the toilet, used it (all in the dark), and returned to bed, burying his face in the pillow. Drake waited some moments for him to fall into a regular breathing pattern, then, with great trepidation, he softly tickled the man's ear. The sleeper turned his head slightly, swatting a phantom midge, exposing just enough of his face. Nope. Not him.

As Drake progressed to target four, he heard two barely audible beeps coming from his transponder, which he immediately acknowledged. That was Tara clear. Time was growing short. He walked down a set of steps to a clearing just before his next objective. He paused.

Of the four quadrants, his was closest to the beach where the cliffs of Oxwich Green, above and to the west, began to rise. The ambient sounds would occasionally travel and amplify, giving him a start; water suddenly slapping against rock, the cry of a gull, that sort of thing. He thought he heard something just then and stopped to listen.

“Sir, please do not move. Do not turn around. Comply with my directions and you will not be harmed. Do you understand?”

The male voice, quiet yet commanding, came from approximately four metres behind him. There was no immediate cover to dive to. He was out in the open, and completely vulnerable. The voice was situated too far away to attempt any offensive tactics. One wrong move and he would be dead, or at least, stopped in some way.

“I...do.”

“Sir, please follow my instructions to the letter. Now slowly, and I mean *slowly*, with your left hand, divest yourself of any weapons you may have.”

Drake was dubious. This man behind him was exceedingly polite given the circumstances. Obviously military, he thought, a trained officer’s quality to the diction and vocabulary the man was using.

“I am unarmed.” Drake said.

“Any form of weapon sir. Blades included.”

“I am unarmed.” Drake repeated.

“Very well. Now slowly, unharness your backpack and let it slide down to the ground.”

Drake did as he was told.

“Now gently kick the pack some distance to your left.”

He complied. The man quickly picked up the pack and moved back.

“Thank you. You are obviously aware that you are here illegally in a restricted area. You are here intentionally, with cause. Is that correct?”

“It...it is.” He had to play along with this. Cooperating meant time for something later.

"Again, I will in no way harm you if you continue to comply with my directives. Do you understand?"

"I do." Good God this man was being thorough!

"Please turn to your right and begin walking at a leisurely pace. Walk straight ahead, look straight ahead, and do not turn around. Walk until I tell you to stop. Begin now."

He and his unseen "host" walked for sixteen paces when the man directed, "Stop please. Turn to your right, and we will proceed for another nine paces." They did so. "Now stop, turn to your left. Walk four paces. The door in front of you is your next stop."

Drake walked to the door, which automatically opened. "Enter the doorway and walk five paces." He complied. As he reached his third step, lights automatically switched on. At his fourth step, he could hear the automatic door close behind him.

He turned and regarded the closed door. Metal. The man behind him had stayed outside. He turned and regarded the room. Square, with metallic walls four metres high, a clean concrete floor, a tiny air vent at the top middle of the wall to his right.

He had merely been unceremoniously dumped in a completely empty square room.

32

Emma Peel; North-West Quadrant Four

A standing reading lamp dimly lit the lounge chair and man sleeping in it, a blanket covered his lap and legs. A book lay haphazardly on his lap, his black heavy framed glasses slid down to the tip of his nose. His hair was full, but neatly trimmed, as was his beard and moustache.

Here, in the third building she searched in her quadrant; here, of all possible places on *Earth* he could have been, here, in a *billion* to one gamble, was the man this mission was all about. The man she had found herself referring to in these past weeks as 'Prisoner Six'! He *was* a twin of John Drake, though more gaunt and perhaps a bit older. It was difficult to say for sure from where she stood outside his window.

Emma realized that she'd been, to be honest, totally beside herself with the discovery. 'Get *on* with it!' she scolded, snapping out of it.

It became suddenly and vividly apparent to her that, had she not been in such reverie, she might have noticed a presence just behind her. Her peripheral vision might have caught a glimpse of a man's hand moving toward her. It wasn't until she concurrently heard the words, "Miss, please come with me..." and felt a strong tug on her upper left arm that she snapped fully back into the here and now.

Rather than defensively pulling away from the tug, she immediately relinquished to it. This allowed her the freedom to perfectly pivot anti-clockwise, thrusting her open palmed right hand to grasp the back of her assailant's head. In continuation of the full circular motion, she had simultaneously raised her right knee to the small of the man's back, adding her momentum and weight to his, causing his face and body to *smash* into the masonry of the building with full alacrity. He slid to the ground completely unconscious.

She leapt away from the unfortunate fellow and quickly found that he was not alone.

Two others orbited her, one deciding to rush her, unfortunately with his arms outstretched toward her. She simply sidestepped him, and with a shove, added to his momentum so that he crashed head long into his companion, knocking his companion backward as he fell to the ground.

She instantly made a forty five degree turn, then jumped and landed with both feet squarely in the middle of the fallen man's back, crushing the wind out of him. Then, using his back as a makeshift springboard she leapt to the other foe who, though stunned, had remained upright.

As she landed, she kicked out her leg, catching her third foe at the side of his knee. She heard a 'snap' as he collapsed to the ground sideways.

The man only had time to yelp in pain once, as she turned, stood, and let loose a flurry of Kung-Fu punches to his face and head which rendered *him* unconscious.

Side-stepping him, she returned to the man whom she'd used as a trampoline. Groggy, stunned, trying to catch his breath, his body caught in an awkward half-crouch, half-kneel, he struggled to get back up. She denied him that opportunity with a swift strong sideways kick full in his face. He fell backward to the ground, done in.

Three down. Emma turned to see what else was in store.

A large white pliant sphere bounced in place not more than three metres from her. It was making a sound similar to that which one hears when wearing scuba gear. She stood shocked, but only for an instant. A connection quickly clicked in her brain. 'Weather balloon equals 'bubble ghost' equals I am in dire danger'.

Rather than attempt to fight the thing (which she somehow instinctively knew would've been useless – How does one render a weather balloon 'unconscious'?), she ran.

She got all of perhaps six metres before the thing came upon her, enveloping her from toe to just below her nose. She could breathe, but she couldn't move. The thing toppled such that she was being held parallel to the ground.

It was at that point when she saw the Mini Moke driving slowly toward her. She felt tears of frustration starting to flow from her eyes, one thought running through her mind, 'No! Not when we were *so* close...!' She commanded herself to stop the tears, blinked her eyes and furrowed her brow.

A man dressed in a charcoal grey uniform parked the cart four metres away, and stood beside it, hands on his hips, appraising her. He removed his hat and twirled it in his hands for a few seconds, staring at it. He was about two metres tall, and stocky, with white, or light grey hair. He put his hat back on, moving it to the back of his head. From his shirt pocket he pulled out a pack of cigarettes, took one out, put it in his mouth and lit it.

He moved closer to her. From his pocket he pulled out a small box and tapped it twice. The sphere-bubble-balloon thing shrank away from her mouth and neck. She was able to move her head. She felt the thing loosen itself slightly, but she was still securely encased.

"*Who* in *hell* are you? And *what* in hell is this...*thing*?" she roared.

He held his hands up palms out in front of him, "Look, ma'am, there'll be plenty of time for answers a little later, I promise. For right now, I'd rather make a deal with you."

"What sort of 'deal'?" she spat, clearly enraged and frustrated.

"I'll get this thing offa you if...*if*...you promise to settle down and come with me peacefully. No tricks. We'll go for a little ride, and then everything will be explained to you. Deal?"

Emma continued to struggle, but to no avail. "Why trust you? What if I choose 'no deal'?"

He kneeled on one knee. "Well then I'll have to 'tranq' you, dump your ass in my cart, and get you where we need to go anyway." He admitted matter-of-factly. "Look, I can help you get to the bottom of all this. I swear. Just give me your word that you'll behave yourself, and we can get a move on, alright?"

She had little other choice, and, though she felt insane even considering it, this man actually sounded *sincere*! As if she could actually *trust* what he was saying.

Nope! There was nothing sane about that at all; nothing remotely sane about *any* of this! The whole set-up was Kafkaesque! But 'At least free of this... whatever it is' she reckoned, 'I'll have options'.

"Agreed then. We have a deal. A truce."

"Good. Because I really don't want to risk hurting you any further."

"And, frankly..." he admitted, as he flicked his cigarette away and looked to his left, nodding his head toward where she had been prior to the thing appearing and encasing her, "I'd just as soon *not* get my *ass* kicked like my three buddies back there."

He hit a button on the little box he held, and the thing immediately began to dissolve, releasing her, eventually disappearing altogether.

She slowly got up and tested her bearing.

The man got in the driver's seat of the cart, waiting while she slowly made her way into the passenger side seat.

"You're obviously American." she stated, as she decided to 'stand down', relax and try to make sense of things.

"No, ma'am, I'm Texan." he clarified, as he drove off.

33
Checkmate

Tara King waited. And waited.

'Where *were* they?' she wondered, worried. She rolled her sleeve back and checked her watch. 03:32. One of the others would surely have finished their task by now! She'd been somewhat concerned when she thought she spied another flash of white. Or a flash of light. She couldn't be certain. But if was one of the weather balloons, who knew what type of spying devices were being utilized? There was just no way of telling.

At one point, she thought she heard a cry. A human voice crying in pain. But then again, she had heard the cry of a gull occasionally as well, which was similar.

Besides, what if it *had* been a human voice? What could she do about it? She'd gone through a plethora of possibilities in her mind. Every single scenario her brain entertained always ended up with the same solution.

Follow the plan. No matter what, follow the plan.

Just then, a Mini Moke drove by the section of fence they'd rewired to gain access. The cart slowed down, stopped, reversed, and stopped again. A man in a dark uniform got out, surveyed the fence, nonchalantly walked back to the Mini Moke and drove off.

'Well, that tears it!' She thought. 'One thing more before following the plan.' She transmitted a beep from her transponder. She waited twenty seconds for a response or acknowledgement. Nothing. She repeated transmission, then waited, keeping an eagle eye on the fence, and keeping her sharp ears open. Again, nothing.

She heard one, perhaps two Mini Mokes being driven. Soon, she heard another sound, as though someone was using an oxygen tank. 'Possibly something to weld the fence? No, that wouldn't be it. Time to away. Follow the plan.' she concluded.

Extraction had failed, now the plan called for any or all team members to get back to Three Cliffs Bay as quickly as possible, send word to Steed, and get back home.

She stood, stretched, shook herself loose to limber up, and exited from the middle of the group of trees. She crouched down, turned left to proceed west, and took five steps before stopping stock still.

She straightened herself and stood at attention, looking straight into the eyes of a tall black haired man dressed in a charcoal grey uniform. Directly behind him was a white amorphous sphere that hovered above the ground. The man's arms were spread, his hands palms out.

"I am unarmed. I will not harm you. Do you understand me?"

She nodded. Her eyes began to water slightly, but she took hold of herself.

"Your colleagues are with us. They are alive and well. Please accompany me, and I will prove that to you."

Frightened, Tara slowly pointed to the sphere behind him. "What is that?"

"That? Well Miss, '*that*' is doing as I ask the 'hard way'." he smiled. "Please simply walk toward me and we'll go about doing things the *easy* way."

She walked toward him. They turned, and, almost as if strolling together, they made their way to the compound, the glowing white sphere following behind them.

34
Room Without a View

It was essentially a long conference room, a door on both ends, with a long conference table in the middle, chairs placed around it. There were glasses and pitchers of water placed on the table, an ashtray at each end. The windowless room was carpeted, with acoustic tiling on the walls that were painted a pleasing shade of mint green. The lighting was subdued, but not dim.

Emma Peel half-sat on the table meditating on the door. She had been there for some time. Far *too* long by her estimation. When the door opened, she would be ready. She'd measured the movement out, testing the sturdiness of the table. The next unknown face entering the room would be enthusiastically greeted by the soles of her feet. There was a slight click at the door, and it began to open. She prepared for the instant when...

Tara King entered, followed by her tall dark haired captor. "Please, sit down and make yourself comfortable." he invited, looking amused. "Ma'am, please?" he indicated one of the chairs to Emma with his hand. "It would've been a nice try, but really, ultimately a waste of your effort." he smiled.

Glaring at him flippantly with tongue in cheek, Emma sat in a different chair than the one he had offered. The man, with a sly smile, shook his head back and forth slightly at an angle as he left the room.

Tara dejectedly half-smirked at Emma, who smirked back, while putting a finger to her lips, shaking her head. Tara nodded and took the seat next to her.

Next entered Mike Gambit, escorted by another man, who simply turned and exited, shutting the door behind him. Gambit nodded to Emma and Tara and sat on their side of the table some seats down from them, dead silent.

Soon, John Drake was escorted in by the man who escorted Tara. Inviting him to take a seat, the black-haired man sat on the other side of the table about two thirds of the way from the door. He glanced at Gambit who sat silently, staring straight ahead.

Drake stood by Emma for a moment. She looked up at him, directly into his eyes and very slightly nodded her head. He dramatically arched one eyebrow, and a faint smirk appeared. He remembered himself, and quickly erased the expression. He then took the seat next to her, closest to the entrance.

Lastly, within minutes, Simon Templar joined them holding an ice pack to the back of his head and neck, being escorted by the same attractive blonde woman who had captured him. Relieved, he looked at each of his teammates, and uttered, "*Thank God!*" and seated himself next to Gambit. The blonde woman sat on the opposite side of the table three chairs away from the dark-haired man.

Within seconds, a white-grey haired man strode in holding some files and sat in the seat between his cohorts. All three were dressed in similar style to Drake's team, each in blue-grey, or charcoal grey pullovers and slacks.

The white-haired fellow motioned to the dark-haired man to pass the ashtray. He took his cigarettes out of his breast pocket and lit one. He stood and leaned over the table, offering a cigarette to any who wished. The team declined, remaining silent, looking defiantly at their captors.

He put the cigarettes back in his pocket and leaned on the table tapping his fingers. He narrowed his eyes at Drake, shook his head a bit, blinked his eyes exaggeratedly, and confessed, "Ya know, when I first saw you; that put a *whole* 'nuther spin on this thing for me."

"My name is Mac McGill." He announced, standing straight.

A bit startled, Tara's eyes widened. 'No it's not! He's lying! He looks nothing like Mac McGill!' she thought. The 'Mac McGill' Tara had 'interviewed' in the newspaper office couldn't have been more physically unlike this man! This Mac McGill, though white haired, couldn't be any older than forty-five at most. He was sharp and very athletically built! She couldn't help herself from staring accusingly at this imposter.

McGill noticed. He had a unique talent for being able to scrutinize a person without specifically looking at them. Something 'clicked' in his brain. He let out a soft chuckle, looked directly at her and grinned sheepishly.

"Yeah, I know. Figure *that*, right?" he agreed, "That was my reaction too!"

Tara gulped involuntarily, bewildered. The dark-haired man glanced at McGill, curious.

McGill turned to him. "Our journalist visitor friend from a few weeks ago. Apparently, this lady knows him too." he said, hitching his thumb Tara's way.

Then the man nodded with gradual comprehension. He also looked at her, smiling, hitched his thumb toward McGill and said, "This is McGill number two."

McGill introduced his comrades. "This is Craig Stirling. And this lovely lady here is Doctor Sharron Macready."

"*Doctor?*" Templar blurted out, rubbing the back of the neck, wincing. He reminded himself to stay silent, but his eyes remained wide with incredulity.

Macready looked down, clearly embarrassed. McGill, grinning a bit sheepishly once again, mumbled "Yeah, well..." as he retook his seat.

"I'm not gonna ask what you're doin' here, because we already know. We're not sure *who* you were after, or *why*. *That* concerns us, believe me. I suppose we'll figure it out before too long. I doubt you'd ever tell us, though it'd sure clear things up a lot quicker.

"I gotta say you folks almost pulled off one slick operation out there. You really did. Ya got nothing to be ashamed about."

He turned his head toward Emma. "And you almost did it without violence. Believe it or not, I respect that. We really respect that here.

"We've got information that leads us to believe this is all one *big* mistake. There's a few people on their way here as we speak, some you even know. These people will be able to clear up this whole thing. We plan to meet later today. Probably around, what, 11:00? Noon?" he asked Macready.

"Yes, it looks like noon."

"Okay." he continued, glancing at Templar specifically, "A few of you got knocked around a little bit." He tilted his head toward Emma once again, "And a few of *us* got knocked around *real* good!"

"It's not what we wanted. Remember that. We gave you every opportunity to do this peacefully. You're here, you're alive, and you're *well*. I'd say we've done pretty good keeping our end of the bargain.

"Don't press us. Until we get things straightened out, you are detainees. Any escape attempts *will* be dealt with! Fully, and with prejudice! Is that clear?"

Drake, Emma, Tara, Gambit and Templar had discussed contingency plans for possible capture and subsequent escape during this mission. With all the variables involved, it boiled down to "every man for himself." A bitter reality, but there it was.

Generally, captors 'divide and conquer'. It is standard procedure to break up any group, to imprison and interrogate individually. It is also a standard practice to try to get them to work against each other. Promise one reward for betraying the others. As they had been taken individually, and incarcerated individually (at first), that was what Drake's team had been expecting, the norm.

To be brought together like this, almost immediately, *that* was very odd! The thought occurred to Drake it would be expedient for their captors to kill them all together right here. By their comportment however, that hardly seemed to be what they had in mind. Again, everything about this place, these people, *everything* was *not* in the slightest what one would expect. It was jarring and confounding.

McGill glanced at his watch as he stood with Stirling and Macready. "Look, I know you don't trust us, but we're *not* the 'Bad Guys' here! What's more, I don't *think* you guys are either. I'm not sure. In about six or seven hours, we'll all have the whole story.

"It's been a long day; we suggest you get some sleep. I plan on grabbing a few hours myself. We've got places set up, one for the ladies, and one for you gents."

Drake stood. "If it's all the same, I believe we'll...rest here."

"Suit yerselves." McGill turned and left, leaving the door wide open.

Macready informed them, "You'll find toilets down the hall. Three doors to your left, and right." She instructed Templar, "Keep applying that pack. Move your head around, back and forth so your neck doesn't stiffen up." She smiled at him as she left. Templar glared at her, watching her leave. She *did* have a *very* nice...smile though, he thought.

Stirling walked over to Gambit. "What Mac said about giving you all a peaceful choice, I didn't give you that option unfortunately. Old habits die hard. I had the advantage, saw an opportunity and took it without thinking. I'm sorry."

Gambit stared back, never saying a word or changing his expression. Stirling turned and left, still leaving the door completely open. The team surveyed each other, *very* befuddled. Drake mumbled in a low tone, "Who knows what devices they have here. Comparing notes will have to wait. Try to get rest."

Emma leaned closer to him whispering, "He's here."

He looked at her and whispered back, "I know. You've already told me."

35
Post Mortem

Drake had tried a number of times to lay his head on the table and rest, but his brain wouldn't allow it. The lights had automatically dimmed, the others were sleeping on the floor, and aside from the soft rhythmic snoring coming from Tara, and the occasional 'eruption' of snorting from Gambit, all was quiet.

It was the contradictory nature of the night's events that kept his mind going full bore. His brain's hunger to analyze, deconstruct, rearrange and reconstruct data with regard to the mission was not to be sated. Specifics of what they had individually experienced were unknown to each other. He tried to tell his brain he hadn't enough data for a post mortem, but his brain wouldn't listen.

It was the nature of the universe that no *one* plan would ever work perfectly. 'No plan survives first contact' as they say...therefore one had to plan on multiple levels, with contingencies at every turn.

They were successful in circumventing the security measures encountered. True, there wasn't that much security to circumvent in the first place.

They had succeeded in avoiding detection. True, except for when each had been detected, exposed, overcome and captured.

He couldn't speak to the experiences of the others. His own indicated they knew he was there all along. They were expecting and waiting for them. They'd been captured within hours after entry.

Of course, one maintained security by assuming there would always be someone trying to circumvent it. That cyclic thinking is what essentially grew technology after all. A better wall begets a better ladder and so on.

So, perhaps no one was expecting 'him' per se. Solid measures would presume an intruder present, and once found, a policy or plan of action would be followed. A controlled non-escalating interaction with said intruder would be attempted. He decided that perhaps his first view was a bit paranoid. It took hours for their captors to capture *them* was another way of looking at it.

They had succeeded in finding 'The Prisoner'. Emma confirmed it. Thus, 'Prisoner Six' *was* being held here. No getting around that fact now. All of their 'shots in the dark' had paid off. 'We're not the 'Bad Guys'' McGill had said. Oh so? Then why was this man here? There was no '*big* mistake' about *that!*

It seemed Emma was also responsible for some type of damage to personnel and/or property. He allowed himself a grin. 'Figure *that!*' he thought. Thus she, Templar, and Gambit all had altercations. Templar obviously, and Gambit apparently, based on what Stirling mentioned. Yet, outside of Templar, none were bruised or wounded. Emma's hair wasn't even mussed!

In his case, he'd had no choice but to comply with his captor and bide his time. He'd not been mishandled. He hadn't even been touched! That was noteworthy of itself. Thus, their captors' repeated 'desire' to do no harm appeared sincere. Again, why?

The five of us brought to this room. That went a long way in supporting his earlier thought they wouldn't be killed. At least for now. They surely could have, one by one, or en masse in this very room. Gassed, for example. So, they wish to keep us alive. Why? That was obvious. To find out who we are. Find out what knowledge we have. What we might know about them.

To see if we can provide them with something they can use. Simple ransom perhaps? No, that didn't make sense. Political blackmail? A charge of espionage made against us, we are then 'spies', to be used in trade for the release of others? *That* is certainly feasible. Keep us fit and well for that purpose.

Their captors; one American, one either American or Canadian, the doctor was British, and the man who captured him was British. The American, McGill, seemed to be in charge. Even so, he didn't fit as head of the *overall*, his comportment not being that of a 'Boss', a 'Number One'. Thus, we have International 'staff' to some degree. Do we then have an International organization running this place? An international 'clearing house' with spies available for trade for a fee?

Mm, no, too convoluted. The cost of running such an enterprise far exceeded the profit one could reasonably expect. Besides, every country had a few 'spies' tucked away in some prison or another hadn't they? Unless something changed during the year he'd been 'Joey Wolf', were things different now? That seemed *very* unlikely.

Still, megalomania had little regard for accurate accounting. He hadn't run across very many 'evil masterminds' in his career, but he was aware, from tales they'd told these last few weeks, that Emma, Steed, Tara and Templar had! Common thugs with outsized egos and bank accounts who thought themselves master criminals of the 'Dr. No' variety, all with ludicrous plots of needless complexity and expense. Was *that* the situation they were in? That idea didn't fit either. Again, very little 'fit'.

Very puzzling too, was the fact that their three captors were unarmed, or ostensibly so. One would have thought there would have been some form of armed guard protecting them. Three against five in a narrow room? Aware of the degree of havoc Emma alone could cause, as McGill seemed to be, one would expect an armed guard at the door. Their three captors had all behaved as though the considerable physical skills of the five were of no concern.

Of course, they assume we are defenceless; in an unknown place in enemy territory. But it would have been a small matter to take one (or even all three) of them hostage and force a release. It was as if we were 'trusted' not to resort to that type of desperate act. That and/or their captors held a trump card they were absolutely certain of. *That* was the most likely scenario.

Finally, there was Steed. With one call, he could have set all this in motion. Betrayed us. Could have been his plan all along. Possibly even with Gambit and/or Miss King as moles. That theory was entirely feasible. That allowed pieces to fit together. 'People we 'know', on their way', what did *that* mean? Suspicion buzzed through his brain. He tried to quash it, but...He felt sick to his stomach even considering it.

Drake *had* had his own 'Secret Plan B', of course. Just in case trusting Steed had been the wrong move in the first place. He *knew* he could trust Keith Turnbull, and two others. They had worked very successfully as a team many times in the past, on extraction missions like this one. This was the reason he'd approached 'Tom' at the café.

The 'framing' he was referring to with Turnbull would have constituted a shadow group to follow him, Emma, and the others after some time had passed. Turnbull and crew would be the 'cavalry' in case they were captured. None of the others would even know about Turnbull's crew. Just in case...

Unfortunately, one *really* needs both arms and hands to do that type of work. So his 'Plan B' flew out the window, due to Keith Turnbull's busted 'wing'.

'Let's be blunt, old boy. This...relationship with Emma, whatever it might be, is certainly playing a part in your thinking. Whether you want to admit it.' He steeled himself. No, he thought; stop this train. Let's not bring any more into this than is evident now. It was at that point that Drake cradled his arms on the table, rested his head on them, and was finally able to sleep.

36
The Morning After

The knock on the unclosed door had startled Drake awake.

"Good morning." a woman's voice rang out.

Looking immediately to the door, he saw Macready along with another young woman, a brunette dressed in a simple sweatshirt and jeans (Of all things! In *this* place?). Macready was dressed in a blue grey pullover and grey skirt.

He quickly scanned the conference room. Templar was seated at the far end of the conference table with Gambit. Emma was up stretching, and Tara was (comically) on the floor propped up on one arm, still half asleep, trying to figure out where in the *hell* she was.

The brunette announced pleasantly, "Breakfast has been prepared for you in the dining room at the end of the hallway."

Macready instructed, "You'll be joining us. We've arrangements made for you to freshen up a bit later." Then she and the brunette simply left the room, leaving the door still open.

Emma stood, hands on her hips, and theatrically sniffed the air, waving her hand in front of her nose. "I'm for *that!*"

Gambit and Templar sniffed themselves, Templar saying, "I concur."

Drake stood. Controlled fury in his eyes, he thought 'This is preposterous!' He looked at his team murmuring, "I don't understand...any of this. We may as well do as asked. It would do us no good I can think of to defiantly decline."

Gambit concurred, "I'm in complete agreement. In a manner of speaking, they're holding a gun to our heads. They could kill us now, or in the middle of coffee or a shower. I'd prefer doing anything other than just sitting here."

Emma chimed in. "I'm famished. The floor was uncomfortable, and I positively *reek!*"

She took the lead as they started to file out of the room. "Doctor Macready" she called as they began to enter the hallway, "might we freshen up prior to breakfast?"

Macready turned to them, seemed to weigh the request, and then decided, "Of course, one moment: Alison? Would you please get Mister Stirling?"

They all waited until Stirling approached them from the dining room. "Good morning, ladies. If you'll follow Doctor Macready we can accommodate you. Gentlemen, we'll accommodate you after breakfast."

He paused. Then, with complete conviction and confidence, he warned, "I would remind you that despite all evidence to the contrary, you *are* our detainees, at least for the time being. Any escape attempts will be dealt with. Again, you won't be harmed in any way if you simply enjoy our hospitality." The courteous smile returned to his face as he bid "Would you follow me please?"

Macready led the two women through a door to their right off the hallway.

The men followed Stirling, Templar saying just loud enough for Drake and Gambit to hear, "This is *extraordinary!* I've been treated worse in some French resorts! Escape warning excluded of course."

They entered into a comfortably sized dining room with all the accoutrements. Daylight shined through large windows. Set up by one wall was a breakfast buffet. Classical music played at a low volume from speakers in the ceiling.

Four square tables had been brought together to form a large seating arrangement for twelve. Already seated at this were McGill and two others, one of whom had escorted Gambit into the conference room earlier that morning. Stirling walked over to the table as the men stood. McGill greeted Drake, Gambit and Templar then introduced the others, "This is Nigel Porter and Rick Barrett. Please, help yourselves." he indicated the buffet, and the three along with Stirling sat back down, McGill and Porter huddled in conversation.

Drake, Templar and Gambit, baffled by it *all*, slowly moved to the buffet. "This is insane!" Templar whispered harshly. "Glass, china, cutlery..." Gambit nodded once as he dished out some eggs. The room held plenty of options for weaponry to aid in escape.

"Mm." Drake grunted, both as acknowledgement and a warning not to try anything. He finished dishing out some eggs with a few sausages, poured some orange juice, then went to the table, seating himself directly opposite McGill.

The man named Porter addressed him pleasantly. "A beautiful day isn't it Mister...?"

"Wolf. And you are, again?"

"Nigel Porter" he answered as they shook hands.

"Our itinerary for today will start right around noon. For now, we all just plan on having a relaxing morning." McGill said.

Templar and Gambit joined those seated and began eating when suddenly Templar paused. He stared at Porter for a few moments. He set his fork down and sat back in his seat. “Mister...Porter, is it?”

“Yes sir.” Porter affirmed, though both Templar and Drake noticed a subtle difference in his demeanour. Porter was nervous, attempting to avoid Templar’s gaze

Templar was in no mood to be avoided. “I’m sorry for staring Porter, but the resemblance is uncanny.”

Now it was McGill’s turn to show a subtle change in demeanour.

Templar went on. “You remind me very much of a very good and Godly man of my acquaintance from years ago.”

Porter fidgeted, smiled nervously and attempted to deflect, “Well, I’m glad I resemble a good guy then, Mister...?” Then Porter looked like he knew he’d made a mistake.

“Tombs, Sebastian Tombs.” Templar answered, still scrutinizing Porter.

McGill suddenly suffered from a slight coughing spell. He reached for his water glass, taking a small drink. Putting the glass back down, he held one hand up, palm outward, “Guys, *please*, can we cut the bull-shit?” he pleaded, coughing and chuckling simultaneously. “‘Sebastian Tombs’, huh?” he laughed further, lightly slapping the table with his hand. “Okay! ‘SeBAStian’!” he mocked, stating the name with *extreme* emphasis on the second syllable.

Drake, Gambit, and especially Templar were genuinely taken aback by his bizarre display! Templar sat fully back, a bit angry, and a bit befuddled. He decided to go ‘all in’. “I was involved in some relief efforts in Africa...” Porter looked down at his plate, silent. He went on, staring directly at Porter, “Given the warring factions at the time, humanitarian efforts were outlawed. I was involved in smuggling medicinal supplies into..."

He leaned forward in his seat pointing at Porter, "It *was* you! You ran interference for us! Made connections with the tribal leaders...You risked your life *numerous* times! To warn us...you hid me, hid the four of us! Diverted the authorities from finding us so that we could escape...Good Lord, you *are* Father Ignatius Loyola!!"

Templar sat back, stunned, and after a moment or two, leaned forward again. "Father, what in *God's* name are *you* doing in *this place?*" he asked, almost pleading, his voice full of emotion and confusion.

Porter looked up at Templar, and eventually admitted with a sad smile, "Simon, my name actually *is* Porter, and...it's a long story, but...it is *good* to see you. Maybe we'll catch up a later, eh?" Porter stood, nodded to each at the table, and left.

McGill had taken out his cigarettes and was tapping one against the table staring at it in contemplation. "Like I told you Templar, we ain't the bad guys. And I'm no idiot. I know the 'famous Simon Templar' when I see him."

Drake hadn't moved one *molecule* during the entire exchange. 'McGill knows who Simon is. Simon knew who 'Porter' actually is', he thought, putting what pieces he could together.

Simon never reacted at all to McGill's 'blowing his cover'. Drake's brain was attempting to play a game of chess, and *somebody* kept coming by *upending* the *entire* board amid *moves!*

Gambit had watched the whole thing while continuing his breakfast. He'd reached the conclusion that things would only get weirder. Next thing you know, he surmised, there'll be a dwarf clown riding a penny-farthing bicycle in between these tables, juggling. A marching band will follow, and then a hula dancer, who will no doubt turn out to be Steed's Aunt Penelope, who is secretly a Russian spy.

'And if I'm to deal with *any* of it' he concluded, 'it *won't* be on an empty stomach!'

Just then, Emma and Tara arrived with Macready, the doctor pointing out the buffet and where they would be sitting. They looked refreshed, both wearing light blue-grey pullovers and slacks. Macready sat next to Stirling but looked at Templar with some concern. "Are you all right?"

Templar, staring ahead, cleared his throat, "No...No, I'm not. But there's nothing you can do for it, Doctor."

Drake abruptly stood up. He didn't care *who* was listening, watching, recording, filming, or *anything!* Leaning over the table so that his face was only inches away from McGill's, he challenged in a low rumble "McGill, if you are half the man that I'm beginning to get the impression you are, you will take me to a place where you and I can talk freely and alone. *Now!*"

Stirling started to rise when McGill halted him with a hand to his arm. After a moment, Stirling sat back down. McGill sat for a moment, one hand covering his chin, index finger rubbing his top lip, looking directly at Drake. "Alright," he finally said.

He stood motioning to Emma and Tara, "Please sit down and enjoy, ladies. If you'll forgive us, Mister...Wolf and I will be going for a chat. We'll be back shortly."

37
Hammer and/or Anvil

Drake and McGill walked to a patio which was just outside and around a corner from the dining room. A table and two chairs were situated by a far wall, but neither man sat down. Rather, they stood at opposite corners of the patio, looking like boxers in a ring. McGill took out his cigarettes and lit one. He took a deep drag, blowing the smoke out with some force. Drake asked, "Might I have one of those?"

McGill looked at him with controlled anger for a few seconds. Then he gave one to Drake, lighting it for him. "Obliged" Drake mumbled.

McGill pointed his finger inches from Drake's face. "You *don't* do that to me again. You forget yourself, *Wolf*, or whatever the hell your name is. I could lock you up, throw away the key, and you'd *never* see the sunlight again, *Capiche?*"

"I don't believe you." Drake stated bluntly. "You haven't the pull. You are not the 'Boss', not 'Number One'. You're under orders to treat us humanely."

"You really think that?"

"I do."

McGill grinned. Eventually. "You busted in here last night with a team of some pretty heavy hitters. Yeah, you put us through our paces, but nothin' we couldn't handle. I recognized Templar and your Mrs. Peel, and I knew somethin' was *waaaayy* off base here. Last I knew neither one of them were dangerous enemy agents. 'Course I suppose they could'a got turned around, but I doubt it."

"*You* think *we* are enemy agents?"

"I *did*. I still do in a way. Some of you. One of you. Maybe."

"What do you mean?"

"You're here for a reason. We're pretty sure we know why, but I ain't a hundred percent convinced."

"What *is this place?*" Drake abruptly yelled. "What is its *function?* Who do you *serve?* Who is *involved* with you? *Why* do you hold an innocent man *captive* here? From what I've seen you could be holding *dozens! Why?*"

Drake's voice had grown louder with every question. McGill stood directly in front of him, silently staring him down. The meaning was clear; shut up, and calm down. Now!

After a moment, McGill looked at his wristwatch, and said "In a few hours we'll be starting the process of getting the whole story. At least, I think it's the whole story."

"What do you mean?"

McGill shrugged.

"You don't want us to know the... 'whole story'." Drake accused.

"That's not true." denied McGill, as he walked over and half sat, half leaned on the table with his arms crossed. "I don't know who you are. Yet! I can't figure out your angle. I've got a few guesses. So, here's the short answer version. This is a maximum security compound that serves a number of functions. I serve a board. There is no 'Number One'. And that's all I'll give you, for now." McGill moved from the table. "You look just like one of our people, and that gives me a creepy feeling."

"One of your... 'people'?"

He nodded. "Spittin' image! You sound like him. You even act like him. You already knew that I'm bettin'."

He walked directly up to Drake and once again stuck his finger in his face, "And until I'm *certain* about you one way or the other, you'd better believe I'm watchin' you. One wrong move and I'll come down on you like a ton of bricks. That's *all* I'm gonna say."

He looked at his wristwatch again. "Let's get back inside, Mister...'Wolf'."

As Drake and McGill returned to the dining room; Stirling, Macready, and Barrett arose from their seats. Barrett instructed, "Gentlemen, you'll accompany me now to showers and fresh clothing." The men left with him.

Stirling and Macready stood by Emma and Tara, Stirling stating "We four will adjourn to the patio."

Arriving at the patio, Macready instructed Emma and Tara to "...simply try to relax and enjoy the surroundings. We've a busy day ahead of us. Please, go no further than the hedge. You both understand why." She then returned inside with Stirling.

Emma decided to take Drake's lead in being indifferent to whatever surveillance might be observing them. "I take it you met up with the 'bubble ghost monster', or whatever it is?"

Tara nodded her head.

From around the corner, the young brunette they knew by now as Abigail, appeared. asking if either would like coffee. Emma accepted while Tara declined.

"This is...I feel as if I've been drugged!" Tara confided.

"Mm. I can see why." Emma acknowledged. "It truly is bizarre! I don't feel drugged, but our sense of logic has been assaulted. Everything here is topsy-turvy." She looked at Tara hopefully. "Don't let it defeat you, Tara. Roll with it.

Rely on what you know. Be the eye in the storm. We will get out of this!"

Tara nodded once again reassuring herself... "Yes. Thank you, Emma, I'm aware, and of course you're right. We have encountered the inexplicable before. Many times, in fact."

"...And are here to tell the tale." Emma concluded Tara's thought. "We are anvils being hammered. But the hammers *will break!*"

38

Once Upon a Time

Breakfasted and refreshed, the five were escorted by Barrett and another man to the first floor of one of the complexes Gambit had investigated what seemed like days ago, but in fact had only been nine hours earlier that morning. This complex had been designated as 'A' on their maps of the compound.

Once inside, they walked to a set of double doors which, upon approach, automatically opened into a large circular room. A large round conference table was located in front of a large curved screen that covered approximately four by three and a half metres of the wall. A hand railed ramp extended from the entrance, sloping gradually into the room. The room was well lit, but not harshly so, having the atmosphere of a rounded theatre.

They walked down the ramp, automatic doors closing behind them. Two men stood together by one section of the table. One man had long hair outlandishly styled (almost comically so) and wore a Fu-Manchu moustache. He was dressed stylishly in a three piece tan suit, with yellow shirt and tie. He stood out like a lit candle against the subdued reds and maroons of the room and was quite a contrast to the blue-grey pull over and slacks the man next to him wore. The man turned, smiling. It was John Steed!

While Tara, Gambit and Templar reacted with surprise and confusion, Emma was *very* shocked, hurt by his seeming betrayal. As for Drake, it took all he had not to leap forward and strangle him.

Steed immediately moved toward them. "Thank *Heavens!* I was assured you were all well. I've been anxious to confirm for myself." he confided, his face a mixture of joy and relief while his eyes sent each of the five a warning to exercise caution and restraint. He had just enough time to flash a silent message to Drake and Emma, 'This is *not* as it looks'. Drake stayed his hand, barely.

Emma was about to speak when the doors once again opened as Mac McGill and a large immaculately dressed black man strode into the room. "Folks, if you'll be seated, we'll get this under way." announced McGill, as both men quickly made their way to the table.

"I am Sir Curtis Seretse." the man announced. "Some of you know me as we have worked together before. I ask that you please have a seat. We have much to do together."

They stood slack jawed. It took a moment for Drake to react. 'It cannot be *possible!*' he thought. The six 'detainees' moved to the tableside opposite McGill and Seretse. They sat as Seretse remained standing, continuing, "To those of you who don't know me or about me, let me just say I hold a number of positions in a number of areas concerning government, commerce and so forth. I will also state with all humility that my work is esteemed and is without blemish. I take pride in that. My time with you today is short, so I will simply ask for your attention.

"Major Steed, once again you have my sincere apologies for the manner in which you were brought here. Had there been another way I would have readily embraced it. To the other five of you, the Major and I have had discussions which have illuminated some of this for him." Seretse moved his arm as to indicate the room, building, compound, and the situation itself. "It will shortly be illuminated for all of you. I ask you all to keep open minds. I ask that you listen to us and refrain from asking questions of us for the time being. We do not wish to confuse matters more than they already are.

"You are not in danger, but you are being detained. As you sit with us now, you *are* being investigated. There are certain details about you that we must clarify. We believe interrogating you would serve no good purpose other than to heighten mistrust and misunderstanding between us. With the information we have thus far concerning you and your mission here; we have decided to proceed explaining our side of the story to *you*.

"You are among benevolent souls here, but we appreciate you are highly suspicious of us, and perhaps cannot believe that. Our hope is that by today's end, we will have all that is required of each other for complete comprehension. I must take leave now and turn things over to my colleague, Mr. Jason King. I wish each of us well, and I hope for peace."

The Six; Steed, Peel, Drake, Gambit, Tara and Templar, were well and truly impressed. However, the fact that *Seretse* was *here* in this peculiar place confounded them!

The admiration felt toward Seretse was incredibly palpable. His sterling reputation of benevolence and vision was known the world over. King stood, watching Seretse leave, saying quietly. "...whose shoe's latchet I am not worthy to unloose..." He then turned toward The Six announcing, "I am Jason King, and I am that man's friend.

"You are here because you held a number of unfortunate misconceptions, theories, and miscalculations. As simply as I can put it, you are right, and wrong, yet right again, and not. After we present the following facts, we hope we'll all have a better understanding as to how best to proceed."

The screen behind King illuminated, as a filmed presentation began. It showed footage of what looked like the compound, only larger, with some differences of layout. There were many more buildings, a number right next to each other, not as spread out as they were here. A good number of structures were exact duplicates of those located here. The topography was somewhat dissimilar, the terrain having much greater elevation in spots.

Jason King began a presentation. "This is 'The Village', as was located in Stolford, England. The Village was built in 1948 as a holiday camp and resort by private concerns. Its design was patterned largely after the resort known as Portmeirion in Northern Wales, a spot favoured and patronized by a chap who invested heavily in the construction of this village in Stolford. There were other designs and architecture included here based on gardens and the like from such places as Dorset and Gloucestershire, etcetera.

"Only ever moderately successful, The Village as a business concern became insolvent in 1957. It was then donated to the National Trust. In 1959 it was "bought back," as some might put it, by the British government as a retirement community primarily for low income veterans and government workers.

"One of the lesser known scandals of the early 60s was the uncovering of the fact that the vast majority of 'beneficiaries' populating this retirement village had familial ties to a handful of members of Parliament. In itself that would seem unimportant, but it is the seed of a pattern of corruption that would come to a horrid fruition in the years to come.

"The Village gradually became recipient of military and Intelligence personnel who were put out to pasture, people deemed too problematic to be loosed in the general populace. People who might not be trusted to keep secrets, either through illness, incompetence, or what have you.

"This *had* been done to an extent after the war, in large buildings or camps where necessary security concerns could be easily addressed. But it had not been attempted in a facility of the size of The Village before, some treble the size of any used prior.

"By 1962, low to mid-level incarceration gradually became The Village's primary purpose. Even so, there were still retirees and the like residing. Thus, the need for unobtrusive methods of surveillance and security grew, as did the technology for them. The Village became a testing ground of sorts for various systems and methodologies.

"By 1964, it was a 'model for the future'. An out of the way place largely undetected, where those in power had control over who went in and who might be allowed out. A place where they could hold problematic undesirables, giving them the illusion of a life of leisure, indeed fool them into thinking they should be grateful for being there!

"In 1966 the model that was The Village almost began to be replicated."

The film had switched to a number of still shots of the very place they were in now.

"Oxwich, Wales, where we presently are, your home from home, so to speak. Though construction had begun, it was thankfully never completed by those who ran The Village at Stolford, for reasons which will become clear to you later. *We* in fact, completed construction of it this year."

Film ended, the lights readjusted while King continued.

"1966: The Village of Stolford was virtually an ultra-maximum security prison. Without walls, yet protected by all manner of technology. That being the overall function, a number of secondary functions began to spring up at this time.

"The study of behavioural science fostered a concept of erasing identity while selling it as a way to insure individuality. There may be hundreds of Jason Kings in the world, but only *one* number 45! Only *one* number 427! With a populace of less than two hundred, numbering its 'citizenry' wouldn't become ludicrous. Thus policy instituted in The Village rid its populace of their names, replacing them with numbers. Anyone strongly opposed to this policy was dealt with quickly and finally, yet subtly. Personally, I would assume The Village had the bad luck of a higher than normal 'attrition rate' that year.

"Concurrently, the British government was switching hands. Things were changing, our Empire was shrinking, our economy volatile, minorities were entering our borders by the thousands, *and staying*, our very identity, disappearing. Certain individuals felt we had to hold onto old 'virtues' at all costs, militantly and draconically so.

"A 'Shadow Government', a cabal, had formed, indeed had begun forming for quite some time, particularly after the death of Prime Minister Churchill; ultra-conservatism, anti-progressive imperialism, militarism and a warped sense of extreme nationalism, the hallmarks of those involved. A secondary function of The Village was to serve as a training ground for those believing in this cause. Recruitment of like-minded Military and Intelligence personnel had judiciously begun.

"Yet at this juncture, all still had to be done surreptitiously, due to the number of scandals we're all familiar with and the investigations going on at the time. This 'cabal' could ill afford exposure. Besides, still present were handfuls of residents in The Village who were unassuming retirees, indifferent to political or sociological ideology. Most could be trusted to simply do as they were told, but there were a few that still needed weeding out.

"In the meanwhile, the experimentation that had been so well utilized in terms of security and surveillance moved to other arenas in our little despotic Village. Drug testing, Genetics, Biological engineering, mind control, methods of interrogation; The shockingly appalling experimentations of the concentration camps of the Third Reich that had been so soundly defeated, found a new home. This was also a secondary function, but it would soon become a priority.

"By middle of 1967 The Village was entirely in the hands of a few, the 'Generals' of this 'Conspiracy'. The number of legitimate officials who even knew about The Village was essentially zero. It ran under the radar, avoiding detection by any legitimate government or law enforcement agencies, as had been the case in other places, towns and villages most of you have had actual experience with; Major Steed, Mrs. Peel, McGill, even Mr. Templar can all attest to this. Actualities difficult to fathom.

"At key points in legitimate agencies, agents of this cabal, this Conspiracy, were in place. Each deflecting and misdirecting, replacing legitimate with illegitimate, moral with immoral, assassinating enemies when they could get away with it.

"As with any form of concentration, the mass grows smaller while what remains grows stronger. By 1968;

through mishap, inner power struggles and assassinations primarily, only a very few 'Generals' of the Conspiracy remained. They were, however, quite powerful, with agents strongly in place."

King finished by saying, "May I strongly suggest we break for a short stroll? My objectivity is being shattered and needs rejuvenation. Were I to attempt more narration of this account of sheer evil without it, I fear I should expire!"

39
King's Gambit

Everyone had filed out from the large conference room back to the patio and yard.

The Six moved to the lawn, where they all agreed that, despite whatever surveillance devices that might be present, their need to communicate superseded those concerns. Besides, discussing matters that had occurred to them *here* would be information already known by the powers that were, so what difference would it make?

It was with that thought in mind that Steed related to them how he had got there, and what he had discovered. "...next I knew, I woke up here! King was sitting in a chair at the foot of my bed. Before I could utter a sound, he convinced me to stay my hand and await further information. It was then that Sir Curtis came into the room."

"The man has *enormous* presence!" Templar related. "I've personally seen him bring a total calm to the General Assembly at the U.N. It was remarkable! But I can't for the life of me fathom how *he* is somehow involved in this!"

"Indeed, and indeed again, Templar; my very thought. In any event, Sir Curtis informed me you all were safe and being held elsewhere, that we would be united at some point this morning, and that he *personally* had taken care of sewing up the remainder of our mission, calling back our drivers and pilots and so forth."

Drake couldn't help himself. He had a million questions. For now, these would have to do. "Who is this King person? How would he know Sir Curtis? How did they know *any* of our business? Why abduct you and bring you here?"

Steed revealed he had sought out King purely as a consultant. He went on to relay what Seretse had told him. Seretse had formed a specialized law enforcement department last year with King at the personal recommendation and urging of the Home Secretary. Seretse said that King had an uncanny ability of making sense of the senseless. Steed had recognized that himself, which motivated him to reach out to King in the first place.

Drake was furious. "Damn good work, reaching out to this man who turns out to be part of this senselessness!"

Steed couldn't help Drake's anger now, so he decided to press on. "As far as my abduction, they'd hoped to consult with me, or us for that matter, before any mission was attempted. At the very least King had gambled that I would contact him once more before we'd try anything. He lost that wager. All I won from it was a crashing headache." Pulling on the back of his neck, he said. "My. It *does* feel better. That Doctor Macready of theirs is *really very* good!"

"To the tale, or rather, 'tail'. Put simply and embarrassingly, Jason tailed me from yesterday noon on. I hadn't an inkling. He'd even gained access to the grounds at Department HQ! He's incredibly resourceful! He watched me see you all off in helicopters complete with gear, put two and two together and concluded it was too late to stop our operation. It took him a bit of time to contact Sir Curtis."

"And by that time..." King, having ambled over to the group, continued the explanation, "...it was close to midnight. I contacted McGill and told him to be on raised alert. I relayed to him that, though I couldn't be certain precisely the type of operation you intended, I believed that your aims were likely peaceful as I saw no weaponry that I could readily discern. Our policy here is to stop anyone as peacefully as humanly possible."

Emma furrowed her brow, skewed her mouth to one side and stepped menacingly toward King. "'Humanly' is *not* the way I was stopped!" she stated accusingly.

Drake quickly moved to step in between them. The last thing anyone needed now was for Emma to get involved in an altercation.

"Yyeess" hissed King taking a step backward. "*That* will be explained to you as well dear lady." Facing Drake he remarked in a stage whisper, "Good *Lord!* She's an absolute *Amazon!*"

Taking a further step back, King went on. "Given the heightened fear of conspiracy you all rightfully had, Sir Curtis and I felt it would be of no use to merely knock on Steed's door and bid him come with us. That might have gotten us shot! Were it not for a miniature tranquilizer device, we almost 'got shot' as it was!"

Steed grimaced.

"We couldn't put him under arrest or under guard for reasons you'll understand later. Besides, we needed clarification on any number of points, not that we got it." King said, somewhat chagrined.

"As your operation was well underway, there was no subtle or safe way we could think to stop you in transit. Cancelling your mission had to be accomplished *here*. Thus, we abducted him, and brought him here to be reunited with *you*, so that we could control the situation, and best understand matters."

"What matters are to be understood?" Drake asked.

King looked at him directly. "I trust, to a degree only, that we are on the same side in this. But until I know who *you* are, and specifically *who* you might have been after, I will stay the course with the methodology we are currently utilizing. Sir Curtis has agreed with this course. *You* will not cause me to deter from it."

Steed drew up to King, "A word, Jason?" They moved ten paces away from the others where he asked, "*You* handed me this location. Why?"

"Recall, Steed, I gave you four, Oxwich being the last on the list. Simply put, I gambled that you would waste time investigating the situation at Stolford. There *is* a cover up going on there after all. But it's ours."

"Which side is 'ours'? Whose *side* are 'we' on?" Steed asked snidely.

King answered in earnest. "The *right* one Steed, as you will see. After our first meeting, I suspected it would simply be a matter of time before you'd made certain connections. Further research confirmed, at least for me, that I should stay connected with you in this investigation of yours. That I should attempt steering the course of it. Remember, I had *no* idea the identities of your compatriots, and only some notion as to where their loyalties might actually lie. What *true* motivations might've been at play I hadn't the foggiest. You would have suspected me if I hadn't tried to help you. You have extraordinary instincts, so I had little choice. If you'll recall, I *was* doing my utmost to subtly stall you. As it was, I got the impression you were beginning to suspect me."

"You're right about that." Steed admitted.

"I was convinced, and still am, that *you* had noble intent. I could not, and cannot at this time, say the same of your people here. You could have been fooled. I was stalling for time, that my enquiries might give me information necessary to move one way or another. Invite you in, or cut you off.

You ignored Stolford, my time was up, and *you* decided to expose the wrong conspiracy!"

40
Bizarre

They'd been escorted back to the circular room and found sections of the large round conference table had been removed, opening it up to form a semi-circle table facing a slightly elevated head table. Both of these sections had seating for ten, and were both placed in front of the large viewing screen. The Six were seated at the curved table, while Jason King, Barrett, Macready, Stirling, and McGill were seated opposite at the head table.

"Oh my!" exclaimed Tara, pointing to a man who then entered, making his way to the head table, followed by two others. Though not wearing a bowler or twirling a brolly as he walked, he was stylishly dressed in a three piece suit and could have easily been an older brother or relative of Steed's. The resemblance was striking, though not exact.

'Goodness!' Steed thought, 'another doppelganger?'

By now Drake had made every endeavour to stop being shocked by the constant barrage of surprising occurrences and revelations encountered here. His recognition of two of these three men foiled those attempts.

They took their seats as a professorial looking gentleman stood at the head table.

"I am John Alexander Templeton-Green, head of Diplomatic Intelligence. You all may address me as 'Temp'. I don't like it, but what can one do?" This brought a few chuckles from those at the head table.

"I attempt humour here to lessen the tension in this room. To you, Steed and your compatriots, I remind you that you have been well treated, with courtesy and respect.

You are being detained here until certain questions have been answered to our satisfaction. Until then, we endeavour to answer *your* questions regarding *us*. Allow us your continued cooperation, and all will become clear."

'Continued cooperation!' thought Gambit, 'As if we had any bloody choice!'

Steed's 'doppelganger' announced "Good afternoon. I am Sir John Raleigh." He walked to the curved table, leaned forward, and looked at each of The Six for a moment. "Major Steed we know. Mrs. Emma Peel, Miss Tara King, and my dear chap Simon Templar, we know you too. Frankly, I'm a bit relieved Mr. Templar is still here! He's a hard man to keep hold of."

Templar permitted himself a small self-congratulatory smile. And, *yes*, he did *indeed* know Sir John. Another connection at the U.N., though, once again, how *this* man came to be *here* was very confounding!

'Temp' muttered sardonically, "Yes. Templar has much in common with a certain antiques dealer of my acquaintance."

Raleigh stared a bit harder at Gambit. "We don't know you young man, and you sir..." he bore down on Drake, "...are an enigma. Would you gentlemen care to enlighten us as to your true identities?"

Drake and Gambit stared straight ahead, their faces as made of stone.

Raleigh sighed "Very well. You might have saved us some time, but here we are. I'd like to remind you what I believe my friend Sir Curtis Seretse asked of you earlier. Keep open minds, eh?

"We believe we are getting the picture of you six in clearer focus. In the meanwhile, we're having a go at making our side of the story clearer to you. It's not a simple story, nor is it easy to tell."

Raleigh returned to the head table, where he placed his hand on the arm of the third man who had entered the room with him and Temp. Raleigh patted the unknown man's arm and sat down.

The unknown man spoke next.

"I believe you all have heard of me. I'm pretty famous, or infamous depending on how you look at it. I've been in the papers quite often, until relatively recently. I've been known by many names; Dr. Leo Royston, Dr. Benjamin Fotheringay, Professor Patrick Charlton and so forth. Most likely you know me as head of the British Experimental Rocket Group, Professor Bernard Quatermass."

Drake, Steed and Emma *now* recognized him. The man present was but a shadow of himself as they could recall him. He had lost a great deal of weight, and had aged considerably, terribly so. Templar and Tara had only known of him through reputation and news accounts, while Gambit had no knowledge of him whatsoever.

"In the overall, my actual name is of no consequence, save to a number of people or forces who would seek to imprison me, enslave me, or kill me."

"We scientific types can simultaneously be extremely bright and woefully dim-witted. Our opening of the atom, heading into space, heading into the unknown opened up new vistas for us, but also introduced us to inexplicable terrors.

"Oh, these events were kept hush-hush of course: a group of strange children all being born at the same time in Midwich, England, exhibiting amazing powers as they grew; my confrontation with the unknown that ended in

Westminster Abbey itself, my involvement at Lochmouth, Scotland, and later Inverness with a prehistoric intelligent mass which fed on radioactive isotopes, the list goes on.

"Particularly kept hush-hush was my discovery of an extraterrestrial invasion taking place in Winnderden Flats...speaking of evil villages! The alien life forms there had actually *enslaved* the minds of the people populating the *entire* area, their mind control spreading to the highest levels of government within the locality! Normal law enforcement agencies had *no* idea anything insidious was going *on!* There had even been reporting on that event that had reached the newspapers, though the story was quickly rescinded, 'explained away' by some nonsense or other.

"You, Major Steed, Mrs. Peel; you yourselves ran across an extraterrestrial form of plant life in Surrey Green! Yes, a good number of us have encountered the unknown!"

Steed and Emma looked at each other recalling Surrey Green with a shudder, only slightly surprised that Quatermass knew of the event.

Templar whispered "Giant ants?" though no one heard him.

"Templar, how *exactly* did you get stopped last night?" McGill asked quite abruptly.

Aside from getting Steed's account, the other five hadn't had the time or opportunity to compare notes of the early morning prior. McGill's question at this point seemed very out of place. Pointless, especially as he would've known the specifics of their capture. Why would he even ask?

Although clearly embarrassed, Templar muttered, "I was knocked around like a toy by your Doctor Macready."

"*You*, Templar? A big strong guy like *you?*" McGill chided with mock incredulity.

"It's not unheard of." Gambit mentioned, hooking his thumb toward Emma.

"Not that she overpowered me necessarily, it was her..." Templar tried to explain.

"Speed?" Macready finished for him.

Templar glared at her. "Yes. Unbelievable speed."

Suddenly, she was behind him, feeling the back of his head gently. "That's very good. Hardly any swelling at all." Then, just as suddenly, she was back in her seat at the head table, leaning forward with her arms resting on the table top.

Gambit jumped from his chair, knocking it over. He crouched in a defensive karate stance; adrenaline, instinct, and training kicking in on all cylinders, pure fear motivating the action. Instantly, before an eye could blink, Barrett had somehow moved from his seat, and was now standing in front of the double doors at the entrance, five metres away from him.

Drake, Steed, Emma, Tara, and Templar all abruptly stood at the ready. Who knew what this sudden change in situation would bring?

"Please, be calm. No one is in any danger here." Stirling addressed them.

Slowly, Gambit got up from his crouch, gulped, then stammered, "You're...aliens...from outer space!"

There was some chuckling, but Stirling sympathetically understood this was not at *all* funny. He hurriedly waved both of his hands saying, "No, no, no, we're as human as you are! Seriously, please, everyone, sit back down. We know such displays can be, well, 'unnerving'." Barrett folded his hands together, and in a split second, he too was back at his seat, his elbows on the table, hands still folded together.

"Who the *hell* are you people? *What* is *this about?*" raged Drake as he stood, pounding the table with his fist.

Macready asserted, "If you'll take your seats, we'll tell you." Slowly, they retook their seats.

Barrett began, "Craig, Sharron and I, were on a mission. We'd had a serious accident. We were, in fact, the three of us, dead. We were...'resurrected' I suppose is the proper term, by a peaceful people hidden from the world at large. Along with healing, we were given powers which, over time, we've learned how to use. These people requested we try to keep these powers a secret to the best of our ability.

"Only a very few people know about them, There've been times when someone's finding out about them has been unavoidable. We risk revealing their origins to *you*.

However, the greatest concern of the people who gave these powers to us was that we never reveal their whereabouts to anyone. We have resolutely honoured that request. Our 'pact' if you will. In fact, no one on this panel even knows. That we keep to ourselves."

After a moment, Steed surmised "Super speed, strength, hearing and vision I take it? Invulnerability as well?"

Macready clarified, "No Major, we're not invulnerable. We do heal very quickly but we can be wounded. A serious enough wound would kill us."

"Just the three of you? Mr. McGill isn't likewise...enhanced?" Emma had to ask, memories of cybernetic beings now foremost in her mind.

McGill shook his head. "Don't I *wish*? Naw, I can't do any of that stuff. It'd have saved me a hell of a lot of trouble if I could have." he grimaced.

"Our powers aren't always 'switched on'." Stirling explained. "There's a mental process involved that we've...'learned' that enables us to switch our powers on when necessary. Our vision is only slightly enhanced. It's pretty much a 'telescoping' kind of thing, like reading small type at fifty yards or so. Clicking 'on' our enhanced hearing requires a great deal of concentration."

Quatermass interrupted, "Thank you Craig. Jason?"

"Evil comes in many forms." Jason King began, as he clicked a switch on an imbedded panel in the table before him. On the screen behind was a photo of a large white sphere, then film clips of the sphere bounding over grass, skimming on water, floating in the air over trees, and so on. "No Mrs. Peel, Miss King, this is not a weather balloon. Nor is it precisely what you each encountered here as you were being...collected.

"This is a 'ROVER', an acronym for what, precisely, we've no idea, that information has been lost to us. Part biological, part technological; it was used by The Village as security, crowd control, enforcement, and most horrifically, murder."

Film clips showed scenes of ROVER attacking people, suffocating them. Then the screen blinked off.

Emma raged, "You *bastards!* That *thing* almost *killed* me!"

Drake and Steed stared at her in shock, and then menacingly at those opposite them.

"No ma'am! I swear to God! *That* thing has *never* been used here!" McGill held his hands up, palms out in a gesture of denial, mixed with apology as well as an appeal for calm.

King repeated, "He is telling you the truth Mrs. Peel. That abomination is *not* what you encountered early this morning."

Drake angrily demanded, "What *did* she 'encounter'?"

Emma quickly related her experience with the white globe thing that had captured her.

Quatermass let her finish, then verified, "It is as Mac and Jason affirms. That particular creature was used only in The Village at Stolford, never here, or anywhere else that we know of. Let me explain.

"Years ago, my group collected residue samples left aground from the creatures at both of the events at Inverness and Winnderden Flats which I mentioned earlier. Those samples, as well as reports of research we'd intermittently conducted on them were stolen from us by a military attaché in 1966, a man we'd foolishly trusted. He was part of the Conspiracy, this... cabal we've been giving you the history of. He had correctly discerned a military application for our work. Our security regarding the samples and our work was lax as we'd never placed a high priority on the stuff. Until quite recently, I personally had no idea the materials were ever missing!

"We'd later discovered that scientists loyal to this Conspiracy, working within The Village at Stolford, had used our work as a basis for creating that ROVER we saw on screen. Scattered surviving notes of the research and experimentation which created this barely controllable hybrid monstrosity were recovered. I, with a few others here, wished to research it more fully. Having done so, we understood we could 'reprogram' this biological technology. Develop a non-lethal form of it. It has a number of beneficial properties that could..."

"*Who* was it *tested on?*" Drake's voice cracked like a rifle shot, his question hanging in the air.

"Myself." King answered.

McGill raised his hand, "Me too."

"And myself as well." Temp added as he rose from his seat. "Mister...Wolf, was it? I am *fascinated* by things of this sort. I have been friends with...er, Quatermass for a very long time. We see great potential in this technology; peaceful potential. I can tell you without doubt that the bio form used on Mrs. Peel was no more dangerous than Chinese finger cuffs. It is however, just as restrictive, completely incapacitating any adversary, but without maiming or killing.

"I dare say use of tear gas is much more harmful and nowhere near as effective. Yet we commonly expose our military, intelligence and law enforcement trainees to the stuff during basic training. If you wish, I can go over every specific of the technology with you after we are done here."

Steed wasn't satisfied. "With your three 'Super-Guards', why would you need something like that in the first place?

McGill took the question, "Again, it's not 'like that'. It's not lethal. Not near as dangerous as it looks. It's a totally controlled 'system'. We call it 'Guardian', and Guardian is *purely* a security measure. Mrs. Peel was never in any danger."

He paused, rubbed his chin and smirked, "Fact is...Mrs. Peel presented more of a danger to *us* than Guardian ever presented to *her*!"

Macready added "Another factor is, this compound doesn't always have 'Super-Guards' on duty. We have lives outside of this place. As example, I have a small medical practice thirty kilometres from here. We're all here this weekend on 'overtime' per se because of you. Sir Curtis, Sir John, Jason, Professor Quatermass, Temp, others, they're all here because of you."

Raleigh noticed McGill rubbing his eyes. He announced, "We've gone over a lot that is...difficult for the uninitiated mind to take in. We've more to come. We need a recess. Time for tea, I say."

41

View from the Villa

Once again, out in the patio area, prisoners and warders were grateful for the tea and the warmth of the day. A few of the tables and chairs that were in the dining room had been brought out to the lawn. A table of assorted cakes had been placed on the patio itself. Abigail was bringing out more tea when she lost her footing, fell off the patio and landed at John Drake's feet.

Macready and Stirling were immediately at her side, but it was Drake who first leaned down to lend a helping hand. Taking his hand as he helped her to her feet, she looked in his eyes and started thanking him when she froze.

"Are you alright Miss?"

Her eyes widened and her mouth dropped open. This was the first she'd really seen Drake's face up close. She stumbled backwards, but Macready was right behind her, steadying her.

"You?" she uttered, staring intensely into his eyes. "How can...*How*...it's not possible..." she almost whispered. "Cur...Curtis?"

Drake looked at her, confused, "I'm sorry? Who?"

"You *can't* be Curtis!" she cried, her voice beginning to quiver. "Who *are you?*" she yelled, tears forming in her eyes.

Drake looked to Stirling and Macready then back to Abigail, "I...I don't know who you...My name is not Curtis. It's Joseph. Joseph Wolf."

McGill was there now, his hand on Abigail's shoulder. He shot a quick glance at Drake, then peered into Abigail's face, trying to get her to look at him. In a very quiet, strong and soothing voice, he comforted the young woman saying, "Here, Abby, he's a different guy altogether, not who you think at all. Hey...Abby, look at me, okay?"

She tore her attention away from Drake and looked up at McGill.

"Look, honey, this guy" he pointed at Drake, "believe it or not, he's just another guy who *looks* like him, okay? This guy's name is Joseph Wolf, and he's not here to harm anybody, okay? That *other* guy, Curtis, is loooong gone!"

Stirling handed McGill a napkin, which he used to dab her tears. He then put the napkin in her hand. "Are you okay now?"

She nodded, and with a self-depreciating smile said, "Of...of course. Sorry..."

McGill looked at Macready, who gently took Abigail by the shoulders and began guiding her back to the dining room while double checking to see if she hadn't hurt herself in the fall. Abigail turned with an embarrassed 'I'm alright now' grin, and looked at Drake, "My apologies Mr. Wolf, you look like someone..."

Drake smiled graciously, "Oh, no...Miss, quite alright. Don't mention it, no trouble. Really. Glad you're alright is all."

Drake moved away from the small crowd that had gathered at the scene. He noted the various degrees of sincere concern shown to the fallen Abigail. McGill's concern for her was *not* an act, not 'a show'. They *were* sincere. The concern shown was *instinctual!* He was certain of that. When concern is acted out, faked, there is always a 'tell'. Always a hint of the *process* masking the lie underneath.

He concentrated furiously for a span of three seconds.

'No!' he thought, 'that's not the way to go about this.'

Drake had been thinking furiously every step of the way so far. Analyzing level upon level of every aspect and word, every event. It suddenly struck him that he wasn't grasping something that was simply *there*!

He let his brain calm down. Let it transport him to another place, another time. A Villa from long ago, a place that looked quite similar to the place he now found himself in.

He'd found a woman there in the villa, she being the last piece of a puzzle. After he'd solved the puzzle, he solved the mystery. Closed the case. He rescued a woman who then wound up rescuing him.

'It's alright. You had to do it. He'll live. And now, so will you.' he'd assured her. They'd found tranquillity for a short time afterward. They found peace there.

Could that be a clue by itself? One he'd missed? The instinctual compassion for Abigail shown...Was there peace *here*?

'I hope for peace.'

He allowed his mind the objectivity it needed, allowed the peace it required to simply sort through, without the need to reach conclusion or form hypothesis.

Yes. This could well have been an act put on for his benefit. Another total flipping of the chess board amid game. Another seemingly benevolent tactic to win his trust.

Win *their* trust. Trust for what? To keep their secret? Secrets.

What are they building here? What, if anything, are they planning to destroy? The Village as a model. A template? Under the radar. Whose side are they on?

Raleigh, Templeton-Green, King, Seretse, Quatermass...God knows who else is involved. *All* gotten to somehow? *All* turned? 'I hope for peace.' Experiments. Torture. 'The wrong conspiracy'. Super powered soldiers. Extraterrestrials. 'The Guardian'. Showers, breakfast, tea, a hero priest! Shadow Government Cabal Conspiracy.

This 'Prison', this whole 'presentation'...more like a weekend course at University. A training conference. Good-natured laughter. ROVER killing those people...

'I hope for peace.'

Emma came beside him. He turned and looked into her eyes intently.

"*You* found our man. *How* did you find him? Precisely?" Drake asked quietly.

"Asleep in a lounger, a blanket covered him waist down. He'd been reading. His book was in his lap. His glasses slipped down to the end of his nose."

A pause.

He signalled the other four to gather with them.

"It so happens that Sir John Raleigh and I *are* related, though in shirt-tail fashion." Steed related loudly as he sauntered over, sensing planning was afoot, trying to keep a 'garden party' atmosphere about them to avoid suspicion.

"They want to know who I am." Drake put it directly. "If I give them that, they'll give us something in return. Freedom for some of you, or perhaps all of you."

Templar drew his head back a bit, "A gallant proposition, but as I told you from the first, I'm with you till the end."

Gambit asked "Sir, *why* don't they know? I mean, if they truly *are* what we *think* they are, why don't they already know who *we* are?"

Another pause.

A rakish grin grew on Drake's face, "In for a penny, in for a pound?"

They all nodded affirmative.

"Then here we go."

"Mr. McGill!" he called out.

McGill walked over to The Six. "Yes?"

Drake inhaled deeply, and slowly let the breath out.

"My name is Drake. John Drake."

McGill's entire face grinned as he rubbed the back of his neck. "Yes sir, it *suuure* is."

The Six stared at him, once again completely stunned!

"Yeah, we just got word about a half hour ago. Temp verified it."

"But...you told the girl my name was..." Drake stammered.

"Yeah, I did, didn't I? Well, you told her first. She was already a little unsettled. Tell ya what; you can 'make amends' later."

He slid his arm *carefully* around Drake's shoulders.

"John Drake. Huh! You're not gonna believe this, but you're part of our Charter!"

42
The Pit

They filed back to the circular conference room in a more relaxed manner. The atmosphere and furnishings of the room itself had changed once again. The lighting was brighter, and the slightly raised table before the viewing screen had been extended to allow for more seating. Newly arrived were two men; one elderly man was seated in a wheelchair, being tended to by the second, a young man with longish blonde hair in a simple black suit, white shirt, and black tie. Overall the room had changed in character from one of inquisition to one of conference. One of gathering.

Jason King, presently sitting at the curved table, absent-mindedly lit a cigarette which McGill immediately took from him, crushing it in his hand as he admonished, "Dammit King! That's three times now. If I don't smoke in here, *you* sure as hell don't smoke in here, Capiche?"

"You are a horrid, despicable man McGill" grumbled King wanly. Looking up and seeing that Drake had arrived, King arose, smiling. "It all fits now. Damn inconsiderate of you to be so good at what you do, Drake. A shame really...I do *so* enjoy a good mystery, and yours really had me going!"

"Okay!" McGill got the ball rolling. "If you'll all please take a seat..." He looked at The Six, once more seated together at the curved table. "I remind you what Sir Curtis mentioned about keeping an open mind, because, we're entering a *very* strange area here."

"Oh *good!*" proclaimed Templar loudly. "Because everything we've witnessed so far has been uhm...so run of the mill!" After laughter from Templar's comment had died down, Sir John Raleigh stood and addressed the room at large. "Our 'crisis', if you will, is over. We're in 'Stand Down' mode. We have pieced together enough of the puzzle to conclude that you acted out of purely noble motivation and intent, and that you have never represented a danger to us, or to our operation here. Misperception remains however, and we fully intend on clearing up any of that in these next few hours, if you'll be patient with us a little longer.

"Craig, Sharron, Rick; you are relieved of duty with our obvious gratitude."

Stirling, Macready and Barrett had (surprisingly) decided to seat themselves *with* The Six at the curved table. Stirling stood, smiled and declined, "We'd like to hang around if you don't mind Sir John. To be honest, I'd like to talk with Mr. John Drake myself at some point."

"Splendid!" Raleigh nodded, returning his attention to The Six.

"Very well, then! Quite obviously, what you've seen, what we've shown you, and what we're about to show is of a very sensitive nature. We believe you can be trusted, and that your proven discretion regarding matters of this sort in the past assures us no other soul will hear of it. Unless otherwise released from that bond, we will hold you to it. Fair enough? Quatermass? If you'd be so kind..."

Quatermass took the baton. "Thank you Sir John. Our Rocket Group eventually realized our mission of experimentation and research was being 'edged out' in favour of military expansion into space." He grimaced, "A few botched missions, a few nasty surprises, overall shrinking of funding, all of it carving away at the more noble aspirations of our work. In '67, we were so involved with plans for colonization on the Moon that we had not been paying much attention to what was going on around us. As I mentioned, we were woefully dim-witted. At least I'd been.

"I was called to a meeting at the undersecretary's office. With no prior discussion or warning, I was told that our funding was being drastically cut back and that we were being handed over to *military* control, our plans taken over for *military* purposes, much to my disgust! Command was handed over to a Colonel Breen, and though I'd be left on as his subordinate, I knew it was only a matter of time before they would force me out! Oh, I tried to fight it, once it was too damn late!

"Like a *fool*, I believed the undersecretary, whom I'd had no reason to mistrust, when he told me this decision came from the very top. Confirmation came from this man." The screen flickered on showing a photo of a dark haired man in suit and tie. "Kiernan McLeod of the Ministry of Defence, as he was then." A second photo flashed. "This is also him, little more than a year later."

Tara gasped. The change in the man's appearance was palpable. The trim, amiable, clean cut image of the first looked almost completely different from the overweight, scowling, longer haired and bearded image of the second.

"Had I fought just *one* level higher, I would have exposed them. Yes, military takeover of my group was being discussed, but *nothing* had been *officially* decided. All three of these men, McLeod, Breen, and the undersecretary were part of this Conspiracy we've been telling you about. *They* decided to force the matter.

"I was disheartened, feeling old, feeling more and more useless. The Americans were making such huge strides in rocketry; our group was redundant. I hadn't the energy to fight or even care any longer."

He stood, walking over to the curved table and leaned forward looking directly at Drake.

"Mister Drake, I know how you must have felt this past year or so. What's more, you've been absolutely correct in your belief that you had great need of anonymity and secrecy. You'd barely escaped an insidious evil; a Conspiracy of savage, sadistic, megalomaniacal tyranny."

Drake was moved to his core. Quatermass' eyes were full of self-recrimination, a tortured sorrow, and a righteous fury.

Quatermass returned to his seat. "I'm certain many of you will recall the event occurring in Knightsbridge, London in fall of '67. Work at an expansion of the London Underground at Hobbs End had uncovered an amazing find of prehistoric bones. Doctor Matthew Roney, an old chum of mine, in charge of the excavation that proceeded, estimated the bones to be some five million years old!

"Well, there were already cross purposes at work. Roney worked desperately to excavate the sight while the London Underground expansion was halted. The pressure to continue the expansion was enormous, and he asked if I might be able to help him publicize the importance of his find. I wasn't sure what help I might have been to him, feeling impotent. My group had been taken away from me the very day Roney contacted me. Regardless, I went to the excavation site. I found what they'd uncovered fascinating. What Roney showed me was something that would drastically realign evolutionary theory forever.

"It was then we had uncovered something else; something purely *evil!*"

"Good Lord, *yes!*" Templar interrupted with growing astonishment, thumping the table with his fist. "*Martians!* First the weird ape-men, then the Martian craft, and then the Martians themselves! I *vividly* recall now! I marvelled at the newspaper reports, the photos of the Martians..."

He stopped himself. Seeing this man Quatermass in front of him, seeing the obvious pain he was going through in the relating of events, he swallowed.

"I, uh...my apologies Professor, I followed the story very intently. I, uh...couldn't help but appreciate the, uh...what I thought...forgive me; at the time I thought it was a... an ingenious scam. I'm sorry."

Quatermass smiled sadly, "Oh, don't concern yourself Templar. You were far from alone in that regard. I *do* appreciate the apology. Yes. We had uncovered a Martian craft that had imbedded itself in the sight millions of years ago. As it had been thought to be a V2 rocket or unexploded bomb left from the Blitz, Colonel Breen was called to investigate, he being involved with unexploded ordinance earlier in his career.

"We found the Martians themselves, long dead, shortly after his involvement. At that time I thought Breen was simply being a close minded militaristic *ass!* Despite the mysterious phenomenon Breen had seen with his own eyes, he and minister McLeod had cooked up a cover story that it was all a Nazi propaganda attack which had failed.

Well, given the depth we found the craft itself that was *impossible*. But we hadn't time to prove our case. Martians had landed here millions of years ago as a way of colonization, had experimented with humans to 'recreate' themselves...at least that was our hypothesis, but it all turned out to be a frighteningly correct hypothesis..."

He lifted his hands sighing "It's an amazingly complex story, and of little value to you to go over those details now.

"As Temp is willing to show and discuss details regarding our Guardian, I am likewise available to discuss these specifics with you at a later time, should any of you wish.

"When all was said and done, Roney, Barbara and I were right, Breen and McLeod were wrong. Devastatingly so."

"Barbara?" interjected Emma

"Yes. Roney's assistant. Barbara Judd. Roney died heroically defeating the Martian force responsible for the devastation that occurred. The fires, the quaking ground, the rioting of the people overtaken by the Martian force...Barbara and I were there with him, right at the source. We've never been the same because of it."

Quatermass started to drift in reverie when he abruptly snapped himself to. "Breen was killed, standing in front of the craft itself. You realize that Breen and especially McLeod had risked their reputations promoting this rubbish about unexploded bombs and a Nazi propaganda plot. All done, they said, in the name of 'National Security'! 'We needed' the populace to be kept in the *dark*, to prevent 'panic'. Controlled, more like it! As I said, at the time I simply chalked their actions up to colossal *stupidity!*

"As it stands now, I firmly believe they saw something in the alien craft that they could use. Some power or force in that thing that could be *controlled*, much like the samples they used to create their ROVER monstrosity. With Breen dead, of course, we'll never really know. But that alien power was an uncontrollably evil force. Barbara and I myself fell victim to it. Only Roney was somehow immune to it.

"Of course a cover story had to be created for the masses. God forbid we tell the *truth!* We need to protect our people from *thinking* beyond comfortable boundaries! McLeod had much to answer for. Hundreds dead, many more injured, the entirety of Hobbs End and the surrounding area a burning rubble. Someone had to pay for it." Quatermass began to tear up. "Jason, would you mind terribly?"

King walked over to Quatermass placing a comforting hand on his shoulder.

"The story that accidental detonation of those unearthed, but still active, Nazi bombs causing all that destruction became the 'official' story. Thusly, the 'history' you've all heard, and I suppose, had no reason to disbelieve. The earlier reports of the finding of 'Martians', which Mr. Templar so obviously recalled, having been falsely discredited."

He walked to the table and tapped a few buttons. The screen flashed on once again showing a variety of film clips of activity in The Village, Stolford.

"In the meantime, The Village at Stolford was humming along. A place of deposed Shadow Government Conspiracy Generals, criminals, forcibly retired inept officials and operatives, malcontents, and a training ground for agents of the Conspiracy.

"As its Generals were slowly losing ground, so to was it losing illicit funding. Again, due to scandals of Parliament and the like, eagle eyes were catching up to questionable government and military accounting. It was becoming difficult to divert and hide a billion or even a million pounds here or there.

"The Village powers opened their doors to foreign enemy concerns. For a fee, we could break an enemy; hide a deposed or exiled political or military leader, etcetera. You can all imagine the ways in which this might work.

"As people of The Village, were known only by numbers, not names, The Village was a perfect sanctuary for this ilk. All unbelievably undetected thus far, though, that would soon change.

"Consider; a 'Number Two' would never fully be in charge of anything, would he? There would *have* to be a Number One above him who was *'really'* the head, wouldn't there? Plausible deniability, diffusion of responsibility, disengagement of morality; call it what you like, it was rather ingenious. There were a number of 'Number Twos' over time. Boss, Governor, Mayor, Chief...call them what you will. This group of 'Number Twos' controlled The Village. They were 'Number One'."

King continued, "Back to the Hobbs End debacle: Indeed someone did pay for their despicable performance and dereliction of duty regarding the menace Quatermass and his colleagues had discovered. Defence Minister Kiernan McLeod was immediately forced to resign in disgrace, never to darken the halls of power again, though it was reported that he'd resigned due to 'health reasons', which may actually have been closer to the truth regarding his mental state.

"Afterwards, in a manner of speaking, this highly placed agent of the Conspiracy fell off of the face of the Earth. But allow me to rephrase that." The screen showed side by side photos of the drastically changed McLeod.

"Let's just say he went under the radar, shall we? Specifically, he went to the Village. Though disgraced and stripped of position and power in legitimate government, he would be a General of great power there. The fall from legitimacy obviously affected him to a very large degree however, both physically and mentally. He essentially went mad. In a Village madhouse of deranged Number Twos, he was the most psychotic and dangerous of all.

"Professor Quatermass and Dr. Roney's assistant, Miss Barbara Judd, suffered physical injury and great psychological and emotional trauma from the event at Hobbs End. Quatermass retired quietly and secretly to an 'unknown' location. Miss Judd was hospitalized.

"Within weeks, his Rocket Group was disbanded, with only a few key people being 'invited' to stay on as subordinate military adjuncts. Which brings us to *this* man." The screen showed a new photo.

The man in the photo was John Drake.

'*Finally!*' Drake thought. '*Now* we're getting somewhere!'

43

Who's Who?

Jason King heard the murmurs.

It had surprised him at first as well. He was only somewhat aware of who John Drake was, a top agent with some notoriety, but had never seen a photo of the man.

How had connecting these two dots eluded him? Eluded *them?* Until, finally, just minutes ago? It seemed so obvious now.

Well, to be fair, it was only by 05:00 that morning that they had a sketch of an idea whom Drake and his crew might be after. By process of elimination, it had to be one of six of their people.

And, after all, King hadn't been completely familiar with the histories of every person housed in the compound. Had he been, perhaps he could have made a few more connections earlier. Besides, they had no idea Drake was even involved! Why would they? *How* would they? He had no idea it would be Drake who was leading the charge! He had assumed Steed would take the lead in their operation. It confounded him to no end when he watched Steed bid his 'commandoes' adieu, then huddle himself in his apartment!

Photographs had been surreptitiously taken of each member of Drake's team while they were in the first conference room earlier that morning. The photos had been wired to those who might have known best who these people were. Drake's 'hippy' disguise served him well!

McGill had immediately recognized Emma Peel and Simon Templar, Tara King's identity was confirmed by 07:20am.

It was of no use at all to try sodium pentothal on Steed, as Steed (like King himself) had most likely received the mental training necessary to resist its effects. Most senior operatives had. Besides, King and Sir Curtis were loath to resort to that extreme.

11:00 that very morning, as Quatermass arrived and had received the photos of Drake and the others, a possible connection was made. Quatermass gave King a file for a quick study. It was only then that King had any idea who 'Prisoner Six' actually was.

At that point, King, Sir Curtis, and McGill had begun their presentations to The Six.

Later on, when Temp arrived, it was Temp who put the final piece of the puzzle firmly into place. He'd made a call to a trusted associate. After a few hours, the associate's return call identified and verified Drake and Gambit's identities, settling matters.

Thusly, at this juncture, Jason King's job was to fully demarcate the line between the dots for everyone.

44

The Conspirators

"No, the man pictured in this photograph is *not* John Drake."

Professor Bernard Quatermass rose from his seat, addressing The Six. "This man you see is perhaps my closest associate. He started the Experimental Rocket Group with me. In fact, he started the idea with me. He has been with me all over the world. He could build anything. I have known many geniuses in my time, but he tops them all. He is a brave and resourceful man. Back in our younger and wilder days, he was a good man to have in a brawl. It was he who acted to end the danger of the isotope eating creature we faced at Inverness.

"During the war he achieved the rank of Lieutenant. He enjoyed a great number of pursuits, but it was his love of science that drove him. He has no honorifics, no 'Doctor' or 'Professor' before his name. Oh, he'd been offered honorary degrees from various universities before. He'd refused them, saying he hadn't done the work necessary to earn them. He had very specific standards of morality; he utterly refused to be a 'fake', as he put it."

"His name is Victor Ives. He can be damn near impossible to like, but he is my friend and I love him dearly. I also feel responsibility for almost killing him. Victor Ives is the man you plotted to rescue from an evil prison Village. For that, you each have my gratitude and respect. He is alive, and he now resides here, in *our* 'village'."

Quatermass slowly paced around the room as the screen showed photographs and film clips of Ives and others during their incarceration in The Village. He never once glanced up at the screen.

"It was weeks after Kiernan McLeod had been forced to resign that my group was shut down. I had been hospitalized, and upon my release I 'escaped' to...well, I ran, to be by myself, to shut everything out. The toll the Hobbs End event took on me was formidable and I could barely function. Ives stayed on as military adjunct, doing his utmost to honour our work. Had I been able and present, I could have advised and convinced him not to even try. The military was hell bent on bringing the war machine into space.

"Victor's ego and temperament were not a good mix in that environment, which was of a different nature than the more noble military philosophy of the RAF during the war. "His conscience could no longer tolerate the situation, he had had enough! So he loudly, defiantly resigned."

Temp asked that material running on the view screen be stopped, noticing it was a discomfort to Quatermass. "I'll take it from here old boy."

"It was about a month afterwards that...er, Bernard contacted me. He had been recuperating and wished to get in contact with Miss Barbara Judd, Ives, and a few others. I told him I'd do what I could.

"I'd found that Miss Judd had been moved to a very specialized hospital by members of Scotland Yard in conjunction with one of your old doctor colleagues, Steed. She'd been moved as an attempt on her life had been made. The Ministry had been keeping an eye on her as she was a 'loose end' from the Hobbs End event. She would need to be 'brought onboard' once she was healthy enough to comprehend the importance of her discretion.

"Now, let me humbly say I'm a man with very few enemies. I've gotten along with most everyone during my career, as I suppose is a trait of a good diplomat. It's not egotistical of me to mention, it just is simply so. I am not known as a firebrand, I am 'steady as she goes'. Ergo I can usually get any information I need without much cajoling. I knew all about the event at Hobbs End. I knew the truth about the aftermath. I helped Bernard get away from it all.

"I was *Goddamned furious* when I heard the news about Barbara. I partnered with Steed's doctor colleague and we moved her to an even more secure location. I immediately began seeing to Victor, as I felt he could be in some sort of peril.

"I personally drove to Victor's home at 1 Buckingham Place. Saw his beloved car sitting out in front of his home. He had built it himself, every bit of it. I thought, 'Good, he's safe.' I felt relieved. That all changed when his door opened. A lovely woman was living there. She told me she'd been living there for quite some time and had no idea who Victor Ives even *was!* This was absurd of course! The woman was lying through her teeth. Well, I stuttered and stammered something about the homes looking similar in that area, so I'd probably mistaken the address and I calmly got the *hell away* from there.

"I was spooked! Obviously concerned. Who would come up with such a preposterous lie? I immediately began unobtrusive investigation as to Ives whereabouts. I found out that he'd resigned and that the military was frankly glad to be rid of him."

Quatermass, *finally*, smiled at this.

"Some weeks further on I'd been able to gather bits and pieces of information. I wasn't certain how to put it together.

A chap I would occasionally employ mentioned another fellow who might be of help, someone on the 'outside'."

Mac McGill intervened, "Someone who charged you three hundred dollars a day plus expenses." McGill addressed The Six. "Temp contacted me. We met, I hit the ground running, and after about a week I'd found out Ives had been taken from his home, in a friggin' *hearse!* But there were no reports or records of a death at 1 Buckingham Place. No burial or hospital or morgue records. No records from any undertaker going to that address at all. Well that pointed to two possibilities; criminal or Intelligence activity!"

Sir John Raleigh chimed in, "Thank you for trying to maintain a distinction there Mac."

This brought forth some chortling in the room.

Raleigh continued, "In my spheres of influence, we were hearing reports, unverifiable mind you, of a troubling nature. Sir Curtis was running across the odd whisper here and there as well. The Conspiracy Mr. King has so well outlined for you was beginning to surface. Primarily due to the foreign entanglements financing it. A thread here, a thread there, bit by bit."

McGill nodded his head, rubbing his hands together. "Things for this Conspiracy were startin' to unravel. The criminal element I was familiar with didn't know Ives at all. Never heard of him. The guy was above board, so any possible connection to criminal activity was out. I told Temp if we were gonna find Ives, it'd be through his intelligence connections rather than my street guys."

At this point, the blonde-haired man with the elder man in the wheel chair situated a microphone closer to the elder man. He addressed The Six in a weak voice. 'Ladies, Gentlemen, my name is Alexander Waverly. I am a member of the board of this Village. In the time frame these gentlemen, my friends, are speaking of, I was the head of an international law enforcement agency, with ties to the United Nations, NATO, and Interpol among others."

"Without us all getting caught in the weeds here, let me simply tell you that we too were involved with investigations that inevitably brought us to action with British Intelligence in regard to this Village we've been discussing." He pointed to both his assistant and McGill. "My young friends here were both involved in the ultimate action that was unfortunately necessary.

"Previous covert actions resulted in the loss of some very fine people. Temp, Sir John, Sir Curtis, I, and a few others found our choices extremely limited, much as I gather you felt Mr. Drake, Major Steed, with regard to whom you knew you could trust. I realize you are each aware, even you Mister Templar, that our lot is a tricky and sticky game. A word in the wrong ear can bring about devastating consequences.

"Thus, it took us time to proceed, as surreptitiously as possible, with an operation that would take out as many of these Conspiracy Generals as we could in one attack. To my last day I will regret we could not act sooner."

McGill motioned for King to begin a particular film clip. The various clips were disjointed; some had been damaged, but apparently had been restored. Scenes of people running, smoke pouring out of buildings, men and a few women firing machine guns, ROVER jutting in and out of view, a helicopter landing, people fleeing. It was evidently film of a battleground.

McGill narrated "The Village had eyes going constantly. Everything you're seeing here is from their cameras. An awful lot of it got damaged in what Mr. Waverly referred to as the 'Ultimate Action'. We were able to recover about half, plus files and computer reels, etcetera. He then clapped his hand on the shoulder of Waverly's assistant. "This is Mister K. He was the genius who got us as much of these records and data as he could. There were rooms full of it. What we know about The Village, ROVER, the numbers, is due to him."

McGill nodded to King, "Okay, cut Jason, please?" King stopped the film clips.

McGill resumed presentation, "So, what happened was this. It took a few months, but we found out Ives was being held in The Village. Temp found out about others. Waverly's organization had lost a few guys tryin' to get in and outta the place. Other intelligence investigations, like Sir John's, were kinda prying the place open. The Village was suddenly on the radar, a small blip, but still there for us to see!

"It was decided to form a team with guys we knew were clean. In a way, we were like another conspiracy. We couldn't go with British or U.N. troops or the like because we felt that was too risky. The Conspiracy had a strong presence in the military, and not just in Britain's either! We *were* able to get some help with British Intelligence. There again, we had to be very particular about who knew what.

"We limited the team to fourteen, and we hit the place. We tried to be as surgical as possible. We had a list of ten people we had to locate and get the hell out of there. We only found seven. Five made it. Our team lost one guy. A ROVER got him."

Emma had to find out, "Did you dispose of this ROVER?"

"Yeah."

"*How* did you dispose of ROVER?"

He grimaced and scratched the back of his neck. "We *think* it was a lucky combination of napalm and a few frag grenades. We're not exactly sure; at least that's what the Professor thinks." Quatermass nodded his head, affirming.

"We grabbed who we could, Ives being the last, prepped and Medevacked them, grabbed what tech and records we could, then we blew the place to Hell, where it belonged!"

"How many others were you able to get out? People not on your 'list'?" Drake interrupted.

McGill's face flashed with a mixture of anger, guilt and pain. "One!" he spat.

45

The Man Who Wouldn't Talk

Jason King proceeded. "McLeod, and others, held position as The Village's Number Two, in an odd sort of succession, with no particular rhyme or reason we've been able to discern. Among these Number Twos, a man named Cargil, an 'acquaintance' of our own Mr. Stirling's. Another, a man of interest to you, Drake."

"Hobbs." Drake croaked the name.

"Precisely, your 'superior' in M9!" King spat out the word 'superior' as if it were a bug that had flown into his mouth.

King continued. "Other Number Twos would be familiar to a few present here. Two from your own Department, Steed. Two who were once highly placed enemy agents familiar to our Mr. Waverly. One who faintly resembles myself shorn of my moustache, and another faintly resembling Temp here...Drake and Steed not the only people here with doppelgangers it seems.

"We return to the reason why Victor Ives was brought to this hell in the first place. As stated, the disgraced Kiernan McLeod had gone utterly mad. He required retribution against those that had been responsible for his fall from grace, those who had 'stolen' his power. From his position as The Village's Number Two, he still had handfuls of agents in place. He sent them to seek out Bernard Quatermass with the plan to capture him and bring him to The Village."

"Not being at all able to locate him and being aware Doctor Matthew Roney had perished in the confrontation with the Martian force at Hobbs End, McLeod sent an agent to kidnap Miss Barbara Judd. The incompetent tried to seize her from her hospital room. He was accidentally stopped by a member of the hospital staff. The agent tried to kill Miss Judd, but was killed himself by a member of British Intelligence who had been assigned to watch over her, all, thankfully, before any harm could come to her, without her ever being aware."

"Having failed in that, McLeod decided to go after members of the Rocket Group. Even though disbanded, the few members left were now attached to the military, Victor Ives being head of that sub-group. McLeod still had people in the military, and it was a simple matter for them to kidnap him. Horribly, and incredibly, Ives inadvertently put himself right in the crosshairs of McLeod's plan, making himself the easiest target on Earth. He loudly resigned in a fit of pique and drove straight into the trap that very day.

"Abducted and brought to The Village, he was given the number Six, which he obstinately refused to answer to. He became McLeod's 'plaything' for the next *eighteen months.* I doubt that Victor Ives even recognized the source of his Village number, that being one of McLeod's twisted 'jokes'.

"McLeod and his psychotic comrades played with him, tortured him, drugged him repeatedly (damn near constantly), experimented on him in horrific ways and did their best to shatter him. The terrifyingly outlandish schemes they devised staggers the imagination. One Number Two after another, after another, after another plied their 'trade' on him. Yet the obstinate and incredibly strong will and mind of Victor Ives withstood everything they brought to bear.

"McLeod's insane scheme was to get him to tell them the reason why he had resigned; apparently hypothesizing that if that could be accomplished, if he could be broken, then it would be a simple matter to get the whereabouts of Quatermass out of him. Ives, Number Six, stubbornly would tell them nothing.

"The sad truth of this is there was never a 'secret' here. Never a need to go to these lengths to find out why he had resigned! That was all spelled out in his letter of resignation which he'd angrily delivered himself. McLeod knew why Ives had resigned before he'd ever been captured!

"Getting Ives to break became an obsession with McLeod. As the cabal that was The Village was faltering due to any number of factors, insanity of the leadership being just one, his *one obsession* began to override every other consideration.

"Eventually, the psychotic rats knew when to leave the sinking ship. A very few of the truly faithful were barely able to maintain The Village, the vaunted security that had been its hallmark was slipshod. Outside forces were on their way in."

46
Fall Out

King turned to McGill. Both men looked at Quatermass.

"Go ahead. I'm all right." Quatermass answered their silent question.

"Yer sure?" McGill asked.

"Yes Mac. They need to see this."

"Okay. This footage is from our 'invasion' of The Village at Stolford, when we got to Ives." McGill said.

The screen silently showed Drake's double crawling in front of a cell, in a large room with bizarre furnishings, or rather, placement of objects. A rocking horse, a toddler's bassinet, a chalk board fallen to the floor, other items, broken, tossed about.

Ives was crawling from one sprawled body to that of a dwarf's dressed in a butler's uniform. Ives was yelling or screaming, crying. Blood was flowing from a cut on his forehead. He was shaking the dwarf, whose head had blood flowing down one side. One could make out blood on the corner of a table right next to the dwarf. Ives appeared to be caressing the dwarf's face. One could see Ives' hands covered in blood.

Suddenly two men came into frame; a bald man and a uniformed man. The uniformed man blocked the view for a few seconds and then fell from view. The bald man ran across the frame yelling or screaming, both hands holding one side of his face, blood gushing from it.

Ives backed away, while the uniformed man followed him. The uniformed man's arm raised a truncheon. Suddenly, the uniformed man's body seemingly hurled into the recording device then dropped out of view. The device shuddered, tilted, settled, and then continued to record.

From the decidedly distorted perspective, the device recorded Ives, standing legs apart, fists raised, eyes wide open and tears flowing. He was bloody, clearly shaking with rage, and he appeared to be howling.

The footage, mercifully, stopped.

The room was dead silent, save for soft sobs coming from Tara King and Sharron Macready. The lights in the room automatically adjusted. The Six could see both McGill and Temp standing by Quatermass as he remained seated. Both with one hand on each of Quatermass' shoulders.

"I had abandoned my *friend* to *that*!" Quatermass choked.

King moved on with his narration.

"McLeod somehow knew time was running out. Thus he attempted one last ditch effort to break Ives completely. Degree Absolute: one week in a locked chamber, or 'Embryo Room'. Only one would walk out. Nonetheless it was *two* against one from the start as McLeod had his dwarf 'henchman' with him.

"Ives was peripherally familiar with the dwarf, and somehow viewed him as an unfortunate servant, an 'innocent'. Ives couldn't have known, but the truth is the wee man was a sycophantic murdering *thug*, a faithful under lieutenant to every Number Two ever in power there.

"As fate would have it, Degree Absolute was about to end just as McGill's raid began. Knowing the end was upon him, McLeod fully snapped, attacking Ives in desperation as the seconds wound down.

"Ives then too, snapped, and strangled McLeod to death with his bare hands. You witnessed Ives crawling from

McLeod's body in the film clip. The dwarf had tried to stop Ives, was knocked backward, and fatally struck his head on a table corner.

"As Ives came out of the 'fever', as I would put it, he realized what he had done, what he had been *pushed* into doing. Killing the dwarf, a man he had considered an 'innocent' drove him over the edge. His mind snapped. He slipped into a catatonic state. Thankfully, temporarily.

"What I've told you is based on security footage, taped records, journals McLeod kept, and from Ives himself. I personally wasn't aware of his entire story until a number of hours ago, as I studied his file."

"Steed, we were *correct* in our assumptions." King continued. "The reason for Ives resignation had always been clear and concise, written in a letter and angrily delivered by his own hand, *completely superfluous* to what McLeod was actually after.

"Agent Drake, Ives' *loyalty* was *never* in question. You were morally right in refusing such a repugnant '*mission*'.

"Victor Ives was the victim of a mad, sadistic homicidal maniac; a man who pledged allegiance to a sick and twisted ideology.

"It is *imperative*, that each of you *fully* understands that strains of this Conspiracy, remnants of this cabal, are *still* at large! *Still* active in key positions. Fewer in number yes, but there. It is for that very reason we shroud ourselves in secrecy. The reason we could not readily give you information concerning us or our mission here. We could not be certain *why* you wanted to 'rescue' him, no idea what you may have wanted him *for*, do you see? We weren't *sure* your intentions were noble.

"Our mission here is to heal and protect Ives and others like him from further harm. We are a conspiracy of care. A maximum security hospital if you will. We are a sanctuary for very special people. Our people are *not* here because they cannot be trusted in society. They are here because our society could not be trusted *by* them!

"We have the finest physicians and psychiatrists helping us here, physical therapy specialists, dieticians, etcetera. Each of whom can be trusted implicitly. We are attached to no one particular arm of any one government. We are governed by a board, a number of whom, as you see, are present today."

"We strive to be agents for peace, for what is right and just. What is *compassionate!*

"We hope we have presented our case to you. We've gone through this laborious effort as we *strongly* feel you six could be allies. At the very least we ask you for secrecy, extreme discretion and silence. The lives of the people we care for in this place *demand* it.

"Oh, yes. One final note; should you wish to 'visit' us again, might we suggest you merely ring us and ask?"

47
The Man from UNCLE

Alexander Waverly once more addressed the gathering. "As you can see, I am unwell, and need to follow a certain regimen. I desired to be present here among you once certain identities of you six 'scallywags' became known to me."

Templar couldn't help himself. Despite the gloom they were all feeling due to the sheer power and poignancy of what they'd just seen and heard, his smile at being called a 'scallywag' turned into a mild laugh. "Forgive me sir. I haven't been called that in ages."

Waverly nodded, "Oh I can imagine Mr. Templar. You more so than your colleagues I'd wager." This gave license for more mild laughter, which helped lighten the mood in the room overall.

Waverly held up a hand signalling 'okay, enough'. "My friend and I must retire to my needs. For the rest of you, I suspect dinner will be ready for you at some point, not that many might feel like eating right at the moment. Before I leave, however, I'd like to ask a favour of Mr. Drake in particular?"

Drake surprised, stood. "Certainly Mr. Waverly, what can I do for you?"

"Would you make yourself available to meet with me for breakfast in the morning? I'd appreciate it, and I'm certain you'd find a bed here preferable to napping at one of our conference tables."

Drake smiled widely. 'In for a penny, in for a pound' he thought. "I...I'd be honoured sir. But...if you'll pardon, I have a choice?"

Waverly waved his hand dismissively, "Oh, I believe we're long past that nonsense, agreed?" Every person seated at the elevated table nodded in agreement, McGill enthusiastically so.

"Splendid. Say, 08:00 tomorrow, Mr. Drake?"

"08:00, sir."

The young blonde-haired man moved the microphone and began preparing the wheelchair for transport. McGill walked up to him. "Mister K?"

The young man looked up at him smiling as they shook hands.

"Do svidániya, buddy." McGill said.

"Very impressive, Tovarich!" Mister K. smiled, "Very good indeed. Adios, y'all!"

McGill winced, grimaced, and then grinned as Mr. K. escorted Waverly out of the room.

Tara, with her acute hearing, overheard the exchange, and whispered to Steed, "McGill spoke Russian to that blonde-haired man!"

Steed smiled pleasantly, murmuring through his teeth, "Just so long as it's not Martian."

Raleigh stood. "You are free to go. With regard to your actions, this never 'happened'. You were obviously on a rescue mission, however misguided. That much has been made clear by Mr. King, and other information we were able to gather. You know, the fact is, I wish I could officially commend each of you."

Gambit accepted loudly, "Suits me! It'd look great in my file."

The laughter resulting from that remark completely took the gloom out of the room.

"We will arrange for transport home within the hour for any of you who wish. We *do* however invite you to stay for dinner, and a good night's rest. It has been a long day, for all of us." Raleigh closed.

48

Danger Men and Women

The Six decided to stay for diner, at least. Most of the group had adjourned from the conference room. Sharron Macready offered to give a limited tour of the compound and a few of its facilities as dinner was being prepared, Tara accepting. Richard Barrett and Sir John Raleigh bid their farewells and left the premises. Emma remained and was in deep discussion with both Temp and Quatermass.

The rest retired to the patio and lawn for drinks and/or a smoke or three. McGill was continuing a discussion with Drake regarding Guardian.

"...the thing is, ever since we first opened up here, we've had to deal with a small number of attempted break-ins. Most of them were nothin' really, but in more than a few, Guardian did the trick. In two cases, the culprits were particularly nasty. Some of our people have enemies we need to be on the lookout for."

"I'm still not convinced." said Drake. "Any 'system' can be shut down, or circumvented, or worse still, perverted. Especially by an 'enemy'."

"Well, we're sure we've got safeguards for that. But maybe you're right. I'm open to discuss it more with you some time."

Jason King was slumped down in a lawn chair to the point where he was nearly horizontal. "Constant re-evaluation is a necessary function of maintenance for any system, I concur," he announced.

A rich lilting voice approached them, "A meeting of minds?" Emma joked. Having brought a chair, she plonked it down between Steed and Drake, joining them.

Craig Stirling was looking at Drake as if deciding whether he should say something. Finally, he decided. "We'd talk about you, you know. Back when I was in the CIA. When you worked with NATO. You're like a real James Bond."

"I'm nothing of the sort!" Drake snapped.

"*Not* a good comparison!" Emma advised good naturedly.

"A ridiculous character!" Steed opined.

"Not *fit* to polish Mark Caine's Smith & Wesson!" hissed King.

McGill jumped up from his chair, arms flailing about "*Holy cats* folks! Stop ganging up on the kid!"

Emma laughed, rich, deep, and lilting, it infected those around her. Drake flashed a smirk at Stirling. "Sorry, bit of a...sore spot." He looked at Emma, his smirk evolving into a warm smile.

When the laughter died down, Simon Templar asked, "I've got most of the connections clear, though I'm wondering how you were brought into this mix, Stirling."

Stirling cleared his throat, "Well, it was a package deal really; Sharron, Rick and myself. Like Jason, we're connected through Sir Curtis." he paused, considering.

"Umm, okay. What the hell. Earlier this year, I was captured after I got back from a secret mission in Hong Kong. I was held in a cell where I was subjected to interrogation. I was mentally tortured. My interrogator wanted details about the Hong Kong mission. I wouldn't tell him a *thing*. He was using methods that pretty much kept me from getting to that mental place where I could utilize my powers, even though I *thought* I'd used them to try to escape, which would have been a mistake if I *had*! I'll tell ya though, I swear to *God* I thought I was a *dead* man."

King clarified a point, "This 'interrogator' was the 'acquaintance' of Stirling's I'd mentioned in our presentation. Cargil, one of The Village's Number Twos; a sadistic coward."

"Right, yes. Cargil. Anyway, I got near breaking point, I *really* did. I was about to tell this bastard *everything*. Then I caught a break. I was able to escape. I was only a few yards out when I started to recognize the building I was in. It turned out I was in our *own headquarters!* Cargil was head of our own internal *security!*"

"What happened was, during the Hong Kong mission I'd used my powers twice. Because of our pact not to mention them, I fudged a few details in my report. Our superior, Tremayne, cooked up this whole scheme just to get at the *full* details of the mission!

"Cargil caught up with me, but by that point their plan was blown wide open. He and Tremayne argued about it, but Tremayne called the 'internal investigation' quits."

"Tremayne...Tremayne" Steed repeated, his eyes widening, "Of 'Nemesis'?"

"Yes." verified Stirling.

Steed exclaimed, "Good heavens! The three of you were in *that* soup? Nemesis was disbanded by the U.N. and *Interpol!* With prejudice! I recall Sir Curtis being involved with that action! Tremayne is now in an American federal penitentiary! There've been agents tracking down a few ex-officials of Nemesis for months!"

"Right." Stirling confirmed. "I immediately resigned! So did Sharron and Rick when they found out about it. Less than a month later Sir Curtis himself got in contact with the three of us, through Rick in London..."

"...then through me, then I contacted Craig." finished Macready, she and Tara having arrived from their tour of the grounds. "We've been 'agents' of Sir Curtis for quite a while now."

"Wait till you see some of the facilities here Steed. *Very* impressive!" said Tara, until she realized she was interrupting. "Oh, sorry, *do* go on."

"Because of my experience with Cargil, Curtis felt I'd have 'affinity for the experiences' of our people here. When he invited us, this place was finishing construction and hadn't 'opened for business' yet. Doctor Sharron here, was one of its first staff physicians. I'd like to think I'd have jumped at the chance anyway, but the three of us working together again in such a noble effort *certainly* sealed the deal for me."

"Had he known of your powers when he contacted you?" asked Templar.

"We get the impression he did, but he's never mentioned them." Macready answered.

McGill opined, "I think he did. Craig was with us on the Village raid. I was gonna put him in charge of three MEDIVAC choppers we used, because he's a *hell* of a pilot, but Sir Curtis strongly suggested him for demolition. I'd seen Craig's file and I'm thinkin', 'this guy doesn't have much experience with explosives'. I let Sir Curtis know my feelings about Craig, so he says, 'You'll need a fast man. Stirling *is* that man. Trust me'."

Stirling addressed Drake, "I'm still a little confused about your involvement with Ives. You had an assignment at The

Village or something? No, you refused, so they were after you?"

Drake thought, once again, '...in for a pound'. He related a basic version of his story. "...turns out I may have been mistaken in thinking my report on Colony Three had something to do with The Village."

McGill said, "Well, we don't know. If they did use any of those suggestions, they perverted the hell out of them. But I know for a *fact* that a few of those suggestions had something to do with *us!* Like I said, you're part of our Charter."

"Yes, and I...I'm still...How do you mean, exactly?" Drake asked

King answered, "Roland Hardy, your retired superior, the man who told you to run. He thought highly of your suggestions. You see, Drake, the 'Captains' of our own little conspiracy here have been knitting it together for quite a few years."

Drake was struck speechless, though he eventually uttered, "Hardy!"

"Yes." King continued. "One of our founders, a close associate of Sir John's, and an old classmate of Waverly's I gather. I'd only met the man twice myself. I'm sorry to say he'd passed on in February of this year. We've incorporated many concepts in building this place. Those suggestions of yours played a part. You're something of a visionary I daresay."

"Obliged." mumbled Drake, embarrassed by any accolades. "I *am* still unclear on one point. Have you any notion as to why I was...manipulated to get myself out of Hobbs' way? Hobbs and whatever cronies he had in M9?"

"I think you just got railroaded." McGill opined.

"You were a danger to them." Emma stated.

King admitted, "I'm not certain. The truth of the matter died with Hobbs. My hypothesis would be you were too interconnected with people the Conspiracy needed to avoid. Consider, this was a group fuelled by paranoia and delusion, desperately holding onto vestiges of power while suspicious of everyone not firmly ensconced.

"I believe both McGill and Mrs. Peel are correct. They couldn't kill you outright, nor could they attempt a frame-up of any kind. Those actions would require a full range of control they no longer had. The wrong 'type' of disappearance would've been suspect."

"I *had* disappeared! I ran like *blazes!*" Drake declared.

"Maybe they thought you were one guy not even The Village could hold." Stirling offered, as his admiration (almost hero worship) for Drake was made very clear.

King went on hypothesizing, "Personally, I think Hardy covered for you. Your running was the 'right' type of disappearance, allowing for alibi rather than explanation. Hobbs and his people certainly wouldn't be raising any questions about you, would they?"

"That would go a long way in explaining why no one was after you, at least in any official capacity." Steed theorized.

"Maybe they figured they did a good enough number on you. You took yourself out of the game." McGill suggested. "Huh! *That* sure sounds familiar!"

King concluded, "Whatever actually occurred, Hardy, though officially 'retired', was still active behind scenes. Steed is correct. Hardy's involvement explains a great deal."

Drake was awed. "I *am* sorry to hear of his passing. A good man, a better...friend than I ever recognized."

There was a brief moment of silence.

King upended his now empty flask. "Has anyone thought to bring champagne?"

"No alcohol, mate. You know the drill." McGill mock scolded. "Ale and wine with meals only." he explained to the newcomers.

"'No Smoking' areas, 'No Alcohol'. What an unpleasant resort! Little wonder I so rarely stay here." King groused facetiously.

Tara asked, "Mr. King, how are you connected here? What's your 'story'?"

"Oh, I've no story, dear girl. I write novels." King smiled enigmatically.

"I mean it. I'm dying to find out! Notwithstanding the sharing of our surname, I find you a fascinating man!" she insisted.

"Th'nk yoh. You're very perceptive." King murmured, shooting a sly glance at Steed.

He took a long drag from his cigarette, and slowly exhaled. "Gregory Francis Halliday, a disgruntled chemist involved with our chemical weapons program at Lansdowne Park, ...God's sake I *despise* how *easily* that just comes off the tongue! 'Chemical Weapons Program', as though we're discussing the manufacture of *textiles!* Terrifying!

"Halliday stole a deadly nerve gas of his own creation, Otriox Five, and went on the run after testing the gas on himself. He was dreadfully ill for two weeks. He was captured by enemy agents out to obtain his lethal product with the intention of selling it to the highest bidder. I and a partner from Department S 'intervened' in their scheme, freeing Halliday. However, he managed to escape our intervention and absconded to London, where he planned to unleash the gas, killing a million people, to prove a point to the world governments.

"With the horrid event of a million dead firmly in their minds, perhaps then they might listen to his plans for cessation of chemical warfare and weaponry. Hopefully outlawing its use. Perhaps even, God forbid, bringing about peace.

"We intercepted him where he was about to drop a fragile vial of Otriox Five from a high window. I caught the vial, averting the catastrophe. He was a sick, beaten, lost, tired, disgusted, and tortured man, every bit as disturbed as we saw Ives in the film.

"I promised Halliday we would help him. I frankly *demanded* of Sir Curtis we find a place for him where he could actually *be* helped, not simply 'stored away'.

"He currently resides one residence away from Barbara Judd here in our sanctuary. And that is my connection. You are correct Steed. What we do should be about *saving.*"

Steed had never been one for showing strong emotion; 'stiff upper lip' and all that. Now, the lump in his throat was such that he couldn't utter a sound.

There was another long moment of silence.

Slowly, McGill noticed eyes turning toward him. "Hey, no fair; I already told my story."

Steed said, "I think some of us know better than that, McGill."

McGill let out a long sigh. "Okay. My turn." he conceded as he lit a cigarette. In a nutshell, I got screwed good! All in the line of duty, for the good of a mission.

"1962, I was third from the top in my division at CIA. I was beginning to enjoy not risking my ass in the field on a regular basis, but I'd still dabble in a case or two.

"I'd discovered that a top scientist named LeFarbe was gonna defect to Russia. I was just about to intercept him when I was *ordered* by my boss, Harry Thyssen, to stand down. I argued the point till I was blue in the face. Didn't do any good. Sure enough, within *one day*, LeFarbe went over to the Russians.

"Next thing I know, I'm charged with *complicity* in the defection! No sweat I figured, Thyssen will clear things up. Problem was Thyssen *'drowned'* in a sail boat accident!

"There was a lot of bad publicity about the case. My name and photo, my *face*, got in the papers somehow. What with Kennedy's Bay of Pigs cluster- hump and all, the CIA was a nice big target for the press back then. Anyway, turns out the 'Company' couldn't make a case against me. They had no proof. So, I was forced to resign. Blackballed from workin' for *any* intelligence organization for *any* country.

"So, I skipped to London as a base and hobnobbed around, pickin' up jobs here and there. Bodyguard, PI stuff, that kind of thing."

"Mercenary." Drake inserted.

McGill smirked at Drake, testily. "Yeahh...yeah there was a little of that. So, early last year, I discover my old boss Thyssen is *still alive!* His death was faked! He's workin' as a sailor on a Russian freighter. He's actually a courier for secret information from LeFarbe, who turns out to be a double agent highly placed in the Soviet scientific community to get valuable intelligence!

"In '62, my initial investigation nearly blew this important operation, so I was made a *very* public scapegoat, to maintain the illusion that LeFarbe's defection was the real deal. And in '68 I find *out* about this but I don't dare *say* anything cause of how 'vital' this whole set up is supposed to be for democracy and apple pie and whatever the hell. So, I go back to 'self-employment'.

"Later in '68, I get a telegram in London from Thyssen. LeFarbe is dead. He had a stroke! Come on back to the U.S.A.! All is forgiven. My name is cleared. My dossier wiped clean! Publicly! Not that anybody reads where your *proved innocent*, but they *sure* as hell remember reading about you possibly bein' *guilty!* The CIA would even give me a job! Not my old job, mind you, but a decent job!

"I figure everyone here is smart enough to know where I told 'em to *stick it!* A few weeks later I get contacted by Temp regarding Ives' disappearance, and you know the rest."

Steed recalled "Tara and I had a case where the only way she could prove her innocence, was to show how easy it was to frame another! *Myself* in fact! Only *then* were we able to convince superiors that they were looking for other culprits. After hearing your tale McGill, I shudder to think what may have happened to her, to *us* had we not been able to..."

"'Used up and spat out'!" Emma interrupted, finding her hand already on Drake's. He looked at her, uttered a light 'grunt' of appreciation (perhaps something more) and patted her hand with his other.

"A bunch of us have been through a wringer, haven't we?" commented McGill. Steed nodded. "Inexcusable. Petty. Short-sighted. I'd go as far as saying criminal."

"Amen, brother!" agreed McGill.

"It is a case of...forgetting why we got in this business in the first place." Drake concluded. "We have dealt with truly dangerous people, got bitten, and are walking around like wounded animals. We become like walking dead after a while. It is why you have a ninety eight percent dropout rate of trainees, Steed. It takes a certain kind of person to be able to handle it."

Templar stood before this gathering, and spoke with great admiration, affection, and poetic sincerity. "By Heaven, you are *all survivors!* Moreover, you are *victors,* Mr. Ives *certainly* to the point! I've rarely known people with such *fortitude!* I am beside myself with gratitude for this opportunity to be *with* you all. Your stories, your relating of your pasts have *invigorated* me to demand *better* of myself! No *wonder* someone as sterling in character as Father Loyola is here in this place. Your examples will guide me the *rest* of my days!"

The group was stunned by his speech. Many were touched. A few were amazed that, yes, somebody actually *does* talk like that.

King, being one of the latter, was motivated to abruptly (if laboriously) extricate himself from his seat. With his left arm extending upward, index finger thrust skyward, with as much pomp and dignity as his emptying of his whiskey flask could allow, he stridently announced, "Whilst I...I endeavour to find out *exactly* why our meal is taking so *damnably long!*"

49

A Hard Day's Night

They had all finished dinner. Sleeping arrangements and preparations for departure the next morning were being discussed. Other conversations dotted the dining room. The camaraderie that had been forged throughout the day's events was a moving and tangible thing.

Earlier, just prior to dinner, Simon Templar, being Simon Templar after all, had approached Craig Stirling, enquiring as to the nature of Stirling's relationship with Sharron Macready. Stirling assured him theirs was purely professional, though deeply platonic. He also mentioned he was aware of Templar's reputation with women. He reminded him about the powers he shared with his two friends, and simply gave Templar a friendly warning to 'behave'.

Templar assured, "Oh, I *will!* I still have back wounds to serve as an ever-present reminder."

As good-byes and good-nights were being said, the repetitive tinging of a spoon against a glass called all to attention. Jason King addressed The Six as they stood together.

"You are a group of nasty, horrid and awful people, and I hope our paths never cross again." He said tiredly, holding his wine glass in a toast. "The light that shines from your integral goodness and nobility assaults my very eyes. You unfairly demand of me compassionate labour when slothfulness and apathy would be my want. The virility of your strengths of character wear me to the nub."

King's eyes watered slightly, "Oh *bollocks!* You are remarkable. I wish each of you well. *Cheers!*" He drained his glass.

He then spat and sputtered theatrically with an extremely sour face, shuddered, pointed to the empty glass in his hand and uttered, "Temp, something simply *must* be done about the *deplorable* state of our wine stock!" Laughter ensued as King exited the room.

The flabbergasted expressions on Steed, Tara and Templar's faces were also a source of humour for any watching. "What an extraORDinary character!" Steed couldn't help remarking, Tara and Templar nodding in agreement.

"I like 'im." Gambit commented simply.

Emma laughed aloud, "I think he's *adooorable!*"

As for McGill, his farewell to The Six was perfunctory. "I've got some paperwork to finish up, and then I'm outta' here. It's been a trip, but I'm *really glad* we got to know each other better. I'm sure we'll be seeing each other again. He turned to leave, suddenly halted, turned to face Emma, wagged his finger at her, and grinned, "And *you!* You *behave* yourself and *stay outta trouble!*" He then turned once more, waving and calling as he exited, "Take it easy folks."

Steed, Tara, and Gambit would be leaving early in the morning. Templar chose to stay on, explaining, "I eh, have been invited to take Doctor Macready's tour of the premises. I believe it's a good idea to be under a doctor's care as a man in my...condition...well, one never knows when I might have a relapse."

Gambit smirked, Tara smiled and Steed outright laughed.

"If I can *ever* be of service to any of you, please do *not hesitate* to call on me." Templar told them in all sincerity.

Steed clapped both hands on his shoulders, "It has been a pleasure to work with the world-famous Simon Templar! Rest assured I will absolutely keep that in mind."

Steed next addressed Emma and Drake. "You'll be hearing from us within a few days. There's cleaning up to do. We've left Mrs. Peel's home in a TERrible state!"

Gambit, ever the stoned faced one, was making a great effort to keep in check. He shook hands with each and said, "I very much hope we meet again. I echo Jason King. You are remarkable people. I will never forget this 'assignment'. It's been an honour."

Good-nights said, Steed, Tara and Gambit exited the dining room while Templar moved to the table where Macready and Temp were seated.

Quatermass hadn't been with them during dinner, but he now entered the dining room, accompanied by Abigail. He spoke with Temp at some length, then Temp nodded, rose from his seat, and the three of them approached Drake and Emma.

"Victor Ives would like to meet you." Quatermass said bluntly.

50

The Prisoner

They weren't certain they'd heard correctly. Emma asked, "Victor Ives wants to meet John? Are you sure that's a good idea? Wouldn't it be something of a shock?"

Quatermass clarified, "No, he'd like to meet both of you."

"And it *is* a good idea." added Abigail.

Drake shook his head quickly, trying to clear out some cobwebs. "I...would think that might present a...difficulty for him?"

Quatermass allowed, "You and he, alone? Perhaps. In the company of Mrs. Peel, Abigail and myself, I shouldn't think so."

Temp agreed, "He's come a far way from the man you saw on screen Drake. He's come to grips with a great deal. We have great faith in his complete recovery. I believe it would be good for the three of you quite honestly." he said, looking at Emma.

Drake admitted, "I'm...wary doing so, but, if you feel there's no harm to him..."

"I do." Temp assured, smiling. "I'll say my 'good-nights' as well. I'll be seeing you both in the morning at some point."

Abigail and Quatermass led the way, Emma and Drake directly behind them.

For Emma and Drake, the entire atmosphere of the place had changed. The evening light softened a lot of the mysterious darkness they'd seen before.

"It *is* peaceful here. Rather beautiful." Emma commented.

Drake agreed, "'Tis."

They came to the residence where Emma had been early that morning. She noticed, thankfully, that there was no residual evidence whatsoever of her altercation with the three guards and the Guardian.

Quatermass knocked on the residence door. "Come in." a voice called, loudly yet pleasantly.

The living area was larger than one would have assumed, pleasantly furnished with subdued colours. There was the lounger Emma had seen Ives sleeping in. Opposite that; a couch, a few other chairs, and a large bookshelf which covered one wall.

"It's bigger on the inside." said Victor Ives standing by his lounger. He was wearing a tan pullover and brown slacks. His hair was slightly long and neatly trimmed, as were his beard and moustache. Ives stepped directly in front of Drake. Peering into his face Ives raised his glasses slightly. "Well I will be damned!" he muttered softly.

Drake had concentrated hard during the walk to Ives' residence. He'd been told in the past that he often looked angry, mean, or harsh. That he could be too imposing, too...intense. Too egotistical and dismissive. John Drake wanted to present as kindly a face as he could toward this man.

He was almost successful. Sheer amazement was clearly on his face as he peered into Ives'. "Mister Ives, my name is John Drake." was all he could think to say. He held out his hand. Slowly, Ives took it, shaking it firmly.

They were precisely the same height, though Ives stooped a tad more. Drake's hair was longer and styled differently, his beard and moustache shaggier. Ives was approximately fifteen pounds lighter, and he appeared to be ten years older than Drake but was in fact only a year older. Ives smiled, patted Drake's somewhat wider shoulders, turned and looked at Quatermass. "I seem to be the economy pack this time around." he commented as Quatermass grinned.

He extended his hand toward Emma, "And this, the young woman responsible for the tumult outside my window early this morning?"

(Drake couldn't help himself from thinking, 'Good *Lord* she's made an impression! I'm sorry I missed whatever it was that people keep referring to!')

"Emma Peel, Mister Ives. I'm honoured to meet you." she greeted him winningly.

"'Honoured'? Good Lord!" he turned his head toward the kitchen, "Do you hear that Abigail? 'Honoured'!" Turning back to Emma, he kidded "As for you, disturbing my rest, assaulting my guards..." he leaned closer, "Good for you! Nicely done! Give 'em Hell!" he mock whispered, winking at her. She rewarded him with her rich laughter.

"Where in *hell* are my manners?" he scolded, turning and indicating the chairs and couch. "Please, take a seat." he called as he proceeded to his kitchen. Emma and Quatermass sat on the couch, while Drake seated himself in a chair opposite Ives' lounger. Ives brought out a tray stand and tray, set them up, and returned to the kitchen. Within minutes, he and Abigail returned with cups along with packages of biscuits.

"So! I'm told you came to rescue me!" he asked as he sat in his lounger.

"We did." Drake affirmed.

"And found you were a bit late in the game?"

"We were."

"Well, as, Jul...ah, Bernard there, illumined me, you've all spent the day trying to get at the...bottom of things?"

'Good Lord' Emma thought, 'even his voice and vocal inflections are similar to John's'

"Yes." Drake answered.

"Have these...'things' been explained to your satisfaction?"

Drake paused, then answered, "Yes, almost entirely."

Abigail returned from the kitchen with a large full pot of tea and began pouring. Emma stood, passed full cups to Drake and Ives, and took one herself as she returned to her seat. Abigail handed a cup of tea to Quatermass, took one, and sat next to Ives.

"Oh? Not completely satisfied?" Ives asked.

"Aihhm, not quite, but no matter. A few minor details."

"The devil resides in those ya know..."

Drake smiled, "So I've heard."

"Might I be of any help, do you suppose?"

"I don't see how you could, sir."

"I see." Ives sipped his tea. "Would you mind if I asked *you* a few questions, Drake?"

"Not at all."

"You were an agent sent to impersonate me?"

"Well, no sir. I'd been given that assignment, but I refused. I found the idea detestable."

"Did you? How do you mean?"

"Well...the...whole idea, it sickened me." Drake wasn't exactly sure what Ives knew, or where this might be leading.

Quatermass clarified, "I've told Victor of your refusal, Drake. They had attempted it with another. Surgically altered the man. Victor foiled them though. Almost escaped too!"

Emma noticed that Abigail had begun to look very sad, but then stopped herself. '...that scene on the patio, when she'd called John 'Curtis'...had that something to do with this? Had she somehow been involved?' she wondered.

"Yes, yes I did." Victor smiled, a bit sadly, "Almost."

"Mr. Ives, I don't wish to speak about things that may...trouble you..." Drake tried to divert the conversation.

"Oh, don't let that concern you Drake. I've come to terms with much of it. Examination of aspects of it actually does me good. Part of my 'therapy'. The road back, if you like."

"I see."

"Drake, had you any idea *why* I'd been imprisoned?"

"No, sir. I mean...I was told a lie. I had no idea who you might have been, or why they wanted you."

"Mmm. Drake, you're a 'special' agent, true? Not your run of the mill?"

"I was an intelligence agent. I am no longer."

"Ah. Tell me, in your career as an 'intelligence' agent, had you ever occasion to impersonate another?"

"I had, though not in the sense we're discussing. I've impersonated persons unknown to other persons."

"I'm...not quite sure I follow you."

Drake gave an example, "Let's say you'd never met Quatermass before, but you were to receive information from him."

"Information? Regarding what?"

"Oh, like the combination of a safe you wanted to break into. You would only know his name or know him through some type of identification, a secret signal perhaps. The two of you would meet, he'd identify himself, you'd receive the combination from him, go open the safe and steal something."

"Go on."

"Well, I would pretend to be him, give you the wrong combination, and foil your plan. Do you follow?"

"Yes. But you'd in fact look nothing alike."

"Correct. Of course you wouldn't know by sight if I was him or not, you see?"

"I do! Clever."

"I suppose."

Ives thought for a moment, then asked, "Had you ever occasion to rescue prisoners?"

"I did."

"Dangerous stuff I'd imagine."

"Very"

"Say, from behind the Iron Curtain? Berlin, perhaps?"

"Yes"

"Many times?"

Emma began to feel uneasy. She noticed a heightening of tension in the air. Alarms were starting to go off in her head. This was not simply teatime conversation, Ives was interrogating John!

"A number of times, yes," Drake answered.

"Almost killed?" Ives continued.

"Yes. Wounded several times."

"Were you ever captured and held prisoner yourself?"

"Yes. Twice."

"Yet you escaped obviously."

"Yes. Barely."

"And you continued to perform missions like that?"

"I did."

"Once? Twice?"

"A few times."

"Even though you'd almost been killed? Captured and imprisoned?"

"Well I..."

"John," Emma warned as both men's voices were getting louder.

"Victor..." Quatermass leaned forward as he, too, began to notice a change in the room.

Ives continued undaunted. "Did you have to change your plans?"

"I...I'm not sure what you mean."

"When you were captured. When you were caught, did you have to change your plan? Have another in mind while you proceeded with the former?"

"Well...of course! One always has more than one pla..."

"Oh, what am I saying? You're a clever chap! Of *course*, you had an alternative plan!"

"One *tries*, they don't always work, but..."

"But what?"

"Well...one *has* to be able to...improvise..."

"Why, Drake?"

Drake was suddenly a bit confused "I...I'm sorry, why? Why improvise?"

"Why did you continue going on these missions?"

"I don't...It was my job..."

"Your job?"

"...Yes."

"You were good at it!"

"Yes, I suppo..."

"No 'supposing' about it! You were very, *very* good at it!"

"Yes! Mr. Ives, I'm not sure what you're getting at, but..."

"Very good at going on a mission, failing, formulating another plan on the spot!"

"Well, aihhm, one *has* to, yes."

"Going with other plans already in mind!"

"Yes..."

"Go no matter the danger! Go. *Improvise.* Do your *job*! *Recover* the prisoner!"

"I...yes."

"Then *why*, Drake? Why *not* go on *this* mission? The one to impersonate *me?*"

"I...it was immoral, it was...the whole idea disgusted me!"

"Why? You went on those other missions! *Why* not the one for *me?*"

Ives was yelling, Quatermass stood.

"*Why? Why not* come, with an alternate plan? Turn the tables on them! You *knew* it was wrong!"

Drake couldn't think straight. He'd only gotten a few hours rest at that table in the conference room early in the morning, the information kept coming at them, the barrage of twists and turns, the shock of seeing who was involved, seeing the horror show on the viewing screen...

Emma stood abruptly, "*Ives! Stop this!*"

Quatermass sided with her, "Victor, you can't *possibly* be angry at this man! You haven't the right. He *did* try to find out about you! You know that! That is the *only* reason he's here *now!*"

Ives got up from his chair, like he wasn't hearing them.

"*Why not* come for a man wrongfully imprisoned? *Why??*" he yelled, looking down at Drake.

"Why *couldn't* you have come and *helped me? When I truly needed it?*"

One could have said the silence in that room was deafening.

All were standing save Drake, who was still seated, staring at the floor. Ives stood over him, staring at him. Waiting.

Abigail was behind Ives, rubbing his back and shoulders, "It wasn't his fault Victor. Please..." she was saying quietly, trying to soothe him.

Quatermass attempted to guide Drake upwards by the arms, intending to get them out of there. This had been a *terrible* mistake!

"No." Drake whispered, gently resisting the tugging. "No." he stated, in a full, calm voice.

Drake looked up at Ives. "No, you're right."

Emma immediately kneeled by Drake, putting both hands on his upper arm "No, he's *not!* He doesn't understand..." She then stood face to face with Ives "That is hardly *fair*, or *accurate!*" she snapped. "*All* of John's support was leaving him. People he would *need* for a mission like that were proving themselves untrustworthy. He was *alone!* How could he *possibly* have accomplished *any* of it?"

Drake raised his hand, "No, Emma. It's alright. I didn't understand before, but Victor was the one truly...alone.

"Victor, I could have...tried." Drake admitted, looking directly into eyes that were very much like his own. "Tried to get you out, but I was scared. The...*immorality*, coming from my superior...in what they wanted me to do...*that* stopped me. Something evil had come to M9 and that's all I was concerned with. That shook me to my core. I'd...felt it coming for quite some time. Couldn't admit it to myself, but there it was, right at my doorstep, and..."

"Yes?" Ives asked, his voice a gentle croak.

"...and you, as a *person*, vanished from my mind. The horrors you went through no longer my concern; of no consequence whatsoever to me.

"I *had* been clever enough. No supposing about it. I could have gone along with them, come up with a counter-plan as I often had before. I could have...done my job. It would've been risky. The chances of a scheme like that working, a million to one."

"But you had done so before." Ives affirmed, speaking gently, returning to his chair. Not an accusation, just a statement of historically recorded fact.

"Yes. I had. But this time, *fear* stopped me. Concern for *my* safety...*overrode* concern for an unjustly imprisoned man. I failed to do my job. When all is said and done, the fact remains; I was too scared to do my duty, my...mission. I ran."

Emma emphatically defended, "You were *told* to run, John. Advised to run by the *only* person you could *trust* at the time!"

While that may have been true, Quatermass understood, it didn't quite '*square things*' as he felt *both* he and Drake saw it. Both had become...prisoners! "True, Mrs. Peel. I'd been given similar advice. Go! Get away from *everything*. Drake, we both faced a *terrible* unknown, had reality *pulled* out from under us. We *both* ran. Me after the event at Hobbs End, and you with... what was the name of your...?"

"M9."

"Yes. You after the 'event' with M9."

"Victor...I'm..." Drake started to apologize.

Ives swiftly interrupted, "*No* John, *stop it! That's* not what I'm *after!*"

"Oh? What...*are* you after then?"

After a moment, Ives asked, "Tell me, what finally happened that caused you to try, John Drake? After all this time, why try now?"

Drake stood silently, his fingers moving, as if counting numbers rapidly ('Good Lord!' thought Ives. We even share *that!*').

Finally, Drake's fingers stopped. He turned and looked directly into Emma's eyes.

"*Emma*...convinced me. Reminded me I had to. She said *we* had to. She helped me escape my own...prison. I didn't realize...I had run into my own cell...as fast as I could. Slammed the door shut and tossed the keys."

Quatermass quietly interjected, "Just as I had, Drake."

Drake turned to Ives, "Emma had the courage to care more about my problems than her own. Her concern for me made it possible for me to see a way that it *could* be done. That we *could* find you, and...'*rescue*' you."

Ives peered at him, a small smile on his face. "Quite a woman. You should've seen her...*dispatch* my guards. Most entertaining!"

"I would have...loved to." Drake said with a slight smile, risking a glance her way.

Ives smiled and spoke warmly. "John, you and, er, *Bernard* here, both of you are *free* now, do you realize that? I needed to free *you*. *Both* of you. Free for all! It would've worn us all down if I hadn't. Would've whittled away at us. *That* is why I wanted to meet with you. It is *unfathomable* the prisons we put ourselves in. Now, you are free to *do* your *job!* From one rescued prisoner to another, I want to thank you. Thank you for your failed effort. Thank you for caring enough about *me* to try."

After some moments, breaking the mood, Ives spoke in more strident and pleasant tones. "What first motivated you to pursue this job of yours, Drake?"

"POP."

"Pardon?"

"POP. Protect Our People." he replied with a half-smile.

"Ahh, 'Protect Our People'." Ives contemplated. Then, "Drake, I hear you'll be breakfasting with Waverly tomorrow."

Somewhat surprised, he confirmed, "Yes."

"POP, Drake. They're making us all numbers, working to make us not *care* about *people.* They're getting us to stop *trying.* Do this, do that, don't question, don't ask, be *'safe'*, don't *risk!* It's getting worse every day!"

Ives arose from his chair once more, extending his hand to him. John Drake took Victor Ives hand in both of his. "Thank *you.*" he said.

"Breakfast tomorrow, Drake. POP. Never give in. Never stop trying. *People* need to *fight*, and if they *cannot*, they need a *person*, not a number, to fight *for* them!"

He turned to Emma, pointing his head in Drake's direction, "And as for you, dear lady...again, Good for you! Give 'im Hell!"

51
Living in Harmony

08:00. Drake strode from the residence where he'd slept, to 'Complex A', where the dining room was located. His stride was quick, determined. The weather had taken a turn for the worse, raining fairly heavily. Thunder cracked just as he reached the handle on the door leading from the patio to the dining room. He walked in and saw Alexander Waverly sitting in his wheelchair, beginning breakfast. His aide, the mysterious Mister K. was in a far corner, reading.

Drake sat opposite Waverly, snapped the napkin open, dabbed his face and wiped his hands, placed the napkin in his lap, placed both hands on the table and announced firmly...,

"I accept!"

Waverly smiled, and slid his hand forward, lifting it to reveal a calling card which read, 'Sir John M. Raleigh'. Drake knew from experience a little lemon juice applied gingerly to the card would reveal a telephone number of a secured private line. "We had a feeling about you Drake."

"We?" smiled Drake

"Your old boss and I, among others. We'd had our eye on you."

The breakfast meeting proceeded for close to an hour.

After the meeting, the rain now a downpour, Drake ran to the residence where Emma had stayed. Entering, he saw that she had just got done with her breakfast and was about to tidy up the dining area. She looked at him and smiled warmly.

"My intuition tells me you are once again gainfully employed."

"Yes. I told Waverly I would need about one month to settle my affairs. He said there'll be a few weeks of preparation and organization with McGill, Sir Curtis and others."

"I like McGill."

"I've grown...'accepting' of him. 'Fond' will take a bit of time."

"Mm. You know, one thing we never found out bothers me."

"Oh? What's that?"

"In Stolford, it was 'The Village'. What do they call *this* place? I hope it's not one of those awful acronyms."

Drake smiled, "No, Waverly refused to agree to any of that. Said he'd had his fill."

"Mm. So what do they refer to it as?"

"Pax."

"Hmm. I reserve judgment. Oh! By the way, Abigail came by with a package for us. She put it in the fridge for me while I was eating. Said she'd forgotten to give it to us last night. Little wonder after the scene we went through."

"Oh? In the fridge is it?"

Emma laughed, "The box with a card."

"Curious." He retrieved the box, carrying it to the table.

"A cake of some kind?" she guessed at the contents as she stood, holding a napkin she'd folded. "I'm glad we went through it, though, with Ives. Abigail thanked us again, said it was important to him."

"Mm. To me as well; a catharsis for both of us, I'd say. Quatermass as well."

"Let's open the card, shall we?" Emma asked.

He pulled the string tying the card to the white box, took the card from the envelope. The front of the card read 'Welcome'.

She moved closely to his side.

Inside, the card read simply 'Be seeing you.' and was signed 'Ives' and 'Quatermass', each apparently by their own hand, as well as 'Waverly and Hardy, among others', likely signed in Waverly's hand.

She asked, almost in a whisper, "How could they have known last night that you'd...?"

He smiled. "What was it McGill said, something about entering a *very* strange area?"

After a few seconds, she put her arms around him, looked into his eyes, and softly said, "There will always be prisoners in need of freeing. Evil forces to combat, the obvious and the hidden. I believe they chose the right man for the job. And I believe that man chose the right people to trust."

He likewise put his arms around her and looked at her for some moments, then said gently, "Mrs. Peel, you're needed."

"It's 'We're needed'," she corrected coquettishly.

John Drake had never been more serious in his life.

"Fair enough. Suit's me!"

Sometime after, Emma opened the box.

It contained something wrapped in aluminium foil.

Drake smelled an aroma that was faintly familiar. He sniffed the air, trying to conjure up what it might be.

A note taped to the inside of the box top read, 'In case you're staying for lunch.'

She unfolded the foil and the aroma hit them full.

Stunned once again, as they had been so many times before in the last forty hours, they stared at each other in wonder.

The foil contained four Spiedies.

At that moment, Elsewhere

He awoke, his head pounding. The ringing in his ears was excruciating. He could taste blood in his mouth. He tried to focus his eyes, but it seemed like there were explosions of light everywhere.

"Ahh, good to have you back with us!"

A voice, amplified, reverberating...a woman's voice.

"Wh...where am I?"

"Right where you need to be."

"Who...who are you?"

"*That* is none of your affair!"

His hands were, tied? Chained? Yes, chained. The lights weren't so bad now, but the swirling...Were his eyes doing that, or the lights?

"What do...what do you want?"

"Oh, come now, you *know* what we want!"

Of course. Of course he knew. And he knew that they couldn't know. If they ever found out...God, the smell! The smell here was putrid!

"You...you won't get it! N...Not from me!"

"Really? What makes you think there are any others *left?*"

No! That couldn't be true! Could it...? True, they'd lost so much, but... No! He'd have to hope. Hold out. Hold on.

"Don't care! I re...refuse to talk!"

"Well then, dear boy, prepare to get very, VERY uncomfortable."

The woman's laugh went on, and on, and on, and on, and...

Prisoner

Information

I hope you enjoyed my tale, and if you have comments or questions my email address is:
djcookirk0@gmail.com
(Please be sure to type the *numeral* '0' after the second 'k', not the capital letter 'o'.)

To keep up-to-date with all things
The Prisoner and Portmeirion, visit:
www.theunmutual.co.uk

Two great books readers may find of interest concerning characters and events in this book are:

The Prisoner Dusted Down by David Stimpson
and
Playboys, Spies and Private Eyes edited by Alan Hayes and Rick Davy

Both of these books are also available through:
www.quoitmedia.co.uk

About the Royal National Lifeboat Institution

As characters in the story stated, their work is about saving lives.

A percentage of proceeds from sales of my book will do precisely that as they will be donated to the Royal National Lifeboat Institution.

As stated on their web site:

"Every day of every year, people of all backgrounds get into danger in the water. Today, with your support, we are working harder than ever to end preventable drowning. In addition to our 24/7 search and rescue lifeboat service, we operate a seasonal lifeguard service. Every year, our volunteer lifeboat crews and lifeguards help and rescue thousands of people and have saved over 143,000 lives since 1824. Countless more lives are saved through our youth education and water safety work.

In an ideal world, no one would suffer the devastating loss of a loved one to drowning. We'd reach everyone with our water safety advice. If anyone got into trouble, they'd know what to do until help arrived. And our lifesavers would always have everything they need to reach them in time and save lives."

For more information, please visit:
https://rnli.org/about-us

About the Royal National Lifeboat Institution

[illegible]

[illegible] Royal National Lifeboat Institution.

[illegible]

[illegible]

[illegible]

For more information, please visit:
https://rnli.org/about-us

Acknowledgements

To my wife Kathleen, daughter Karen, and sons Ian and Colin who helped me mould the first roughs into something cohesive, and followed me through this trip every single step of the way. You are my heart.

To my granddaughter, Rowan Dawn Cook, who helped me design the cover for the book ("It needs more orange up in that part, Grandpa. Make sure you do that!"). Thank you, honey.

To Jackie Albano Johnston, a dear friend, who graciously accepted the task of sifting through my story with a perspective of intelligence, wit, and care that was outside of mine, and not "locked in." She is very much a partner in this endeavour.

To Al Jones, editor supreme: A great chap and friend who suffered the slings and arrows of dealing with matters of English versus American English in his exhaustive work on this book. Al's a brave lad - *much* braver than I.

To Glenys, Allan, Isobel, Dwyryd, Paul, Anne, Colin, again to Al, and many others who helped navigate our way to and around Portmeirion, and who helped make it more magical than it already is (especially the staff).

To Rick Davy and Alan Hayes and the rest at Quoit Media for making this book a reality, and to many other authors who have written books and essays about *The Prisoner* and other series over the years (Rick and

Alan themselves, David Stimpson, Dave Rogers, Cat Frumerman and Tina Jerke to name just a few), who have kept the conversation and debates alive.

To Patrick, Dame Diana, Patrick, Peter, Sir Roger, Steve, Richard, Leo, Gareth, Linda, Jane, Mary, Stuart, Alexandra, William, Barbara, Warren, Paul, Sue, Colin, James, Julian, Andrew, and other wonderful actors who breathed life into amazing characters, and all of the other "magicians" involved in the production of the wonderful British television series I've thoroughly enjoyed over my years.

About the Author

On Saturday, June 1st, 1968, at 7:30pm, author David John Cook (then 11 years old) happened upon a TV program that was a summer replacement series for *The Jackie Gleason Show* which normally aired at that time.

David was already a huge fan of every British mystery, spy television program available to view on American television till that point. He loved *The Avengers*, *The Saint*, *Secret Agent* (the American title used for ITC's *Danger Man* series) and, later, *The Champions.* (In fact, each of those British series, along with *Man in a Suitcase*, first debuted as summer replacements series here in the USA.) Those shows keenly shaped the way he viewed the world as a boy, but when this odd short run series, *The Prisoner*, hit the airwaves it frankly changed his life.

The Prisoner put the turbulent year of 1968 into a new perspective and radically opened up his understanding of events, and his place in them. *The Prisoner*, and the subjects addressed in the series, informed his philosophy, actions, and passions from that point forward.

This book is a love story, a "Valentine" if you will, to all those series and the characters that lived in his head and heart then, and still do!

May you enjoy the interweaving of those worlds in the same way the author enjoyed being in "the actual place" of The Village (Portmeirion, Wales) in 2014, and several years since with many happy returns.

Be seeing you.